OCCULT DETECTIVE MAGAZINE

#6 (December 2019)

Edited by

John Linwood Grant & Dave Brzeski

CATHAVEN PRESS

OCCULT DETECTIVE MAGAZINE #6

ISBN: 978-1-9160212-1-1

http://greydogtales.com/blog/occult-detective-magazine/
occultdetectivemagazine@gmail.com

Publishers: Jilly Paddock & Dave Brzeski

Editors: John Linwood Grant & Dave Brzeski

Logos & Headers: Bob Freeman

Cover by: Roland Nikrandt (http://phoarto.com)

Interior design by Dave Brzeski and Jilly Paddock

Sam Gafford sketch © 2019 Jason Eckhardt
Sam Gafford portrait © 2019 Dave Felton
The Rending Veil art © 2019 ODM/Autumn Barlow
The Empanatrix of Room 223 art © 2019 ODM/Bob Freeman
He is the Gate art © 2019 ODM/Russell Smeaton
House on the Borderland © 2019 ODM/Mutartis Boswell

'Komolafe' first appeared in Expanded Horizons © Tade Thompson 2013, 2019
All other material original to this issue. Not to be reproduced in any format without prior permission from ODM.

Published by
Cathaven Press,
Peterborough,
United Kingdom
cathaven.press@cathaven.co.uk

CONTENTS

Editorial — Dave Brzeski   5
In Memoriam: Sam Gafford (1962-2019) — John Linwood Grant   7

FICTION
The Rending Veil — Melanie Atherton Allen   9
Illustration by Autumn Barlow
Komolafe — Tade Thompson   23
The Way of All Flesh — Matthew Willis   28
Blindsider — Cliff Biggers   43
Vinnie de Soth and the Phantom Skeptic — I.A. Watson   57
The Empanatrix of Room 223 — Kelly M Hudson   75
Illustration by Bob Freeman
The Unsummoning of Urb Tc'Leth — Bryce Beattie   91
In Perpetuity — Alexis Ames   111
The Way Things Were — S.L. Edwards   129
Angelus — John Paul Fitch   143
The Last Performance of Victoria Mirabelli — Ian Hunter   157
Occult Legion: He is the Gate — James A. Moore and Charles R. Rutledge. Illustration by Russell Smeaton   175

NON-FICTION
Kotto's Creepies: An Interview With Jonathan Raab — S.L. Edwards   52
Nury Vittachi's The Feng Shui Detective and the Singapore Union of Industrial Mystics — Craig Stanton   122
COLD CASES: Supernatural Sleuths: Stories of Occult Investigators, Edited by Peter Haining — Michael Kellar   167

REVIEWS   192
Describin' the Scribes   203

DEDICATION

This issue is for Sam Gafford (1962 – 2019), dear friend and Occulteer Supreme.

EDITORIAL

Welcome to the first issue of OCCULT DETECTIVE MAGAZINE – or the sixth issue of OCCULT DETECTIVE QUARTERLY, however you want to look at it.

A lot has happened since our last issue. In particular, we lost our publisher, Sam Gafford, to an unexpected heart attack (see John's 'In Memoriam' piece for more on that). We owe Sam an awful lot. He originally conceived the idea for the magazine with John Linwood Grant, long before I got myself involved. He stepped up when our first publisher found himself in over his head, and brought OCCULT DETECTIVE QUARTERLY in under his own Ulthar Press imprint. The problems he inherited in doing this were enormous, yet he persevered right up until his death. Losing Sam looked like the end for us – unless we found a new publisher.

My partner, Jilly Paddock, immediately suggested that we publish it ourselves. My reply was an instant, "No way, no how!" We simply did not have the income, nor capital to support such a mad venture. But Jilly had also pointed out the synchronicity of stories that had been accepted for publication by Sam's Ulthar Press being rescued by our imprint, which happens to be called Cathaven Press. If anyone reading this doesn't get the inference, go look up H.P. Lovecraft's story, *'The Cats of Ulthar'*. It seemed to be fated that we should do this – if only we had the money...

Up stepped Cliff Biggers, of Dr No's Comic & Games Superstore, Marietta. Cliff has always been a supporter, and he loved the magazine so much that he was willing to donate enough funds for us to cover outstanding costs and to finance at least the next two issues (I should mention that Cliff's story in this issue was accepted long before any of this occurred, so he's included on the strength of his work!).

Having managed successfully to format and publish one of Jilly's own books, we felt confident enough to throw ourselves into formatting and publishing OCCULT DETECTIVE MAGAZINE. The copy in your hands will stand as evidence of how well we achieved that task.

I'm not going to say much about the contents of this issue, except to say that we've striven for variety as is our wont. Unusually for us, there are three vampire stories, but they're very different from each other, so we thought it might be fun to include them all at once. We're also delighted that award-winning author Tade Thompson provided us with a haunting piece of his for our relaunch, something which reflects our determination to include authors and subject matter from the widest possible range of backgrounds across the globe.

As I said, we will be publishing at least two issues, and if these go down well, we'll continue as long as we can.

Finally, a few notes on how we approach the editing of this magazine. Our contributors come from all over, but mainly the UK and the USA. We allow the authors to use whichever spelling convention they choose. This gives the Americans the freedom to cope with their national shortage of the letter 'u'. We do try to employ a certain level of consistency, however. Dialogue is done the American way, with "double quotation marks". We chose this because we, along with a lot of British writers we know, were actually taught this way at school. We do title contractions (Mr, Mrs, Ms, Dr) the British way, without a full stop.

We all hope you enjoy this exciting new development – and if you do, please recommend us to friends, acquaintances and, quite frankly, anyone who will stand still long enough to listen.

Dave Brzeski

IN MEMORIAM: SAM GAFFORD (1962-2019)

One of my greatest pleasures over the last few years was my unlikely conspiracy with the American writer Sam Gafford, an old-style fan of horror and weird fiction, a fine craftsman himself, and an earnest, enthusiastic publisher (as Ulthar Press). It was unlikely, because we had no shared friends, very different upbringings, and the Atlantic Ocean lay between us; we never met in person, and never even had a telephone conversation (neither of us were overly fond of telephones). It was a conspiracy, because within a few weeks of getting to know each other we were already hatching up mad ideas together, ready to unleash them on the world.

Our meeting point was the work of William Hope Hodgson, in whom we shared an enduring interest (Sam was a major WHH scholar), but soon we were comparing writing notes, gossiping about weird fiction, laughing about bizarre 1970s comics and collectables, Monty Python sketches, and anything else which came up. His mind was a turmoil of clever, fun and cool ideas, hidden inside a self-effacing guy who often didn't have enough confidence in his own talent.

As a writer, he didn't feel comfortable with the fuss and falseness of marketing, networking and all that exhausting jazz. He didn't show off like so many of us do. Yet his novels *The House of Nodens* (Dark Regions) and *Whitechapel* (Ulthar) – a Lovecraftian horror, and a weird Arthur Machen/Jack the Ripper tour de force respectively, were both superb. His sole collection *The Dreamer in Fire* (Hippocampus) is a wonderful selection of stories both dark and strange; his collaboration with artist Jason Eckhardt, the graphic novel *Some Notes on a Non-Entity: The Life of H P Lovecraft* (PS Publishing) is fascinating. These were just some of his achievements.

As a publisher, Sam was an egalitarian. He didn't care if you were a well-known 'name' or an emerging voice. He wasn't interested in which snarky, argumentative corner of the field you were in or identified with. He published writers who wouldn't even speak to each other – but they would speak to Sam. And if they had a good story, he wanted to help get it out there – he presided over some wonderful Ulthar publications, doing virtually all the work single-handed. That urge to share the sort of stuff he loved was the core of what became *Occult Detective Quarterly*, and what is now *Occult Detective Magazine*.

So much of this is made poignant by his untimely and unexpected death on the 20th of July this year, three weeks after a massive heart attack. It has been a bitter blow to me personally – we are selfish, and we recognise when something unique has been taken from us. Whenever I see something bizarre about comics, or something happening in the horror genre (or even when parts of me hurt more than usual) I immediately want to message or email him – and then I realise he's no longer there. Sam leaves behind him a widow, Carol; for her this is so much the harder to bear, and my heart goes out to her.

We should remember him, and all his works. This issue is dedicated to my dear friend Sam, and he will remain *Occult Detective Magazine*'s guiding spirit.

John Linwood Grant, November 2019

Editorial Note: We are honoured to present in these pages three commemorative pieces of art: a portrait of Sam by Jason Eckhardt (below); a full page illustration of him imagined in an old-style study surrounded by his interests, by Dave Felton (on the Dedication page) and finally, on our back cover, a depiction of The House on the Borderland by Paul (Mutartis) Boswell, to celebrate Sam's fascination with William Hope Hodgson.

THE RENDING VEIL

MELANIE ATHERTON ALLEN

"Pendleton," said Anderson, collaring me as I entered the smoking room of The Anacreon Club. "Got to talk to you." His face was green. That isn't usual, for Anderson.

"Talk on," I said.

"Got a letter." He gulped. "From Simon Wake."

"Impossible."

"Fact."

"How do you know it's from him?"

"It is signed 'Simon Wake,' " said Anderson, with his usual simplicity.

"It must be a trick!" Just then, I happened to catch old General Finsbury's eye. There was a certain reproving something in it that made me realize I'd been shouting. "You know as well as I do," I said, quietly, "That Wake—"

"Got stolen by the fairies?" said Anderson.

"Is in no position to send people letters," I said, firmly.

"Yes. I know. Only seems like he's done it anyway. And – Pendleton?"

"Yes?" My heart thudded uncomfortably in my chest.

"He wants our help. An investigation. We're to make our way to a railway station somewhere in Wessex, called Gorne Halt. He's waiting for us. Says it's urgent."

"No," I said.

* * *

It wasn't much of a station. On the platform, there was a single building, looking forlorn and as if it had in the distant past been partially burned and half-heartedly repaired, and a single bench, on which sat Simon Wake. I saw no evidence of civilization save for the train, which, I could not help noticing, was steaming rapidly away from us. A single dirt road wound away from the station through an autumn-denuded forest.

"So glad you chaps could come," said Wake, springing to his feet. Anderson went to shake his hand, but I remained aloof. I'd allowed myself to be persuaded into answering Wake's summons, but only in order to cut him. Looking at him now, I saw he was sadly changed. His black hair was too long, and terribly tangled. His suit, which had been a good one, bore signs of ill-use. His eyes were wild, as if with the memory of a thousand opium dreams. And he was fearfully thin. Pity warred with sternness in my bosom, and sternness won out. *He may be down on his luck*, an inner voice whispered, *but why has he brought you here?*

"Yes," I said, "here we are. And here are you. But my question is—who are you? A club acquaintance of ours, true, but with The Anacreon, that isn't in itself a sufficient social recommendation."

"Steady on, old chap," said Anderson, turning rather scarlet in the face. I hadn't told him my plans concerning the cutting of Simon Wake, because he'd have tried to talk me out of it. And I didn't let him stop me now.

"Allow me to continue, please. You've got to see this in its proper light. Who is Wake? A man we know from the club, who claims to be an occult investigator, and who has told us, over the years, some rather odd stories, all concerning his alleged investigations. And then, five years ago, he told us a very odd story indeed, implying that he'd—" No. I couldn't say it. It was too dashed silly.

"—been stolen by the fairies," said Anderson.

"Thank you. He then vanished—"

"From under our very noses. As the bell tolled out the hour of midnight," said Anderson.

"He vanished," I continued, "in a flashy, bumptious, ostentatiously impossible sort of way, and at the dramatically appropriate moment. I say he's a charlatan, and an intriguer, and that we ought to leave him to his silly games, and take the next train back to London."

"I like 'ostentatiously impossible'," murmured Wake. "It captures the essence of the situation. Impossible, certainly – yet it happened. Ostentatious is fair enough. I imagine that most miracles, when they occur in surroundings so mundane as The Anacreon, do seem ostentatious." He spoke with sleepy indifference, but I thought I heard a note of danger in his tone, in the slow way he let each word fall into silence.

"As do charlatans' tricks," I said, sneering.

"Are you finished?" asked Wake.

I kept on sneering, for lack of anything else to do.

"I could really use your help," said Wake. "I don't say that the world as we know it *will* end if you don't rally round, of course; that would be the statement of a charlatan. I say only that it *might* end. Still, the world is the world, and it isn't the sort of thing one ought to take chances with."

I wavered. It was nonsense, of course. It had to be nonsense. Worlds don't just end because chaps don't rally round. On the other hand, the fellow seemed in deadly earnest. "Very well. I'll come," I said at last. "Not that I believe a word of it."

"Good," said Wake. "Then let's hurry. We've got to get there by a quarter to twelve. That is when *it* happens." And he stepped off the platform, not onto the dirt road, but directly into the forest. Anderson hurried after him, and I followed more slowly, glancing behind me now and then to watch the little station, and the connection with civilization that it represented, vanish from sight as the forest thickened around us.

* * *

"And here we are." Wake consulted his pocket watch. "And with just over a minute to spare. Excellent."

The forest was thinner here, and a bright moon shone down through the bare branches of trees, giving a gloomy radiance to the scene. In all other respects, this bit of forest looked exactly the same as all the other bits of forest we'd seen lately.

"If you look up to the top of that hill," came Wake's high, precise drawl, "you will see the ruins of an ancient castle." I looked up. He was right. There was a hill, commencing about twenty-five yards in front of us and rising precipitately to a fair height; at its top, a dark bulk of crumbling masonry stood out against the sky.

"And if you look at the bottom of that hill," continued Wake, "you will not see the crude shelter where a poor devil of a poacher once spent part of a filthy night, until he was harried out by the gamekeeper and his dogs. But it was once there, nevertheless."

"Ah." I stared at the spot that did not contain a crude shelter.

"Probably, of course, nothing will come through tonight – but if it does, even if it's only a little one, we might be in danger," Wake said. "Still, I thought you ought to see it happen. No good asking you to—"

"My God!" cried Anderson, pointing up at the ruin.

I had seen it, too. It would have been hard to miss it. Or, rather, her.

She was a moving spiral of dark hair and pale garments, all surrounding a lovely and terrified face, and she glowed, as if the light of the moon had got tangled up inside her. She seemed to have emerged from the ancient castle, and for a few seconds she was perfectly still, as if waiting in terror to see if she'd dodged a pursuer. Then she gave a cry, and started to float down the hill, her dark hair and light draperies streaming behind her like the tail of a comet.

Quite like that, in fact. I wish the reader to understand this. She was just a head and some hair and a few tatters of clothing – not remotely human, not any longer.

I felt rather ill. I wished, on the whole, that I'd never seen her. Still, I had an apology to make, and I started to make it. "Wake," I said. "I'm sorry. I didn't think any of it was real."

"And here's the second one," said Wake. "Base of the hill. Straight ahead. Look."

Another living blob of moonlight and darkness was indeed apparent where he pointed. This one was like an untidy pile of fur, wires, traps, and the corpses of small animals, assembled into a sort of approximation of the human form. He, too, was in a hurry, and, though his run was not at all graceful, it was rapid. I soon lost track of him among the trees – and then saw him again, as he began to scramble up the slope of the hill. I noticed, with the part of my mind that was still thinking at all, that the distance between the two ghosts was closing, and closing fast.

"My god, they're going to..." I said – and then it happened. The two ghosts collided.

What happened next is quite vivid in my memory, and yet I am not sure I shall ever be able to describe it. A flash of darkness rolled over us and back like a breaking wave. But when the darkness rolled back, it seemed to leave a piece of itself behind. This piece of darkness moved, and appeared to stretch too many limbs, luxuriously, as if it stretched for pleasure alone. And then – did it step forward into a patch of moonlight, or did it actually coalesce? – I saw, and finally understood what I was seeing.

A horseman rode forth from the place where the two ghosts had collided. He held a head – his own, presumably, for he had no other – in one hand. The head was faintly luminous, and this was odd, for the rest of the horseman seemed to be made of darkness itself.

Someone screamed. I think it was probably me. At this, the horseman stopped, and seemed to listen. He lifted his severed head high into the air, turning it this way and that, as if by this means he could survey his surroundings. He must have spotted us, for quite suddenly he was moving, coming towards us at a fearful pace, shaking out a long and glittering whip as he came.

Wake swore. "Up this tree, quick! As you value your lives!" he cried, and indicated a nearby oak. Anderson was up in an instant, and in another instant he'd pulled me up after him. And then the horseman was at our tree, and his whip was after us. It seemed to grope along branches, like a blind but deadly serpent. My hope that the whip was immaterial died when I saw it coil around a branch and bring it crashing to the ground. We scrambled higher into the tree, and it was a desperate scramble, too, as branches that looked firm gave way, and as moss and smooth patches of bark shook off our grasping hands. Finally, we reached a place where the whip could not reach.

"Where's Wake?" asked Anderson.

"Did it get him?" I asked.

"Must've done," said Wake from the branch immediately above us. "Poor old Wake. Dead."

"Ass," I said, feeling almost drunk with relief.

"What is that thing?" asked Anderson, pointing down to where the horseman paced restlessly below us.

"A little one," said Wake.

"A little what?" asked Anderson.

"A little forgotten God, slipping back into our world. When you get a case of supernal co-location—"

"A case of what?" I asked, to save Anderson the bother.

Wake sighed. "Did you ever actually *listen* to the stories I used to tell you? Or were they just a sort of background for your own thoughts? Supernal co-location. Two ghosts, haunts, or other non-material entities, coincidentally occupying the same space at the same time. Like if your great-great grandfather's ghost always walks a particular hall in your home, but now your newly-deceased aunt, whom you probably poisoned, has started to walk there too. The two time-tables may well overlap. When your great-great grandfather steps through your aunt, that is supernal co-location. And supernal co-location can tear the Veil. The Veil being—"

"Yes. We know."

"Well, how am I to know what you do and don't pick up?" And Simon Wake paused to consult his pocket-watch. "We have some little time yet, I see. On with—"

"Some little time?" Anderson asked.

"Before what?" I asked.

"On," said Wake firmly, "with my instructive talk. Attend, please. Generally, this doesn't matter. Your great-great grandfather and your aunt probably cross paths but rarely, and they're probably going pretty slowly when they do co-locate. This is unlikely to really wrench at the Veil. If it affects it at all, the tear it leaves isn't big enough to let much through, and it is quickly healed. But just occasionally you get two ghosts – not that these are ghosts, but I haven't time to explain that – slamming together at speed, and that is bad. Especially if it looks like they are going to keep doing it. The ghostly lady is quite an old haunt, and the poacher is a new one – only died a few years ago, and just woke up – but both of them walk whenever there's a bright moon. And so, whenever the moon is bright, they will collide, and the tear in the Veil will grow at every collision. Already, the rent is big enough to let a Dullahan through."

"A what?" I asked.

"An ancient Celtic God. All doors," intoned Wake, "open before him. If he calls out your name, you shall die."

We looked down at the Dullahan. There he was, under our tree, looking up at us. That is, he was holding his severed head so that its death-dulled eyes seemed to look directly into mine. It was, to put it mildly, unnerving.

"Yes," continued Wake, sounding thoughtful. "He's a little one, as I said, but not so little, at that. He can kill, and does, which is a pretty big thing, when you think about it."

"And this Veil-rending business has happened before?" I asked, appalled at the fragility of what I had previously thought of as a fairly solid and certain world.

"Oh, certainly, certainly. That's how Pan got back in."

"Pan?"

"He's not so bad, really. Just don't look too poetic in any wild and desolate spots and you ought to be fine. But my point is—" he squinted at his pocket watch. "No. No time for that. Listen especially carefully now. Tomorrow you've got to go to the glade at the centre of this forest – it is cursed, by the way – and dig up the body of that poacher chap. It ought to be there, I'm nearly sure. The man who killed him – the gamekeeper – wanted the poacher damned, y'see."

"Does that work? Damning a fellow that way, I mean?" Anderson was fascinated.

"No, but no doubt the gamekeeper thought it would." Wake said. "No more questions. No time. Listen. Take the body to the churchyard. Church of the Holy Something Or Other. You'll find it. There's a vault – Gorne family vault – the Gornes own this land, and the poacher was an illegitimate Gorne himself. So was the gamekeeper. Part of the trouble between 'em, I think. Put the body in the vault and say something suitable over the corpse. That should lay the ghost of the poacher. And, of course, without him, there's no supernal co-location. Do all of this before a quarter to twelve tomorrow night. Meanwhile, I will be keeping him," Wake pointed to the Dullahan, "in play. You'll be perfectly safe, digging. And, of course, once you step into the graveyard, you'll be on consecrated ground, so you'll be safe there, too. Remember: if you don't do as I say, it might – just might – be the end of the world as we know it. Goodbye." As he'd been speaking, he'd also been inching out along his branch. Now, he dropped out of the tree. He dropped just over the Dullahan's head, and when he hit the earth and started to roll into the underbrush, he had the head, faintly glowing, cradled in his arms.

The Dullahan roared (though how he managed it, I don't know) and set off after Wake. We heard him crashing about in the brush for a time, and then the sounds died away in the distance.

It was only then that I became aware of another, much nearer, sound. Anderson was laughing.

"Stop it, man!" I hissed. "You're demented!"

"He won't catch him, you know. He won't catch him!" Anderson was examining his own time-piece in a handy bit of moonlight. "See?" He thrust the device at me. "After midnight. Our boy has gone. Poof! Off to—"

"—keep an urgent appointment?" I shrugged. "Perhaps."

Anderson looked at me queerly. "I don't know, I'm sure," he said, "but it seems to me that I am not the demented one up this particular oak."

"Speaking of the oak," I said, "do you think we need stay here?"

"With that Duller-Than thing about? I'm staying put."

"For the whole night?"

"At least."

"I can see a church steeple from here," I said. "Due east of us, I'd say. Not much over a mile as the crow flies."

Anderson gave an uninterested glance churchwards. "Probably the Church of the Great Whatsit Wake was telling us about."

"Probably." After a slight hesitation, I went on. "Where there are churches," I urged, "there are often inns."

"True."

"Inns have food. And beds."

"And drinks." Anderson, I saw, was convinced. He has, of course, no soul, no real sense of the true importance of things. However, at the moment, I didn't give a damn.

* * *

After what felt like hours (and it probably was – neither Anderson nor myself is an experienced woodsman, and heading towards a church steeple you can no longer see in a haunted wood lit only by moonlight would not, I fancy, be a simple task in any case), we stumbled out onto a road. We walked along this for a time, quite without thought, until mean habitations began to be visible ahead.

There was an inn in that nameless (to me, for I never inquired) village. The landlord didn't like being woken up at 3am to tend to the needs of two scruffy and improbable gentlemen, but we made him do it, in the end.

* * *

I must now pause to make a few remarks about digging up corpses in cursed glades. I feel that, having had this experience myself, I owe a debt to posterity – and especially to any unfortunates who find themselves saddled with a similar task. It is, indeed, to these last that my remarks are primarily addressed.

The first point I should like to stress is this: do your digging in daylight. Novices though Anderson and I undeniably were, we did see the advantages in daylight digging ourselves. We meant to be out of that forest again by sunset. Factors beyond our control prevented us from this less harrowing course. We hadn't any actual money, for one thing. The inn had finished us. One look at the proprietor of the local shovel emporium was sufficient to tell us that he did not sell shovels to grubby strangers on tick. We therefore had to steal our equipment. This was made more difficult because some wicked person had of late taken to stealing cows in the district, which meant that each farm we came to was a sort of armed camp, bristling with pitchforks and suspicion.

We eventually got our shovels from the very graveyard that would later in the evening have another part to play in our drama. Anderson got away with the shovels, leaving me to deal as I thought best with the Vicar, who obviously thought I was a Gentleman Brought Low By Drink, and who took me in to tea and blasted me with information concerning the moral habits, hygiene, life expectancy, etc., of The Drinking Man. I did get him onto the topic of Cursed Glades – The Location Thereof, which was something saved out of the wreck, but by the time I left him, the sun was down and the world was decidedly given over to shadows and darkness.

The next point I should like to bring to the attention of anyone considering a go at this sort of thing himself is that it might be as well to know – in general terms, at least – the nature of the curse upon his selected glade. Anderson and I did not know (I tried to get it out of the Vicar, but he seemed to think that telling me would send me screaming for The Bottle – and I cannot say that he was wrong there), and so we were in for some nasty shocks over the course of our labours. It is not pleasant, turning to make a remark to one's friend, to find that the Something you've sensed behind you is not your friend, but an utter stranger, grinning horribly, indicating the various Death-Wounds upon his person, and gabbling at you in (presumably) Anglo-Saxon. It is especially horrid – but I have said, I think, sufficient on this subject to illustrate my thesis. Gentlemen (and ladies of the bold, modern sort), when you go for an evening's digging in your local cursed glade, Know Your Curse!

A final point I would urge upon the interested amateur is that he (or she) have system and method in his digging. Divide the grove up into sensible segments and do the thing methodically. Don't go about it in a casual and slap-dash style – as Anderson and I did. Think the thing out, and don't be hours about it.

Oh, and bring a sack. If the corpse you're digging for has been dead for some considerable time, what you'll primarily be getting is bones. Since we had no sack about us, we used my coat. It was, prior to this experience, a very fine coat indeed, and fit me well (not an easy matter, with my figure) – but I was never able to feel the same way about it afterwards. It, too, seems changed by its trying ordeal, and sags, as if at the memory of the Doleful Remnant it once contained.

* * *

"Thank God," I said piously. It was twenty to twelve, and we'd been working along the woods by the road to the church for the last hour (for if you don't think being observed along a public highway carrying an impromptu sack full of bones would make for an embarrassing legal situation, I envy your innocence). Finally, we were at the churchyard gate. Only the empty road stood between us and it. I took a step forward – and froze.

For I heard, ringing out sharp in the chill night air, the sound of a horse at a gallop, coming rapidly down the road towards us. Anderson and I had just got back into cover when the rider came thundering into view. And the rider had no head. He hurtled past us without pause, and we heard the sound of his wild ride dying away in the distance.

I leaned up against a tree and swore softly; Anderson, presumably, used some similarly primitive form of nerve-restorative. But we dared not tarry. Time was pressing, and I was aware of a strange electricity in the air, a sort of heavy fated feeling about the night that told me that, if we didn't prevent the supernal co-location, something yet more terrible would slip in to this world through the resulting tear in the Veil.

My foot was on the road when the hooves sounded again – and coming from the same direction as before. We dove back into the concealing shadows of the wood, and watched as the thing went by with a rush so swift it seemed to catch at one's breath as it passed.

"He's circling," I whispered.

"Wake said he'd keep him in play," said Anderson.

"Well, I wish they'd go play somewhere else." But even as I spoke, I was aware of a great sense of relief. It was oddly comforting, knowing that Wake was in the vicinity. "Next time he passes," I said, "we've got to make a dead sprint for the gate, just after he goes by."

"He'll see us," said Anderson. "Or whatever it is he does. No head, of course, so makes it awkward, seeing."

"But Wake said that we'd be quite safe once we were in the cemetery. We'll just have to chance it."

"Right." Anderson adjusted the makeshift (read: bespoke, Savile Row) sack on his shoulder, and assumed a ready position.

"If we get separated," I whispered, "it is the biggest, fanciest, tallest mausoleum in the churchyard. All over marble. Can't miss it."

Anderson nodded. The Dullahan thundered past us with his customary breath-taking speed. An instant later, we ran across the road, and I know I hadn't much breath left, myself, by the time we were safely within the cemetery, nestled securely among all those nice graves. I turned to look, hoping to enjoy the spectacle of the Dullahan, baffled and furious, raging on the other side of the gate. Instead, I saw him clear the thing in a really fine jump, to land, his horse snorting fire, a couple of yards from where I stood.

The Dullahan's whip snaked out and seized me about the ankles, and I was sent sprawling to the ground. "Go!" I cried to Anderson. It was, perhaps, the most heroic thing I'd ever done. I wanted to cry, "Save me! Bugger the world!" – but I did not. It is a shame, therefore, that I doubt anyone heard me. Anderson was already sprinting for the tomb. The hot breath of the Dullahan's horse was scorching my face. I felt terribly alone. I closed my eyes and tried to pray. It was, quite obviously, The End.

"Hoy! Dullahan! Head this way," shouted Simon Wake.

The whip ceased to grip me by the ankles. I felt cool night air on my face. I opened my eyes and sat up. There was friend Dullahan, pounding off down the path towards the dim bulk of the church. And upon the church porch I could just see Wake, holding the Dullahan's head high in air.

I didn't see Wake for long, however. An instant of stillness, with Wake and the head posed as for a portrait upon the church porch – then Wake had

Occult Detective Magazine #6

vaulted the railing and was in among the graves, moving at a dead sprint. The Dullahan, roaring with rage, followed him. I rose slowly to my feet, watching in fascinated horror what I took to be the final moments of Simon Wake. I mean, the fellow hadn't a chance. I saw Wake take cover behind a gravestone, and saw the gravestone shatter all to flinders a second later, at the impact of the creature's dreadful whip. Granted, Wake had somehow contrived to no longer be behind that particular stone, but that, I felt, was incidental.

"It's locked!" Anderson cried. "The bally tomb's locked. I can't—"

I ran over to see what I could do. I shook the door. Yes, it was locked. Looking up, I perceived that there was an opening above the door – a sort of transom light, I suppose – but it was too narrow to accept Anderson's broad shoulders or my somewhat rotund middle.

"How about pitching the bones in through there?" I said, pointing.

"Won't do. No ghost would be satisfied by that," Anderson opined. I nodded. He was right.

"WAKE!" I bellowed. "The tomb's locked!"

"All doors open before him," Wake shouted. "Remember?" And then Wake came tearing towards us, still clutching the Dullahan's faintly luminous head in his hands. Behind Wake, and gaining rapidly, came the Dullahan.

"Move!" cried Wake.

Anderson and I got out of the way.

Wake pitched the Dullahan's head into the tomb through the transom light. He didn't leave off running to aim, either. He went one way, and the head went the other. It was really quite pretty to watch. Anderson muttered something about getting Wake on his rugger team. I thought this overly optimistic, but said nothing.

The Dullahan charged the door of the tomb – which flew open to receive him. Horse and rider disappeared into the darkness. Anderson and I waited. I felt each second ticking by, felt the air thicken with terrible expectancy, felt, in fact, the coming of a quarter to twelve.

Finally, the Dullahan emerged. He seemed in no hurry to be gone, however. He just stood there, holding his head aloft, upon the porch of the Gorne family vault. He looked like a ghastly parody of the memorial sculptures that surrounded us on all sides. He was posed heroically, I mean, and quite still enough for statuary. But the eyes within his head were not still – they were moving, scanning the terrain, seeking the one he would destroy.

Wake popped his head round a tombstone and stuck his tongue out. The Dullahan was after him in an instant. The doors of the Gorne family vault gaped open and unguarded.

Anderson and I dashed inside and looked round. There were shelves with corpses on them, some more disgusting than others. Anderson cleared a shelf with a single, mighty sweep of his arm. We then emptied our sack (and by "sack," I mean... but enough! One must endure sartorial bereavement with fortitude) onto this shelf and looked at each other.

"Say something suitable," I said. "Any ideas about what that would be?"

"We're sorry you're dead?" Anderson hazarded. Nothing happened.

"Rest in peace," I intoned. Wake screamed somewhere in the graveyard.

"Chap's a poacher, of course. Simple sort of fellow, I expect, without much education," said Anderson, obviously thinking almost unbearably hard.

"Yes, I suppose."

"Latin ought to dazzle him, then. Anything solemn-sounding."

We heard running feet along the path outside. I turned, to see Wake run past the door. Then the dreadful whip must have arrested his flight, for he passed again an instant later, only now he was on the ground and struggling feebly as some force pulled him towards his doom. His eyes met mine for an instant, and there was a desperate entreaty in them. Then he was gone, into the dark. I heard scuffling sounds, and swearing, and, I think, a certain amount of unmanly whimpering and sobbing.

There was a sickeningly final-sounding thud. My brain was extinguished, drowned in a grief keener than I would have thought possible, for the death of a chap like Wake.

Then I heard the sound of running feet once more. Hope surged within my bosom. I could think again.

"In vino veritas," I said, looking pious.

"Cave canem," said Anderson, crossing himself.

"Arma virumque cano," I said, bowing my head. "Facilis descensus Averno," I continued. "Veni Vidi Vici."

There were, of course, other things one could say in Latin. I knew I'd gotten off some good bits myself, on my more intellectually powerful days. But at the moment, that was all the Latin I had. I looked at Anderson – and saw that something was happening in his usually sleeping mind. His eyes were shining. He began to intone. Most of it was muttering, but there were fancy twiddly bits chucked in here and there.

"In nomine patri... mutter mutter... filius est unicorn... pater noster hodie hodie hodie... miserable oculos and nos converte... something something... et in hora mortis nostrae." Anderson took a deep breath. "Amen."

It worked. That was obvious at once. There was a flash of light, and a fizzling sound, and an odd smell. A horse screamed from the graveyard – and the scream was cut off in the middle.

"I think," I said finally, "that it is now safe to go outside again."

We went outside again. The cemetery was bathed in bright moonlight. It was a still, tranquil scene. I liked the look of the place, now there were no ancient Celtic gods mucking it up.

* * *

We found Wake lying in a crumpled heap at the foot of a rather moth-eaten weeping angel.

"Is he dead?" Asked Anderson.

"Yes," said Wake.

Anderson kicked him, but quite gently. "Where'd the Duller-Than go?" He asked.

Wake looked as if he'd rather defer explanations, but we weren't having it. "The Dullahan," Wake said, "was only able to get in here at all when you chaps brought an unshriven, murdered corpse into the cemetery. This de-sanctified the place – well, it would, wouldn't it? – and he could enter. When you re-sanctified the place, he was instantly banished. All clear? No more questions?"

We said we had several further questions.

"I think my leg is broken," said Wake.

We did not care, and said so.

The church bells chimed midnight. I was looking at Anderson's face as the ruckus began, and I kept on looking at it, because it suddenly had upon it a very curious expression. He was staring hard at Wake, and, it was evident, trying not to blink. His eyes, as the chimes rolled out in the chill midnight air, began to fill with tears. Then, reluctantly, the lids flickered closed – and snapped open again at once.

"Damn it!" Anderson cried. "I wanted to see it happen."

"See what happen?" I asked.

"See Wake go pop, of course. But he must've done it while I was blinking."

I looked down. At my feet was a Wake-shaped depression in the grass. But Simon Wake was gone.

KOMOLAFE

TADE THOMPSON

I.

Wake up, Komolafe.
The young men have come for you.
They drag you to the palace.

The king speaks in a whisper,
The crier repeats his words loud.
Explain. Explain!
Your dead friend. Your dead friend!

Then you notice the palace floor.
The remains.
Bloody.
Arowolo was your friend. Now he is a bloody corpse.

You say, he was alive when I last saw him.
As an afterthought you add, Your Highness.

Now you are in jail, Komolafe.
Nobody believes you.
You have been here before,
One score and two years ago.

The last time you saw Arowolo
He enters a hut
As a prelude
To entering a woman.

II.

You and Arowolo, hunters both.
Your shotguns find prey for your sacks.
The forest is full of game.

At dusk you make a fire.
You, Komolafe and Arowolo share roast bush meat.
You talk, you share tales.
Tales of brave men and women of old.
Forest spirits, thunder deities, trickster gods.
Eshu. Oranmiyan.

Arowolo only knows stories of sex.
Men with giant members,
Women of infinite appetite.
Lies, not stories.
There is a difference.

Komolafe,
Belly full, skin warmed by fire,
You fall asleep.
Even mosquitoes stay away.

In your dream,
A woman enters the camp,
Warms herself at the fire
At the edge of the clearing,
A hut that was not there before
Her hut.

She fills your eyes
With her slender neck,
Her wide hips,
Her bosom,
Her lithe walk,
Her lustiness.

She unfolds herself,
And billows towards Arowolo.
He rises to her,
And she leads him to the hut by the hand.

Just as he disappears into the dark maw,
Arowolo looks back at you, Komolafe.

On his face there is no lust.
Instead, fear, terror,
Sweat glistening on his forehead.

You, Komolafe, cannot move to help.
You are stuck to the spot.
A log spits in the fire,
But otherwise all is still.

In the morning,
The fire is out, Arowolo is gone,
Along with his rifle, his gunpowder gourd,
And his catch.

The sun is high in the sky
When you return.
The village is awake.
A child chases a chicken across the square.

Two days after this
You, Komolafe, are in the
King's prison.
Awaiting the King's justice.

III.

After twenty-one days,
You receive a sentence.
A trial by ordeal,
To determine innocence or guilt.

You, Komolafe, despise the king. You always have.
You know.
You know his claim to the throne is spurious.
You know this.
The knowledge will not save you.

The ordeal is a distraction for the village,
An entertainment,

Justice as diversion, as amusement.
Recreational justice.

If you could, Komolafe, you would pray.
You would.
But the gods have never been good
To your family.
There is no kin to pray for you,
Nor any other to mourn should you die in
The ordeal.
You walk alone.

IV.

A crowd.
Roiling, boiling, singing.
The king's executioner,
With his mighty right hand,
He stands ready.
One hundred lashes.
If you cry out, you are guilty, Komolafe.
An innocent man feels no pain.

The crowd counts along,
With the executioner.
He drags out the space between strokes,
Allowing the crescendo of pain
To rise and fall,
Before delivering the next blow.
At his side, a sword.
If you cry out, Komolafe,
He will swap the rod for the blade,
And take your head
In one swoop of his sinewy arm.

You last long, Komolafe.
The pain is red and lingers
Like pepper on the tongue after food.
You bite your inner cheeks,

And clamp your mouth shut so tight
Your front tooth cracks.
You swallow the shard,
Afraid that if you open your mouth,
A scream will sneak out,
And tickle the king's ears.

You are only a man, Komolafe.
You are not stone.
A whimper on stroke thirty-two,
The difference between life and death.

The executioner drops the cane
And unsheathes the sword.
You kneel,
Place your head on the block.
You wait, Komolafe.

The slice does not come.
Silence now.
The crowd parts for a woman.
This woman of your dreams,
She who went with Arowolo.
Even her.

Come, she says.
Your bonds are loosed,
Your tormentors are paralysed.
You go, you follow.
Perhaps she will kill you
Like she did Arowolo.
Perhaps you and she,
Will inhabit the dreams of others, Komolafe.
Perhaps we will see you
In our dreams.

O d'oju ala.

THE WAY OF ALL FLESH

MATTHEW WILLIS

Surely the dead could wait for the noonday sun to soften the frost? Milosova doubted they could have broken out of frozen-solid earth to walk abroad and prey on the living anyway. But none of this made sense. If you were worried about them leaving their graves, why dig them up? The sound of mattocks hacking at frozen earth drove spikes into her ears. She pressed the heels of her hands harder against her head.

It was no good. The dreadful, metallic scraping forced its way past her hands and buzzed right through to her teeth. She shrugged uselessly at the hand clamped around her arm. Rastko and Dušan swung their mattocks into Lazar's grave again, dragging at soil which eventually started to come out in lumps. The sandy, stone-strewn earth was still bound into a solid, icy mass.

The crunch of the tools echoed off the mountains. The grave was scraped into the grassland above the village, at the foothills of the range of peaks which separated the settlement from the nearest towns. It was on the very edge of the parish boundaries. A beautiful place to be alive, a terrible place to be dead. A place for suicides and sinners, and adulterers. For her lover.

She could see the tips of Lazar's fingers poking through a disturbed patch of earth, just by the spot the men were digging. She saw the way the other villagers stared. As if the frost-gnawed flesh would start to move and claw further out of the grave.

Fools. She tried to look away, but the gripping hand jerked and forced her to regard the grave.

"For heaven's sake, I'm not going to run away!" she whispered.

"This is your doing," her mother said. "You need to see what you've done. You and that man. Four people are dead!"

"Five."

Milosova's mother spat. "Thanks to you we could *all* die. Or worse."

Milosova snorted but said no more. She noticed Jelena standing across the grave from her and looked away, feeling the widow's eyes on her like an itch.

The soil began to crack, then a scrap of shroud was visible. A choked-off gasp went up from the assembled villagers. The two men started levering chunks of gravelly earth out of the grave. The dirt peeled away from the cloth with a sound like a drunk vomiting. Dušan gulped, and pulled back the ice-stiff cloth. The huddle around the graveside shuffled forwards. Another gasp punctuated the air.

Milosova forced herself to look. It was Lazar, of course. Hardly decomposed. In fact, his flesh had a sort of sheen to it and a plumpness that had not been present in life. One arm remained raised in a horrible parody of a gesture, where it had been pushed, or dragged up through the earth.

"Look at his nose!" someone cried. Milosova bent forward. The outer layer seemed to be peeling away, and smooth, yellowish skin could be seen beneath. A sharp tang flooded her mouth. She gulped it down.

"Undead!" a man muttered. Someone else muttered another word, and was quickly hushed by his neighbours.

"Check his nails!" The priest insisted. Dušan leant over.

"They are long!" the man gasped. The crowd began to hiss and mutter.

"Oh, the wretch!" said the priest when the din had died down, taking a closer look. "Such wild and filthy signs."

What did he mean? A snigger behind her was cut short by the priest's glare, and it was only then that Milosova saw the bulge in her former lover's breeches. Saints! Did that happen when a man died?

"And his mouth?" the priest demanded, crossing himself.

"Full of blood!"

Milosova was suddenly barraged with shouts and curses, like stepping outside into an autumn gale. A clod of earth hit her. Her mother was yelling too – she could make out the woman's reedy tone, but none of the words came through the roar.

"Cover the creature!" bellowed the priest. The crowd quieted.

"But you must exorcise it Father!" Rastko said. "Protect us!"

The priest turned white, then a shade of green. He shook his head. "This is beyond my... I have not the..."

Milosova felt everyone's anger slipping from her and onto the priest. Coward! He'd whipped them all up and was now too scared to do his job.

"The demon is powerful. The sin that infected him was great," he added, staring at Milosova for a moment. "It is beyond a single priest. If the exorcism was performed without the necessary strength, it could provoke the... creature."

The villagers broke into muttering again, and Milosova felt their fear as a tangible mass.

Branković raised his arms. "We must summon a priest from Belgrade to assist with the exorcism!" Everyone turned back toward him. "There is a man. One who has battled such evils before!"

No one wanted to mention the word which, they believed, might cause a dead man to jump out of his grave and start drinking the blood of maidens. Milosova rolled her eyes. They weren't all stupid, were they? How had a whole village been swept up like this?

"And what about the devil's whore?" Dušan pointed at her, as if there could be any other.

Branković gazed at her. Milosova did not like what she read in that look. "I will go to her this evening, and perform a cleansing rite," he declared.

"How come you can exorcise her and not Lazar?" Rastko asked.

The priest ground his teeth. "I intend merely to keep the beast from doing further harm until Father Solarić arrives."

That might have settled it, but whoever it was behind her who had laughed earlier—probably that tyke Alina – murmured "Looks like Milosova's cast her spell on another. She doesn't waste any time!"

The priest's face reddened. "Enough!" he cried. "The vampire and his *strumpet* will be dealt with. Return to your homes and pray for our salvation." He made it clear the meeting was over by turning and stomping in the direction of the settlement without another word. The villagers began to follow, some extravagantly making the sign of the cross at Milosova, leaving the workmen to cover the grave again. Milosova's mother refused to release her grip all the way back to the house.

Without a word, they began to prepare a meal. Whenever Milosova disappointed her mother, the older woman could refrain from speaking to her for days, which was not to say they didn't need to work together. Milosova thought that would be the end of her troubles, unless Branković gathered enough nerve to drop by and ogle her while mumbling bad Latin. Before the pot had been long on the fire though, the sound of voices began to carry up the street.

Her stomach contracted. She gripped the back of a chair with a sudden swirl of dizziness. They were coming for her. It would just be for questioning by the priest... Wouldn't it? Oh God, what if some of them had decided to take matters into their own hands? "Mother?" she squeaked.

Her mother folded her arms and narrowed her eyes.

They were right outside now. A fist thudded on the door. Milosova's heart leapt in her ribcage. No!

"Milosova Vojinović!" It was the priest. Oh thank God...

She stepped up to the door, willing her feet to make each pace, and opened it.

The priest stood before her, holding his crucifix at her, at arm's length. There was a crowd at his back. "You are to come with us," he said. Before she could react, arms lunged to grab her, dragging her into the street, staggering along with the racing mob. *Saints preserve me!*

"Where are you taking me?" Milosova tried to say but her voice was subsumed in the shouts of the mob and the thumping of blood in her ears. Where? Oh God, the square! She was going to be burned!

But the priest steered away from the centre of the square towards the Cage – a tiny, stone cell standing alone at the back of the square, mostly used to hold drunkards and poachers before a flogging. Hope flared for a moment. No burning! Then the voice of reason overrode it – this just meant she would be dealt with in the morning. The rough hands bundled her in and she barked her hands on the wall. The door slammed shut and she was immersed in black.

She had never seen the inside of the cell, but it was far smaller than she had imagined. The walls must be three feet thick and there was barely room to sit on the floor, let alone lay down.

After the blind terror had subsided a little there was nothing to occupy her but thoughts of the future. She veered between howling despair and incandescent fury. What had she ever done to those bigots and frumps? She'd started to notice the looks on the faces of more than one farmer who would happily have taken Lazar's place in her affections, but she hadn't asked for them to leer at her. Hadn't done anything to encourage it.

Oh God, Lazar! He'd gone, and she hadn't even had time to feel it. Hadn't been able to say goodbye. She'd never see that lopsided smile again, hear the way only he said her name. Even now, after a while she'd find herself in a daydream that he'd be trying to find a way to get her out, just like he'd found ways to have her mother and Jelena distracted so the two of them could snatch a moment together, just like it was all a game... Unless he really was...? No, ridiculous. He was gone. Milosova, in fear of her own life, wept for Lazar for the first time in that cell.

Letting her grief for Lazar wash through her was at least some help in blocking the future out. The future. The only thing left for her outside this cell, and short though it would be, it would be filled with humiliation, terror, pain. Oh Christ Above, how would she confront burning? How badly would it hurt? How long before...? In the black of the cell, she saw the villagers rippling before her eyes, approaching, eyes and torches flamed. Lazar stepped between her and the pack. His gaze was terrible – it seemed to consume her in fire from within. She screamed as her clothes began to flare, but the blaze was like ice.

She awoke to the sound of the door being unbolted. Light burst into the cell and for a moment she was back in the dream, engulfed, burning and freezing.

"Get up." It was Branković. As her eyes adjusted to the light she saw his robes silhouetted. Another, identical shape stood just behind him.

She struggled, creaking to her feet. Muscles groaned in protest.

"Can someone help her?" said a voice behind the priest. Branković growled but seemed to assent. Arms crept under hers, less unkindly this time, and she felt herself borne up. After a few moments, she realised she was being carried into the inn. The dark of the interior was a blessing. She was placed on a bench in front of a table.

"She must have food and water," said the stranger, leaning closer. "I am Father Solarić. You are Milosova Vojinović?"

She looked down, nodded.

"I have come to investigate the… matter," said Solarić. She had forgotten… the priest from Belgrade. She had expected another Branković. Not this. His voice was warm. Urbane, even. She forced herself to raise her gaze from the floor. He was young! In his mid-twenties, perhaps. Not like any priest she had seen before. From his voice she had been expecting an old man. He wore a frown. He removed a pair of tinted eye-glasses to reveal unexpectedly gentle eyes. "Are you hurt?"

"No," she said, her voice a thin scratch.

"The beast must be exorcised," said Branković, somewhere back in the room. "As must his harlot."

"I will establish the facts and proceed accordingly," said Solarić, an edge to his voice that had not been there when he had been speaking to Milosova.

Branković snarled, but said no more. A bowl of soup and a cup of water was placed before her. She ate as much as she could manage. The soup's warmth bloomed in her stomach and she began to feel restored.

Solarić conversed with Branković while she ate, and she was grateful for the attention to be elsewhere, but they could be deciding her future. She pretended to concentrate on eating, but listened.

"The vampire is depraved and filled with desires of the flesh," Branković muttered. "We uncovered the thing, and it was fresh as when it was buried. Its mouth was full of blood, so recently had it supped on the living, and its… parts… betrayed lustful compulsions."

"How do you believe this revenant to have been created?"

"From sin of course!" Branković cried, before lowering his voice. "His adultery with this whore brought forth a demon in him which cannot sleep."

"And there have been more deaths?"

"Yes, many! Four."

"And what were the circumstances?"

"What do you mean?"

"Were they sick? Did they die suddenly?"

"A short illness. Each became unable to breathe and choked."

"And it was the same with this Lazar?"

"The vampire, yes."

"You say he was a revenant himself, yet he died in the manner of a victim?"

"Yes! Exactly!"

"Hmm."

"My own servant girl is among the dead," Branković said, as though proud of the fact. "When I came to give her the last rites she was terrified. Her family said she had been crying for me, raving about a creature that had visited her and pressed himself upon her in the night. You can ask them."

"She identified the man Lazar?"

"Of course it was him!" Branković snapped.

"Hmmm."

Milosova hunched over her soup, even though she had long finished with it. She felt the stare of the two men on her back. Poor Stana, working for that foul priest – the stories she told! – and to die so young...

"I wish to speak to the young lady alone, please Father."

"This strumpet?!" Branković snapped. "Why should we listen to anything that irredeemable female has to say? She surely harbours a demon herself."

"I wish to, and I have authority here, Father." That edge again. "Would you kindly see to the preparations for the hearing?"

Hearing? No! With a huff, Branković departed. The city priest placed a chair at her table across from her.

"Am I to be tried as a witch?" Milosova asked. She tried to keep her voice steady but it betrayed her.

"No," said Solarić, not unkindly. "Will you tell me what happened?"

She looked at him, narrowing her eyes. Did he want a confession?

"Lazar got a cough. It got really bad, and he started bringing up blood. Then he died. Then Vučica, Petar, Rade, and Stana."

"And is it true what Father Branković said? That you had relations with the man Lazar?"

She looked at her feet. He could find that out from anyone. Yes! she wanted to shout, yes! He was everything to me! The marriage to that shrew Jelena meant nothing, and it was me he loved, me, and what kind of stupid world is it where a man has to be shackled to a woman he didn't love! She'd do anything, kill herself, kill the whole village just to see him one more time!... She exhaled. Holy Christ. Could it be true that their sin had... unearthly power? Perhaps. And what of it?

"Yes, Father," she said. "I thought he would marry me."

He said he would leave Jelena. She knew he would, she knew. It roared in her chest and threatened to burst her open. And those villagers treating Jelena like the bereaved widow, as if she cared Lazar were dead, as if Milosova had no right to feel anything.

The priest even smiled at that. She looked at him, and her expression must have betrayed her, for his smile faded.

"It was a sin, of course, but it does not make you a witch. Necessarily. Father Branković believes the man Lazar rose from the dead and killed the others. And you?"

Milosova shrugged. "I believe he was a man, and he died of a sickness. The others, too." She stopped herself. Saints, she was perilously close to blasphemy. "I am just a girl," she stammered, "I do not know about demons and unholy creatures."

Solarić folded his arms. "Yet Father Branković is convinced a vampire is preying on the villagers. Are you not frightened?"

She looked at the floor. "I am, Father." That was true.

"Of the vampire?"

She narrowed her eyes. What was he getting at? Did he want her to trap herself? If she admitted she had no fear, would the priest consider she was calling Branković a liar? Or that she had no fear of the 'vampire' because she was a witch and the creature her lover?

She could say she was frightened of Lazar, but that would be lying to a priest.

"I don't know," she mumbled. She heard Solarić make a quiet noise in his throat. One of confirmation and disappointment. For some reason, it angered her. She looked up and met his gaze. "Do *you* believe these things are real, Father? You're supposed to be some kind of demon hunter, and yet..."

"And yet what?"

"It does not seem that you are convinced by what Father Branković tells you."

Solarić cocked his head, returning her gaze. "You think what he says is not true."

"I didn't say that. Father..."

"Yes?"

She leaned forwards. She had to ask. It was dangerous. It was heresy, for if demons were not real then the devil was not real and if the devil was not real, maybe God was not real. But what did she have to lose? "Do you actually believe in vampires?"

Solarić raised an eyebrow. He almost seemed amused as he leaned forward. "Let me tell you this – my duties have taken me to many places. Vienna. Budapest. Even Paris. In those places there are many who do not believe in vampires. Not all are blasphemers."

"But you have seen them? Exorcised them? How do you know so much about these things anyway?"

"Experience." The priest sat for a moment, calculation on his face. Then he stood, replacing his spectacles. They made him look very modern, Milosova thought, though she supposed he had weak eyes. "Come with me."

"Where?"

"I have to investigate, as I said. And you are in my custody. The choice is to come with me or go back to that rabbit hutch."

Milosova stood so quickly that white fuzz bloomed in her vision and the room toppled without moving.

"Careful," Solarić said, grabbing her arm, but his grip was gentle and he merely steadied her before letting go.

"It's a little late to be careful," she replied, and smiled to hear the priest laugh.

They went to each house, Solarić explaining kindly but firmly that Milosova was in his custody – and under his protection – listening to everyone's recollections. They accepted it, even those who made signs to ward off evil at her when the priest's back was turned.

When they came to Lazar's house – Jelena's house, Milosova corrected herself – she hoped Solarić would instruct her to wait outside. He did not. Jelena glared at her, and recited a detailed description of the acts of the vampire, suspiciously close to Branković's earlier words, repeating it several times in slightly different order like lines from a Mystery Play she was rehearsing.

"It was sin. Sin of the flesh. My poor Lazar was tempted into it," she said during the third cycle, casting an icy glare at Milosova, "and it corrupted his soul and turned him into a... a..." She sobbed unconvincingly. "Foul beast who said terrible things."

What things?! Milosova wanted to shout, but Solarić interjected.

"What happened next?"

"The vampire chokes his victims, as is well known," Jelena replied, as if she had not heard the question. "He also bites them and drinks their blood in his frenzy. He rises from his grave like mist in the night and takes the form of a man. The women he visits, he... violates. All he despoils die or become like him. Then he returns to his grave as mist and cannot be caught."

Solarić tapped his lips with a forefinger. "Pardon me Madam, would you repeat that? Did you see your former... your husband rising from his grave as... mist?"

Jelena looked puzzled. "You have seen vampires before, you know of their ways, yes?"

"I have indeed performed many exorcisms in cases such as this. So he rose from the earth like..."

"Mist."

"Yes. Like mist. But earlier you told me his arm had pushed through the ground, you say. As it had dug its way out?"

"Yes, father, we all saw it."

"Hmm."

When they returned to the inn, Solarić paced in silence for some minutes. Milosova had begun to wonder if he had forgotten she was there when he spoke.

"What do you think, Miss Vojinović? Of what we heard."

She sighed. "Everyone told a different story. Except when they told exactly the same story."

"Meaning?"

She could trust him, couldn't she? He seemed a decent man, not a bit like that bigot Branković. She bit her lip for a moment. "It was as though they had been told what to say."

Solarić said nothing in response to that, but did not appear to be angered. "What would you say explained what we heard today? For example, how Lazar's hand had come out of the earth?"

"Animals. Jackals will dig at a body in the ground. There's only a little topsoil. He wasn't deep."

"Some said animals digging for the corpse are proof that the body is that of a revenant."

Milosova snorted, despite herself. "Then we're all *revenants*."

Solarić smiled a thin, humourless smile. "No. Not all. The body had hardly decomposed, it is said, and did not smell foul."

She shrugged. "It's winter. It's been cold, colder than normal."

"And his fingernails continued to grow."

She almost laughed. "Lazar never cut his nails."

"His mouth full of blood?"

"He had been coughing it up. I think when he..." The moment washed back. Hearing he was dying.... rushing to the house, despite the scandal it would bring. She blinked back tears. "When he died, I think he choked on his own blood."

"Hmmm," said Solarić. "Do you believe sin can corrupt a man and cause him to walk the Earth after death?"

She sighed again. "I don't know what to believe. I saw nothing that wouldn't have happened with a sickness. Anyway, if vampires can rise from the earth like mist, why should they need to dig their way out?"

Solarić smiled infuriatingly to himself. "Quite."

... Unless the sun came up before mist – Lazar was fully back in his grave... She shook her head. Stupid thought. Don't be ridiculous Milosova. She looked Solarić in the eye, pushing the thought away and deciding to face what was coming. "What will become of me, Father?"

The priest pondered for a moment. "There will be a hearing. You must confess your sins – of the flesh, of course, there will be no accusation of witchcraft. This is the 19th century after all, not the dark ages, though others here may not realise it. No, you will be required to undertake a task for penance. It will be difficult and unpleasant. But it is important that the villagers and Branković can be satisfied that there will be no more problems with revenants. There is a ritual for such cases as this. It must be performed exactly, in each step, to prevent a vampire from rising."

"A ritual? Does it work?"

"In previous cases there is evidence it has dealt with the problem. Do you understand?" She nodded, wiping her nose with the back of her hand. It was ingenious, really. The village had gone into a frenzy of superstition with virtually no provocation. They could be persuaded out of it just as easily. A bit of theatre for the rustics. She could go along with that. And perhaps, in her way, say goodbye to Lazar...

Anyway, anything was preferable to another night in the Cage and what might come after.

After hours of humiliating confession before the village, she found herself back by Lazar's grave again as Rastko and Dušan dug at the earth, and Jelena performed the role of keening widow again. Milosova smiled to herself. It was not just Solarić who could turn to theatre to get what he wanted.

The body looked much as it had before except that more of the dry, outer skin had peeled away to reveal the strange, ruddy flesh beneath. Oh Lazar... it was as though he was only asleep and might wake at any moment.

"The sinner shall perform the ritual acts, all of which must be performed to prevent the revenant from rising," intoned Solarić, inscrutable behind the coloured glasses though Milosova thought she could detect a subtle note of amusement in his words. She couldn't help but admire the man. He had them in the palm of his hand. She scrambled into the shallow pit, with the corpse of her lover, catching the unctuous smile on Branković's face as she did so.

"Turn the thing face-down," said Solarić. She heaved at his arm – the arm that had pulled her so tight to him – and eventually managed to manoeuvre the corpse onto its front.

"Now the stones."

Rastko pushed two heavy rocks into the grave, and she shuffled them, a little at a time, onto Lazar's back. Soon she was streaming with sweat despite the freezing air.

"The stakes!"

Two sharpened pieces of hawthorn were tossed down to her. She lowered herself to her knees, and tugged Lazar's hand – the hand that had caressed her – flat in front of her. She put her whole weight onto the stake, and it slid softly into the dead man's flesh. She gagged, and quickly pushed the second stake through his other hand in the same manner.

"And the coin."

Solarić had given her a silver coin, bearing a cross. She took out a gleaming disc from the bag tied about her waist, and pulling Lazar's head up by his hair – the hair she had run her fingers through – placed the penny beneath his face. Soon this thing would end, one way or another.

"It is done. Cover the thing up again."

She scrambled out of the grave even as men hastily shovelled the earth which pattered onto Lazar's back. Milosova's mother grabbed her arm, but she turned defiantly to Solarić before she could be dragged away. "We would be honoured if you would eat with us this evening, Father," she said, so her mother could not now possibly refuse.

As the sun set on the hateful day, Milosova and her mother began to prepare the meal – in silence but together, as if Milosova had done nothing worse than break a milk churn. Solarić sat at their tiny table, fingers steepled.

The pot had not long been on the fire when a sudden chill passed through the room, as though a shutter had come loose in the wind. But the windows were sealed tight – Milosova had closed them herself.

What was that? She listened. A shuffling could be heard from outside. Something bumped against the window. Then scratched against the door. An animal? The scratch sounded again, then became a constant scrape, scrape.

As though a hawthorn stake were being dragged against the door. Clawing to get in.

Milosova reached into the cloth bag tied at her waist, and drew a glinting object from it. Solarić and her mother stared as she placed the coin marked with a cross on the table.

"They said he has... desires," Milosova said. "I wanted to know who he desired – Jelena or me."

Now she knew. Milosova smiled, despite the stab of fear in her chest, as the scratching at the door became more insistent, audible even over her mother's screams. It was real. He was back. "Lazar?" she called.

The sound that drifted back was animal, a piercing howl that was somehow Lazar's voice but not connected in any way to the man she loved.

"You!... You!..." her mother wheezed, and fainted, sliding onto the floor like a sack of turnips.

"You switched the coin!" Solarić finished. He shook his head. "Oh Milosova. I forgot you were so very young."

What did that have to do with it? "I'm not that much younger than you."

"I am ninety-three."

Milosova laughed, despite the situation, but there was something eerie about Solarić's placidity and she stopped abruptly.

The priest opened his mouth a little. At first, Milosova wasn't sure what she was seeing, and then ice gripped her stomach and she gasped. Jesus and all the Saints! His canines were extending like a cat's claws sliding out of their sheaths – and the teeth were as fine and sharp as any cat's claws.

She froze, deathly cold rushing through her limbs. He was... he was...

Solarić smiled, close-mouthed. Then he stood. "Come with me."

"Wha... what?"

"We have work to do," the priest said. "We have to deal with Lazar, I'm afraid. He's not himself – he was reborn improperly. Your lover is gone, what remains must be put to rest." He sighed. "I've been pursuing the vampire that did this to him – to many others, too – cleaning up after him. Usually the villagers are easy to convince. Not you though."

"Oh."

"I suppose it's better this way," the priest – was he even a priest? – added. "If we cut off his head, his soul will be freed. As we'd left it – as I thought we'd left it – it would have been trapped until the body finally decomposed."

"Cut off...?" Milosova's vision swirled.

"His head. Do you happen to have an axe and a large, sharp knife?"

She nodded mutely, pointing to the axe on the wall, and went to fetch the skinning knife, hardly believing what she was seeing, doing, thinking, her head filling with questions and contradictions.

"But you're a priest!" she spluttered after a moment's stunned silence.

Solarić shrugged. "It's very convenient for my work. My real work."

"But all the crosses… the icons… and Holy water…"

He smiled, momentarily revealing those teeth again. "You have a lot to learn, I can see. Belief is powerful, as you've seen. But belief isn't everything."

They clambered out of the window at the side of the cottage, as Lazar was still scraping at the door.

"Call to him, let him see you," Solarić whispered. "He's bound to follow. Draw him away from the village and I'll follow and set upon him once we're a safe distance away." He laid his hand on her arm. "Don't worry, he can't go too quickly, you can outpace him easily. You've outpaced everyone in the village, after all, by a hundred years or so. Well, perhaps fifty."

Milosova wrapped the knife in her shawl and stepped out to reveal herself. The moon was bright, casting a yellowish light on the village. "Lazar," she said, voice cracking, trying to sound alluring. "Lazar, my love."

The thing that had been Lazar looked at her. The lust in its eyes. That was Lazar's. But there was nothing of his wit there, nothing of his love. Nothing of Lazar but his appetites. It shuffled a step towards her, then another. She turned and ran, every so often taking a glance behind her to make sure he was following, but not getting too close. Her heart was running like a hare. The snow-clothed slopes of the mountains glowed ahead. She ran towards them, up the slopes of the foothill, towards the spot that should have been Lazar's resting place. It made sense.

She heard a wet thud and a pitiful whine behind her, and whipped round to see Solarić and Lazar wrestling, the axe jutting ludicrously from Lazar's back. Her lover thrashed, the movements not human, his face a mask of confusion and fury. The axe dislodged itself and flew into the grass, spattering Milosova with droplets of something dark. She tried to take a step but her feet seemed bonded to the earth. "I'm sorry!" she whispered.

"Come on!" the priest shouted, "Help me get him on the ground."

She rushed forward, ducking under Lazar's grasping hands and the stakes still sticking through them, seized him around the waist, and shoved for all she was worth. In a moment the three of them were a scrabbling heap on the ground.

Solarić beckoned with one arm, holding a struggling, wailing Lazar with the other. "The knife! You'll have to cut through his neck"

Milosova grabbed the knife from where she had dropped it a moment before and, gagging, swallowing vomit down, sliced it across the vampire's throat. Dark blood welled up, but the cut was only a finger's width deep.

"You'll have to push harder than that," the priest snapped as the two men – the two not-men – struggled, Lazar groaning and barking mindlessly. Something seemed odd about it, as if the priest was acting the part rather than really fighting. Then she realised Solarić wasn't panting despite the exertion! He looked at her with an eyebrow raised, which sparked her out of her reverie. She tried again, putting her whole weight behind the knife as she had with the hawthorn stakes, and gradually, through flesh, gristle and muscle, sawed down to the bone. Lazar flailed but Solarić had him pinned.

"Now hold him," Solarić instructed as he scrabbled on the ground for the axe. "You won't get through his spine with that."

That time she did vomit, lying across Lazar's twitching form as the axe made wet, crunching noises a hand-span from her head. Finally the vampire stopped moving. She looked up to see his head rolling slowly away from his neck, fluids leaching into the frosty grass. They dragged the remains to the old grave and shoved them in, roughly heaping the earth back over the body. When they finished, Milosova sat, hugging her knees and trying to ignore the slime she seemed to be covered in. "What happens now?" she asked.

Solarić looked at her, calculating. "The vampire that did this is still out there and I could do with your help. You can come with me, or go back to your mother as long as you promised not to mention my – ah, *nature* to anyone. Or, if you prefer, I could just kill you, I imagine that would be preferable to life with your mother."

"Y-yes. I mean, there's no need to kill me."

"Good. I hate waste and you've been useful, despite this little escapade. Now, I have to go and find the beast that's been giving my kind such a bad name and cut his cursed head off. If you're coming along, you must be ready to leave at first light."

Milosova looked down the hill towards the village, where it lay hidden in darkness but fixed in her senses as a compass points north. It had been all she'd ever known. Her mother was down there in the gloom, and for all that they fought with each other, they were each other's only kin. Any fool could run off in search of adventure, but this man... this, whatever-he-was, Solarić – his world was bigger, scarier and much more confusing than anything she'd ever known.

"Why wait?" Milosova replied when she'd got her breath back. "Let's go."

"Recently read Alice Loweecey's (Kate Morgan) *Demons for Tea* and it is a fun occult detective romp that will appeal to fans of John Constantine, Anita Blake and Harry Dresden."
—Brian Keene
DEMONS FOR TEA
1 Best Selling Author
Kate Morgan
OMNIUM GATHERUM

THE BLINDSIDER

CLIFF BIGGERS

"Anyone home?"

The loud voice was accompanied by a heavy rapping on the screen door that caused the wood frame to rattle against the doorway with each knuckled tap. Horace Cole had already begun to walk to the door before the voice or the knock, however. He had heard the thudding footsteps on the wooden porch, telling him of the arrival of a visitor.

"Can I help you?" Cole spoke through the screen door, but neither opened it nor beckoned his visitor to enter.

"You Mr Cole?"

"That's what my pupils call me. Folks your age can just call me Horace, though."

"Mr Cole, I was told you might be able to help me."

"By whom?"

"Bessie Aldridge. She said you was a man who knowed things."

Cole smiled. "I guess I am that. I'm a teacher, Mr…"

"Campbell. Virgil Campbell. Friends call me Verge."

"Well, Mr Campbell, what sort of knowledge are you searching for that brings you way out here?"

Campbell fidgeted a bit. "Mr Cole, would you mind if I come inside? This is a bit of a private matter, and I don't feel right talking about it full-voice through a door."

"I'm afraid not."

Campbell looked a bit surprised and more than a little confused. He was so accustomed to the hospitality of the mountain people that he had never expected anything other than a welcome.

"No? I don't rightly understand. Have I done something to offend you, Mr Cole?"

"Offend me? No, not at all. And it's not you I object to. It's your friend."

"My friend?"

"The one standing on your left, a half-step behind you."

Relief flashed across Campbell's face. "You can see him?"

"Of course."

"Thank God, Mr Cole! Thank God! Bessie was right. That's why I'm here, Mr Cole. I can't get rid of him!"

* * *

Cole wiped the icy water off the six-ounce green glass bottle, popped off the cap using the bottle opener mounted to the wooden porch post, and offered it to Mr Campbell. He then reached into the galvanized metal tub and pulled out a second one for himself.

"Thank ya, Mr Cole."

"Gladly, Mr Campbell. Sorry if I seemed hostile, but if I've learned anything, it's not to invite these" – he gestured towards Campbell's left – "into my house. Once they're in, they're harder than ladybugs to get rid of."

"Well, at least ladybugs are something real. This thing... I'm still a mite surprised that you can see it. Nobody else can – not even Bessie. She seemed to have some idea what it was, but she wasn't sure. Sent me out here. Even with directions, you're a hard man to find, you know that?"

Cole chuckled and nodded, tipped his Coca-Cola bottle in Campbell's direction, then lifted took a sip before replying. "I'm always around people when I'm teaching. When school's out, though, I appreciate the peace and quiet. There's plenty of that out here."

"I guess there is." Campbell shifted his weight from one foot to another. "So what is it?"

"Oh, him?"

" 'Him' makes it sound like a man. Ain't no man, though, is it?"

"No. Not a man. Its real name wouldn't mean anything to you – but over the years, folks who've had the misfortune to attract the attention of one of his kind have called it a Blindsider."

"Blindsider?"

Yep. You don't see it, do you?"

"Not exactly. I get a glimpse of it out of the corner of my eye, like a shade. But when I turn to look, there's nothing there."

"And that's where the name comes from. They live in your blind side. Once these things are attached to you, they're like a tick – only a lot harder to get rid of."

"Nothing as easy as tweezers and turpentine, then?"

"Nope. The thing is, blindsiders don't normally stay in our world for more than an hour or two. They drift over, latch onto someone for a little while and hold on like there's no letting go, but after a while they make their way back to their own reality. This one is different, though. I can see that it's not happy to be here, but you say it's been attached to you for a while now. So I have to ask, Mr Campbell – how'd this happen?"

Campbell looked sheepish. "It's a long story."

"I'd like the one-paragraph version, please."

"Well, I guess it was love gone wrong."

"Maybe too short. I said one paragraph, not one sentence. A little more."

"There was this woman, Caroline. We was dating – thought we was going somewhere. Caroline thought different. Found out that she was seeing a couple of other men at the same time she was seeing me."

"I think I see where this is going, but continue."

"Went to one of those fortune teller places on Highway 53. Someone told me that they could help."

"A word of advice, Mr Campbell: a real fortune teller never needs neon."

Campbell scratched his head and looked at the floor. "Yeah, reckon I can see that now. But I was crazy in love – at least I thought I was – and I wanted Caroline to love me back. This fortune teller said that she could make Caroline come running, and it would only cost me a hundred bucks."

"Bad magic – it never comes cheap, and it never has a guarantee."

"What can I do, Mr Cole?"

"We need some privacy before I can discuss that."

"Privacy? Like you said, there's no one out here."

"Not from other people. From him." He nodded to Campbell's left.

"How? 'Attached like a tick,' you said."

"Pardon me for just a moment." Cole stepped inside. Campbell could hear the creaking sound of a heavy door opening, then heard noises of someone rummaging, moving things around. "Here it is."

A moment later, Cole stepped back through the doorway carrying a bundle of vines with spiky balls attached.

"What's that?"

"This, Mr Campbell, is privacy."

"I don't follow."

"Sweetgum balls. Some folks call them witches balls – and with good reason. They're powerful and protective. Bad things can't pass through. Wisteria vines – they make magic stronger. Put them together with nine pieces of nine-foot finely drawn wool cord, with nine knots along the stem of each witches ball, and you get a pretty good barrier against any bad things. Even blindsiders. At least for a little while." Cole began stringing the vines around the door, tying it to nails driven into the doorframe long ago for just such a purpose.

Once all the protective bindings were in place, Cole opened the door. "Won't you come in, Mr Campbell?"

Campbell stood in place for a moment, then exhaled heavily. "That's it? That's all I have to do to be rid of this thing?"

"Oh, no. This just keeps him from entering the house with us. And he's going to be pretty riled up at being locked out like this. Odds are he's going to make his dissatisfaction known to us before too long, as a matter of fact. But when you eventually leave, the blindsider will be right here waiting for you."

Campbell's shoulders slumped. "What do I do, then?"

"That's what we're going to discuss in private."

* * *

"This thing – this blindsider – it's really that bad?"

"Of course it is. You knew that already, though, didn't you? Otherwise, why go to the trouble of coming here?"

"But it don't hurt me or nothing like that – it's simply right there, looming just out of my line of sight so that I know it's there but can't really see it."

"Of course it doesn't hurt you. It's attached to you. You mentioned a woman—"

"Caroline."

"Yes, Caroline. Did you ever see her again?"

"Tried to. We talked on the phone some, then we said we'd meet at the Waffle House and talk things out."

"How'd that go?"

"Well… she never made it. Drove her car plumb off the road and into a culvert. Ended up in the hospital."

"Of course she did. That's how blindsiders work. They make bad things happen, but you never see their direct involvement. After this accident, did you go to see her?"

"I tried to, but they moved her to intensive care right after I got there – some sort of blood clot or something – and I couldn't get in to see her."

"Exactly. Because the blindsider didn't want you to see her. You belong to the blindsider, you see. This one seems mighty possessive. He stopped the two of you from meeting. Have you tried again?"

"Well, I called a time or two. We'd talk a little, but the line was all staticky. Finally had to hang up, 'cause we couldn't hear each other worth a damn."

"What about the rest of your friends? Hear much from them?"

"Not much recently. Bill wanted me to head down to Panama City with him, but then he fell off a ladder and broke his leg. And I was going to go to hunting with Travis and Leon, but Travis's truck blew up…"

"Are you seeing the pattern here?"

"You're saying that this thing can do all of that?"

"Oh, this thing, as you call it, can do a *lot* more than that. And he will stop at nothing to keep you for his own. What you've described so far is subtle. A blindsider won't stop at subtle. A blindsider will kill if it has to to protect his territory. And I'm afraid that you're his territory."

"But how can it do anything? It's just some shadowy blur — ain't even nothing you can touch."

"That's the way you see it. I assure you, though, it's much more. Claws and slime and tentacles and eyes and orifices... it's quite repulsive. Imagine the ugliest thing you can think of. This is uglier."

"You're shittin' me..."

"Language, Mr Campbell. I overlooked your 'damn' a moment ago."

"What? Are you sh— are you joking?"

"Not at all. As I said, I'm a teacher. Have been for a long time. Don't allow that sort of talk in the classroom, so I've gotten accustomed to not hearing it at all."

"Just what sort of teacher are you?"

" 'Round here, if you're a teacher, you teach everything. The schools are pretty small, so they expect their teachers to teach what needs to be taught. I've become pretty versatile over the years." Cole pointed towards the doorway and its protective bindings "Good for you, right?"

"I guess that's why Bessie sent me your way."

"Bessie. Good girl. One of my best pupils."

"You must be thinking of someone else. Bessie Aldridge is—"

"Seventy, I'd guess... maybe seventy-five. I always have trouble remembering exactly when a student graduated."

"But you're in your thirties — no older than forty at most."

"Thanks. I get that a lot. Took after my Aunt Odessa..."

"She looked young, too?"

"Oh, not so much — 'Dessa was eighty when she died and looked a hundred and twenty. Lived a hard life, and it showed."

"But you said you took after..."

"I did. Ended up in a strange place where time flowed crooked. I made it back. 'Dessa didn't."

"I'm sorry for your loss, Mr Cole."

"Oh, it's all right now. She was sort of aggravated about it for a long time, but she got over it after a while. She eventually came back home to stay."

"Your dead aunt — she lives here?" Campbell's expression made it clear that he realized how foolish that sounded.

"Well, she *exists* here. Right now, she's on the porch, staring down that monster. Around people, blindsiders are real, real terrors. Around the dead, not as much."

As he spoke, Cole walked over to an enormous chifforobe that seemed to take up half the far wall. One door was still open; Campbell figured that was where the teacher kept the protective bindings. Cole reached in, shuffled through some stacks, and brought out one book, which he placed on a round oaken table embossed with ornate decorative carvings. He leaned back in a second time, and came out with a second book. He repeated the process a third time.

"What's all that?"

"This" – he lifted the first book – "is, I suspect, what got you in this trouble to begin with."

"What do you mean?"

The neon fortune teller that you saw – Anya, I bet?"

"Yes – how did you know?"

"Annie – that's her name, but Anya sells well to the people who might be willing to waste money on a fortune teller – Annie's been playing with this sort of stuff for a long time. Her heart may be in the right place, but she was a very bad student, I guess; she keeps doing things wrong. Tell me what you told her."

"Well, I told her how much I loved Caroline, and how I wanted her to love me back. She said that she had a spell that would make Caroline forget those other men and only want to be with me. She had a book – nothing as fancy as all that – and she read some stuff and handed me something she called a medicine bag, and told me to hold it to my heart while she kept on reading."

"*Spells of the Cherokee Shaman* – this is the real thing, right here. I'll bet that she was trying to use the 'separation of lovers' spell. Probably had some cheap printing that garbled everything up, though. Ever heard of the *Book of the Dead*?"

"No, not really."

"Well, the Egyptians had these scrolls called Coffin Texts – they were supposed to contain everything needed for the royal family to take their place alongside the gods after death. They eventually became *The Book of the Dead*. Problem is, word got out and everyone wanted their own copy. Who doesn't want to spend eternity alongside the gods? So a cottage industry grew up around *The Book of the Dead*, with unscrupulous shysters producing garbage copies that looked like the real thing but turned out to be mumbo-jumbo."

"This blindsider is Egyptian?"

"No, it's an analogy, Mr Campbell. What shyster Egyptians did with *The Book of the Dead*, shyster occultists have done with *Spells of the Cherokee*

Shaman. Annie probably bought her copy at one of those magic bookshops in Atlanta – they sell all sorts of trash like that. Like I said, I bet she meant to use the 'separation of lovers' spell to separate lovers so that the object of your love would return to you instead. But she probably garbled the whole thing and opened a gateway for this blindsider to come over – and the medicine bag brought it right to you. Now it's attached to you... till death do you part."

"You'll have to kill it, then?"

"Not even I can do that. Blindsiders are almost invulnerable, and pretty much immortal. They're so ugly that not even death wants them."

"So there's no way out of this hell?... Pardon my language."

"Forgiven – because in this case, 'hell' really is the right word."

A sudden thud on the roof startled both men. A few seconds later, a large limb fell struck the eastern window on its path to the ground.

"That would be the blindsider. It can't get in through the door, so it's trying to find other ways in. Aunt 'Dessa kept it occupied for a while, but in addition to being ugly, these creatures can swell up into something pretty big when they get angry. The longer it's separated from you, the angrier it gets. It'll keep trying to make a way to get in. If that doesn't work, it'll try to make us come out. So we don't have a lot of time."

Another thud. Another limb, on the western side of the house. This one cracked the windowpane as it fell. Cole could see the growing fear in Campbell's eyes.

"You said you couldn't kill it, though."

"That's correct. But I *can* kill you."

Campbell's eyes widened in fear, then narrowed a bit in anger. Cole could almost see the adrenalin pumping through the man's slight frame. "Kill me? How's that any better than living with that thing out there? At least then I'm alive!"

"No, no – I'm not going to kill you for good. We only have to make it appear that you're dead, just long enough for the blindsider to lose the connection. Then it'll go back to the place where it came from, and I'll use a real version of the separation spell to stop it from ever coming back."

Campbell looked only slightly relieved. "How do we make it look like I'm dead? You gonna give me some sort of drug or something?"

"I'm a teacher, not a doctor. No, that's what *this* book is for. This is the *Ascuns La Vedere*. A sort of guide to hidden worlds, and the things that dwell in each. This is the book that we want."

A loud, sharp, resonant crack was followed a few seconds later by a thundering impact. "It's bringing down trees now. We have to act quickly."

Cole opened the book midway through, then flipped back a page or two. "Here it is!"

Campbell began walking towards Cole, who was reading from the text while gesturing with his left hand. Campbell wanted to see the book; instead, he saw a void appear in the air before him—a sort of hole in space. Inside, there were swirling things, coalescing shapes, and indefinable colors.

"Quickly. Step inside. But take this with you!" Cole handed Campbell an object consisting of four birch twigs meticulously bound into an irregular crosshatch pattern with tiny strips of birch bark. "This is a return talisman. Whatever you see, whatever you do – no matter what, don't let go of this." He gave Campbell a push just as the void began to waver... and then both the void and the man were gone.

Another thud – this one shook the house. Another fallen tree, probably a pine, even closer.

Cole strode to the front door, opened it, and removed the bindings, placing them in a pile in the house. "Thank you, Aunt 'Dessa," he said to the apparently empty porch.

And then, even though it was a sunny day, the porch became gloomy, almost overcast. The darkness seemed to swirl towards the door, then into the house.

Cole could see the darkness's face. The blindsider was here, and it was looking for Campbell.

"He's gone. He's not here any longer. Your attachment to this world is broken. Time to go home." Cole began the separation spell, reciting it in the slow cadence necessary for the spell to work.

There were times when Cole wished that he could not see things. This was such a time. A blindsider was horrifying enough; an angry, abandoned blindsider was even worse. Amorphous pulsating tentacle-like projections... blood-red slime that seemed to condense on the walls and run down in viscous streams... eyes which discerned that Cole saw them just as they glared at him – and those eyes were displeased to be seen. Cole forced himself to control his repulsion and finish the incantation.

Sun shone through the western window. A summer breeze wafted through the screen door, which stood ever-so-slightly ajar. There was no sound at all other than the rustling of leaves and the caws of disturbed crows, for they knew what had just occurred here.

Cole picked up another bound-twig object, a twin of the talisman he had given Campbell. He placed it on the floor, exactly where the void had appeared just moments before. He then repeated the incantation as the void thickened, swirled, and coalesced above the talisman.

A moment later, Campbell slumped through. His eyes were wide, his mouth agape as if he had been silenced in mid-scream, but he made no sound.

Cole guided him to a chair, then drew another chilled bottle of Coke from the tub on the porch and placed it in Campbell's hand. The man sat mute, holding onto the drink for several minutes. Finally, he lifted it up, staring at the green glass, the darkly caramel beverage inside, and the patterns of light that shone through both. He put it to lips and tilted it slightly; most of the liquid made it into his mouth, but some ran down his face and dribbled onto his shirt.

"Take your time, Mr Campbell. You've been through a lot. It's over now, though. The blindsider is gone."

Campbell sat mute for five minutes. Ten minutes, half an hour. Every now and then, he would take another small sip from the Coke bottle. Cole sat across from him, waiting.

"You didn't... You never said..."

"You're right, Mr Campbell. I didn't tell you what you would find in the Outer Dark. You couldn't see the blindsider because it wasn't meant to be seen by human eyes. When you passed into the Dark, you were like the blindsider. You were in a world where you didn't belong – where you weren't meant to be seen by the eyes of the creatures that dwell there. For that moment, you were the thing that lurked over *their* shoulders. Well, if they had shoulders..."

Campbell gulped so intensely it seemed as if he were swallowing his own Adam's apple. A few more moments passed before he spoke again.

"Will... will it come back?"

"No. It's gone for good."

Campbell continued to sip at his drink slowly. Now most of it made it into his mouth.

After fifteen more minutes, he finished the last of the drink, He was shaky when he arose from the chair, like a child dizzy from spinning in circles too long. Finally, he stumbled towards the door. "I'll be leaving now, Mr Cole."

"Of course." Cole put one hand on Campbell's shoulder, both to steady and to reassure him. "It's going to be okay."

Campbell nodded. But it wouldn't be okay for a long, long time...

KOTTO'S CREEPIES: AN INTERVIEW WITH JONATHAN RAAB

S.L. EDWARDS

SLE: Let's start out by learning a little more about Sheriff Cecil Kotto. Who is this character? What would you tell unfamiliar readers about the sheriff?

JR: Sheriff Cecil Kotto is a rural county sheriff elected to office on an anti-goblinry and paranormal defense platform — picture a combination of early 2000s Alex Jones and Hunter S. Thompson. He was elected due to a county-wide corruption and drug trafficking scandal that decimated the sheriff's department — and because of his popularity among counter-cultural types as a minor conspiracy theory radio show host. Since getting elected, he's served as both embarrassment and savior to Cattaraugus County, broadcasting his paranoid ramblings and bizarre policy initiatives via his podcast/radio show, and now, his public access television show. He's become embroiled in a number of occult and supernatural conspiracies, relying on his knowledge of the esoteric, his wits, guns, and a liberal amount of drugs and alcohol to help him overcome threats like corporate blood thieves, alien menaces, secret societies, witch cults, and more.

SLE: Elsewhere you've mentioned Kotto's appearance in film. It seems as if this is a character who has been with you for a long time. What can you tell us about his development prior to and during the process of actually writing him into existence?

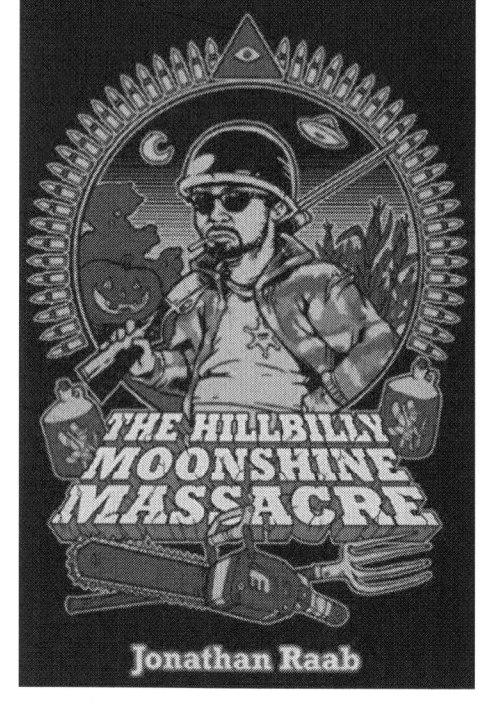

JR: Sheriff Kotto originated in a series of awful backyard monster movies I made with my friends years ago — films that will never see the light of day outside of some private viewings, I assure you. The character was different back then: more crass, more of a crank, less competent, a total degenerate, played more for laughs than anything. When I revisited the character in the novel *The Hillbilly Moonshine Massacre*, I decided he would be a bit different. He's still a booze-fueled madman spouting nonsense about the end of the world and conspiracies behind every major event, but he's got a little more depth and heart to him now. I grew up a little, and so did Kotto.

SLE: Readers of Occult Detective Magazine usually have some fondness for the classics. Thomas Carnacki, Jules de Grandin, John Constantine and others. You've mentioned in previous interviews that a lot of autobiography went into Kotto, particularly your experience in the military and growing up in rural, upstate New York. Was there any inspiration from more classic occult detective fiction?

JR: Aside from Van Helsing and Solomon Kane, I'm not very familiar with some of the classic occult detectives — but I've absorbed plenty of the tropes through more contemporary media. Sheriff Kotto and his crew are inspired in different measures by characters like Hellboy and the BPRD, Fox Mulder and Dana Scully, Dale Cooper, the Ghostbusters, Dr Loomis from the *Halloween* movies, and Batman. These characters are all occult detectives, after a fashion.

SLE: The pitch I've seen for the Kottoverse is 'every conspiracy is true.' Are there limits to this? Is the Earth flat?

JR: I'm a huge fan of conspiracy theories (and believer in some), but there is certainly a dark side to them. They tend to attract people with mental illness who can project their own issues onto others through belief in gang stalking, crisis actors, and racist conspiracies. Conspiracy theories can also be employed to unfairly malign groups or individuals — we've got plenty of that on the nightly news right now, whether it's the Russians or immigrants who are supposedly behind all of America's ills. There's definitely a dark side to entertaining alternative information and ideas.
Then again, the stigma associated with the term 'conspiracy theory' plays into the hands of those in power. I don't believe 9/11 was an inside job or a hologram, but if you start to question whether the attack was blowback or a

response to American imperial aggression, suddenly you're not just crazy, you're un-patriotic. Questioning the government's official narrative makes you a conspiracy theorist

Entertaining conspiracy theories — even and especially the ridiculous ones — allows us to break out of the mental prison in which we find ourselves. I want people to be entertained first of all, but I hope that between the humor and the horror, something sticks with them — something that gets them to question: *what if?*

Yes, certain conspiracy theories are off-limits. I wouldn't write a story about racist conspiracy theories — *The Protocols of Zion* come to mind — as those are memetic viruses meant to foster division and racial/ethnic hatred. And no, the earth is not flat, and Kotto doesn't believe it is. He can recognize a domestic PSYOP meant to discredit conspiracy theorists when he sees one.

SLE: *Freaky Tales From the Force* **came out this year. You've actually invited other creators to take part in Kotto's world. This is pretty big, as many creators (looking at you, Sir Arthur Conan Doyle) have been fiercely and justifiably protective of their creations. Why did you choose to let other writers play in your sandbox?**

JR: In Kotto's world, (almost) every conspiracy theory and Fortean phenomenon is true, which means the storytelling possibilities are wide open. When I wrote *The Hillbilly Moonshine Massacre*, I wasn't sure anyone would 'get it.' Much to my delight, readers — including many talented writers — really like the guy. I can't wait to see what writers like yourself have in store for the good sheriff.

SLE: So far, Kotto has popped up all over the place. He's run through Mer Whinery's Little Dixie mythos, he's shown up in Turn to Ash and a few others. Is there a weird fiction, location mythos or monster that Kotto hasn't interacted with that you would like him to? Are there any sandboxes you

haven't gotten to play in yet that you would really like to?

JR: In *Freaky Tales From the Force: Season One*, I collaborated with Matthew M. Bartlett on a story where Kotto goes up against the satanic forces of WXXT — that's probably the episode I was most excited about whilst putting it together. It's cool to have a character with connections to so many other writers' worlds, and as the character evolves and if more writers like the guy, I'll be happy to have him set foot in some new spaces. There's a lot said about the good of the weird fiction/indie horror community, but it's not always a positive, welcoming place. Having a character who crosses creative boundaries is just a small way of making our connections stronger.

SLE: What can you tease readers with? What can we expect from *Freaky Tales From the Force* and Cattaraugus County PD going forward?

JR: If you haven't read any of the previous books, not to worry. *Freaky Tales From the Force: Season One* can be read start to finish on its own, but of course there are callbacks to *The Hillbilly Moonshine Massacre*, *The Lesser Swamp Gods of Little Dixie*, and the Mississippi Bones concept album *Radio Free Conspiracy Theory* (the album leads directly into this new book). You'll get new takes on the character from other authors, several new stories from myself, plenty of action, adventure, horror, and humor. The Kotto stories are always about the fun side of horror — memorable characters, ridiculous plots and circumstances and gonzo action... with heart.

Buy the ticket, take the ride — and maybe afterwards, think a little harder about what you've been told to believe.

And watch the skies!

Occult Detective Magazine #6

ODQ'S FLAGSHIP ANTHOLOGY OF LONGER SUPERNATURAL TALES

BRAND NEW FICTION
by
Bev Allen, Charles R Rutledge,
Willile Meikle, Robert Pohle,
Edward M Erdelac,
Amanda DeWees, S L Edwards,
and a complete novella by Adrian Cole

PLUS A rare reprint of the classic essay on Occult Detectives by Mike Ashley, 'Fighters of Fear'

ART by Sebastian Cabrol, Yves Tourigny, Jim Pitts and more

AVAILABLE ON AMAZON NOW!

VINNIE DE SOTH AND THE PHANTOM SKEPTIC

I.A. WATSON

"There is no such thing as ghosts," the skeptic told Vinnie de Soth.

"Um…" said the jobbing occultist.

"Any reports of such things are misperception or wilful deception. I'll grant the psychological phenomenon of people in grief sometimes convincing themselves of life after death, but there is not and never will be a shred of evidence to support any actuality of so-called 'phantoms' and 'spectres'."

"Er…" Vinnie responded. He raised a hand as if in class, but Zephraim Holtz was not finished.

"Not only is belief in such apparitions illogical and erroneous but it panders to the lowest denominator of human irrationality, contributing to the decline of respect for science and logic that so besets our society. In perpetuating that superstition you are actually harming the development of the human intellect."

"Okay," Vinnie challenged. "Then why are you transparent?"

Holtz halted his tirade and stared down at his body. He stood in his hallway, next to an opened cardboard box containing copies of his latest bestseller *The Occult Con Trick*, and he could see the pattern of his rug through the trunks of his legs.

"I'm only asking for information," his annoying visitor clarified.

Holtz lifted his hand before his eyes and inspected his palm. He could see Vinnie through it. The skeptic did appear to be insubstantial.

"Alright," he growled in his best I-see-where-you-palmed-the-card-from voice. "Very good. One of the better deceptions I've encountered. How do you do it? I *will* find out."

"I'm not actually doing it," Vinnie promised. "It's kind of a side effect of you being a ghost."

Holtz snorted. "Right. I'm a ghost. Except there is no such thing – as you would know if you had gone to any of my lectures or read my books."

The jobbing occultist stuffed his fists into the pockets of his scruffy denim jacket. "Tell you what then. I'll read your book if you autograph a copy for me. Go on. Pass me one."

Getting more bad-tempered by the moment, Zephraim Holtz snatched up one of the hardback volumes from his box – except that his fingers passed right through the book as if it was not there. "*What?* What is this? What the hell are you doing?"

"Right now, not much," Vinnie promised him. "Just a bit of a divination dweomer to let me see dead people – well just ghosts really. And to hear you. Otherwise it gets to be a mime-show and nobody wants that – you're one step off puppets and Pictionary. But that's how I can communicate with you when the rest of the world can't."

"Divination? What kind of..." Holtz stopped mid-scorn and stared more closely at the dishevelled young man in his hallway. "Wait a second – I *know* you!" He fumbled through his memory. "De Soth! Vincent de Soth. Of the notorious con-artist cult who've been bilking people since before World War One!"

"First off, it's Vinnie, not Vincent. Secondly, my family has been doing bad things to people since long before the twentieth century and so far nobody's been able to stop 'em. So far. And thirdly, I have nothing to do with House of de Soth any more. They think they threw me out and I think I escaped. Right now I'm..."

"You call yourself a 'jobbing occultist'!" the skeptic accused. "Oh, yeah, I know you, bud! You work out of some seedy little brothel in Soho..."

"Bookshop. It's a bookshop, actually. Admittedly, there are some dark corners around the back shelves, but..."

"You advertise yourself as some kind of occult guru, helping people with 'Tarot readings' and 'aura cleansing' and all kinds of mumbo-jumbo nonsense."

"Technically, mumbo-jumbo is nonsense, so that's redundant."

"You bilk grieving relatives out of fees to 'settle the spirits' of their dead loved ones. You perform 'exorcisms' to cast out evil influences. Oh, yes. You were on my list to expose."

"Before you died," Vinnie pointed out.

"Before I decided you were too small-fry and too obviously a fake to bother with," Holtz sneered. "Really, if you were any good, would you be living like you do? Grubbing round selling curse-removing herbal teas and cheap good-luck amulets to brainless morons? No, de Soth, I thought about exposing you in my next bestseller, and decided you weren't worth the ink."

The jobbing occultist winced. "Well, that's just hurtful. I could really have used the publicity. Right now if you google 'de Soth' you get an American basketball team and a public school district. And a place that sells pizza."

"Anyway, don't think for a moment that I'm not onto you, buddy,"

Zephraim Holtz warned. "Once I find out how you pulled this little transparency scam I'm going to take you down!"

"I can tell you how you're transparent," Vinnie insisted. "You're dead. You're a ghost — specifically a transient sentient ectoplasmic soul-waveform reverberating in the six thousand terrathaum range, tethered to your place of death by harmonic imbalance. There are plenty of other kinds of ghost, of course, but it's pretty obvious which you are."

Holtz expressed his response crudely.

"What's interesting," the intruding occultist went on, "is that you are see-through. Most ghosts of your type aren't at first. They appear perfectly normal and solid to people who can perceive them — sensitives and an occasional close friend or relative. It's only as their waveform degrades and they slip out of the arcanosphere that they start to get transparent. Eventually they're just a smudge and a shiver, and then they're gone. But you... you're ghosty-looking right from day one. Well, day two. You get that you died yesterday, right?"

"Once and for all, I'm not dead. This whole scam has gone on long enough."

"My theory is that you're transparent because there's a part of you that believes that's how ghosts look."

"There are no such things as ghosts!" Holtz almost screamed.

Vinnie folded his arms. "Okay. If you're alive, you only have to do one of two things. Pick up an object or walk out of this hall."

"I'll do better than that. I'll open the door and toss you out on your ear!"

Holtz strode to the exit and reached for the door-handle. His fingers passed through it. He reached for the door itself, but his whole hand seemed to dissolve away.

"You're tied to this spot," Vinnie told him, not unsympathetically. "Like I said, you're tethered to where you died."

Holtz punched him in the face. His first passed through the jobbing occultist with an odd tingle.

Vinnie sneezed. "Please don't do that. It won't hurt living people but it's bad for your waveform. Also, I have a few extra defences against spirit attack and they take ages to re-set if some bumbling non-corporeal entity sets them off. Why not just take a breath for a minute, calm down, and then we can talk?"

"You won't get away with this!" shouted the skeptic.

"Get away with what? I've not done anything. The worst I'm gonna do is go into your kitchen and get myself a cup of tea. If you have tea. Do Americans keep tea in their kitchens? Is this the way to your kettle?"

Holtz fumed as Vinnie discovered the way into the neat little kitchenette of his London flat. The jobbing occultist regarded the top-of-the-line coffee maker with some concern and shied away from it.

"Drugs, is that it?" Holtz demanded from the doorway. "I was slipped something in the flunitrazepam range and now I'm extremely suggestible. Very clever."

Vinnie managed to get an only-slightly-baffling kettle going, without having to understand the Bluetooth programming manual. "I honestly don't know how you died," he told the skeptic. "The doctor's report said heart attack, and there'll be a coroner's inspection – standard practice when an only-a-bit-overweight bloke in his forties keels over – but honestly, heart attacks don't usually leave spectres in their wake. Not unless you have some urgent unfinished business. Were you rushing out to finish some vital mission when you keeled over?"

"I. Am. Not. Dead!"

Vinnie found a tiny packet of what looked like expensive designer tea and cautiously dropped it into his cup. "Let's agree to differ on the mortality situation for a moment. What's the last thing you recall before falling over in the hallway there?"

"I didn't fall over. I never..." Holtz frowned. "Unless I tripped and bumped my head? This could all be a concussion hallucination. *You* might be a figment of my inner negative thoughts."

"I'd prefer not to be, thanks," Vinnie admitted. "What can you remember doing? Before you started your sermon to me about ghosts not existing."

"It's not a sermon. It's plain fact, proved by scientific method, that there is no such thing as supernatural—"

Vinnie cut him off. "Hold up! I know mad scientists, chum, and the first thing they say is that the scientific method can never disprove anything. Absence of proof isn't proof of absence. You can verify a theory through experimentation. You can indicate that one explanation is better than another based on the current evidence. You can't ever prove a negative."

"I can point to hundreds of cases of so-called supernatural events that turned out to be categorised in error," Holtz replied, on sure ground in this kind of argument. "Fake mediums, fake faith-healers, fake apparitions. Photoshop ghosts and UFOs. Petty cons to scam gullible believers. Badly-researched events repeated and amplified by cheesy internet hacks. 'Recovered memories' of Satanic abuse publicised by unscrupulous or ignorant hypnotic practitioners..."

"You can point to a million of them," Vinnie agreed. "But it still doesn't prove that the million-and-oneth isn't real. Just because someone sells you a fake concert ticket doesn't mean there aren't any real concert tickets, or that there's no concert."

"But we can prove concerts! And tickets! Nobody can prove an afterlife, or telepathy, or telekinesis." Holtz snorted. "Skeptics have been offering a million dollars for years to anyone who can prove that they can do telekinesis in a controlled laboratory setting. Nobody has ever managed it. Ever!"

"Of course not," the jobbing occultist scorned. "Be real! You think the Great Houses want the modern world to know about magic? First thing the de Soths and the others do on any test of that kind is to fix it with enchantments so that it will never work."

"Oh, that's a clever excuse," the skeptic scorned.

"Or as I like to call it, a reason. It's the same for why nobody has ever come forward to the media to say 'Hey, I'm a werewolf!' or 'Look, a vampire!'. It's just not allowed. Hell, I bet one or more of the Families is somewhere behind your publisher, encouraging your book up the sales charts. There are Powers out there who prefer that magic stays in Harry Potter films."

Holtz slammed his fist at the wall, but his arm vanished before it impacted. He stepped back hastily and was relieved that his missing limb shimmered back to insubstantial existence. "I can't tell whether you genuinely believe your delusions or whether you are a very clever manipulator," he told the man making tea.

He ignored the feeling that he was being watched by more than the intruder. Nothing was behind him.

"Not many people accuse me of being clever," Vinnie admitted. "But Holtz, take a clear look at yourself. You are not-living proof of some kind of life after death. I have no idea what happens once your ectoplasmic echo fades, but right now you pass most of the standard definitions for a sentient being, right? I mean, you think therefore you are?"

"I can see you are ignorant of current scientific debate on that concept," the ghost objected. "'The capacity to feel, perceive, or experience subjectively' is an eighteenth century definition. There's a long road from there to McGinn's ridiculous position and Dennett's clarity." [1]

"Backing away from that swamp..." Vinnie suggested. He sipped his tea and made an unhappy face as he tasted it. "Oh, that is possibly *actually* diabolical!" As far as he understood it, the drink was not supposed to include peanuts. "Anyway, all I'm saying is look at yourself, Zephraim. Assume for a

---

[1] Holtz quotes from the Merriam Webster dictionary definition of sentience, then references the writings of British philosopher Colin McGinn and his 'new mysterianism' versus the work of cognitive scientist Daniel Dennett, one of the "Four Horsemen of New Atheism".

minute that you've not been roofied. What is the last thing you do remember?"

Holtz tried to dredge his memory. "I was here, in the hall. There was a delivery – the box there with advance copies of *Occult Con Trick*. I signed for them on one of those ridiculous electronic pads where you can never write your name properly, and hauled them inside. I needed them for my lecture tomorrow."

"Today," Vinnie advised him. "It's cancelled on account of your death. Go on."

The skeptic dismissed the interjection. "I opened the container, of course, to check that everything was alright. You wouldn't believe the kind of blunders that some publishers commit on your covers. The stories I could tell you…"

"So you opened your box," Vinnie agreed. "What then?"

"I set aside volumes to give to my daughter and son-in-law, and I, um, I smelled a book."

"That new-book smell, right? Nothing like it. I guess it must be especially good when it's your book you're sniffing."

"Um, well… I put the book back down on the box and then… then… You."

"Ah." Vinnie set aside the horrible tea and came back into the hall. "Well then, let me fill you in. At 6:12pm yesterday your daughter came back from shopping and found you on the floor there. You were already dead, no pulse and all that. She called an ambulance and tried to resuscitate you, but the attending paramedics reckoned that you'd been dead for half an hour to an hour before she found you. The police arrived, and a doctor examined you at the scene and offered a tentative diagnosis of heart failure. You were taken off to the nearest hospital morgue for autopsy examination. Well, your mortal remains were removed."

Holtz looked like he might object again but he held his tongue.

The jobbing occultist continued. "There was no sign of foul play, no reason to suspect it. Unless the coroner's inspection finds something there'll be no police follow-up. Why should there be? But this morning, Mrs Ramnarine came to clean up – the agency housekeeper, nice lady from the Caribbean, you remember her? She's slightly psychic, so as soon as she entered the hall she saw you haunting there. She ran out and came straight to me. And here I am."

"You broke into my flat?"

"I used Mrs Ramnarine's key. She's doing you a favour, really. She offered to pay my fee for this." Vinnie sighed. "Unfortunately I can't really charge her. She's on minimum wage so…" He spread his hands out. "Hello, another charity case!"

Holtz regarded the jobbing occultist suspiciously. "What is your angle in this scam?" he wondered.

Vinnie shrugged. "Honestly? I don't like the idea of what happens eventually to transient sentient ectoplasmic soul-waveforms. I mean the 'transient' bit is a bad news/good news joke if you're sentient. Here you are, still aware, stuck in this hallway where you died. You can't leave. You can't interact. Apart from Mrs Ramnarine nobody can even tell that you're here; certainly not your daughter or son-on-law evidently. All that's left is a lot of boring waiting and loneliness as you gradually succumb to a sort of posthumous dementia and dwindle to nothing. Brrr!"

"But you can help me. For a price."

"You did *hear* the bit where I told you it was a freebie? It's not like you can still use your American Express, is it?"

Holtz flung his arms up in frustration. "This is completely ridiculous! As soon as I work out what this trick is I'll be going to the cops! And I'll sue you for every penny you have and expose you to the whole world!"

Vinnie leaned on the kitchen doorframe. "And if it's not a trick? What then?"

"But it is. It has to be."

"There's a couple of things we can try," the jobbing occultist explained. "We could do an exorcism. That would be interesting, because I'm pretty sure you don't believe in them, so would it work? But that's kind of like nuking the problem. I don't really know what it will do to you, as in you the being inside the waveform."

Holtz frowned. He felt uneasy. He didn't like how plausible the unexpected intruder sounded.

"Or, plan B," Vinnie suggested, "We try and work out what **triggered** your ghost-state. Like I said, it's usually some kind of unfinished business or a cause-of-death kind of thing. If you were murdered, we can solve the case."

"Murder? As in... *murder*?"

"Holtz, you made your career out of annoying people who believe in the supernatural. Are you saying you never made any enemies?"

"Well, sure. There are always sore losers and idiots who won't accept plain facts. There are often demos where I speak, or hecklers. I love hecklers, they're great for getting the audience on your side. There are whackos and nutjobs all over: New Age techno-pagans and Roswell believers, fundamentalist fanatics and self-publicising 'whistle-blowers' with no real data."

Vinnie wondered what the technical difference was between a whacko and a nutjob. "I guess we're not short of motives. But what about a method?"

"I don't believe I'm engaging in this conversation."

"See, if I could examine your cadaver I could probably tell if you were hit by some kind of necromancy, or a curse-hex, or whatever. There'll be signs if you were attacked by a shade or a grue. But your body is in the custody of the forensic coroner, and there's only so often I can sneak into the morgue before it gets predictable."

"Sneak into the…?"

"Let's put a pin in that for now. Maybe there's evidence on site? Look around. Can you spot anything different from how you remember it? Anything unusual that shouldn't be here?"

"Apart from you? No. I only use this place when I'm in the UK. We arrived from Dallas day before yesterday – that is, Thursday if I really have lost some time. We hardly had a chance to unpack before we had to go check arrangements for the conference."

"The Skeptic Conference with the American 'k' in it?" Vinnie checked. "For people so sceptical that they need a harder consonant?"

"I'm supposed to be the guest of honour and keynote speaker," Holtz declared, a little plaintively. "Now I suppose they'll get FitzGibbis."

"Is he the one that was a TV conjurer? Or the one who's a doctor of chemistry and is therefore an expert in parapsychology?"

"FitzGibbis is the one who'd be happy to see me on a morgue slab," Holtz growled. "We're suing each other. He plagiarised my research for that rag of a magazine he publishes. He claims that it was jointly gathered data, which is complete bull."

"I'll add FitzGibbis to the suspect list, then. Did you meet him this visit?"

"He was at the auditorium when we were doing sound checks. He got into an argument with my daughter, Florence. She's also my tour manager, with her husband Kenny covering the financials."

"What was the quarrel over?"

"The usual. Lawsuits, threats of defamation. The big issue of seating at the panel table. Kenny separated them and security helped FitzGibbis from the centre."

Vinnie noted it for later. "What else did you do when you got to London?"

"I told you, we checked the venue and then crashed out. Today – yesterday, you say – Flo and Kenny went down to follow up on the prep and I stayed in to polish up my presentation. Also, I knew there'd be a package from my publisher, with the first imprint of my new book to launch at the conference."

Vinnie checked the label on the delivery box. "Thirty copies of *The Occult Con Trick*. I only count twenty-five in here."

Zephraim Holtz reached to see for himself but his hands still passed insubstantially through the container. He muttered another rude word. "I put

Flo and Kenny's copies in their room. There's another one there on the side-table. That's probably the one I was looking at…"

"Sniffing," Vinnie corrected. "And the others?"

The skeptic had no idea. "There must have been plenty of people in here if I collapsed. Medics, cops, who knows? Probably some fortune-hunter stole a couple to sell on eBay. It'll be a collectable."

Vinnie found it hard to accept that people might want to pay actual money for such a book. "This package looks like it might have been opened and resealed. Were the contents complete when you got it?"

Holtz shrugged. "It was stuffed with brown paper and bubble wrap. I didn't count the books. I just grabbed three, set two of them aside in Flo's room, then checked the copy I was holding." He thought he saw something out of the corner of his eye, something skittering fast into shadows, but when he looked round there was nothing to see.

"Can you remember much about the delivery person?"

"Youngish woman in overalls. Brown skin. Baseball cap with the parcel firm's logo on it. I wasn't really paying attention. I wanted to get back to finessing my speech."

Vinnie examined the volume set aside on the table. It lay face down so that Holtz' stern, half-lit face photo stared back at him. 'Another incisive expose of the murky world of supernatural fraud and delusion,' the cover blurb promised, 'from the best-selling author of *The Hoodoo-Huckster's Code* and *Dangerously Deceived: Supernatural Fraud and Fakery*.'

"I think my brother got my sister one of those as a joke birthday present once," Vinnie remembered. "Golgotha stabbed him with a plaguemort pin."

Holtz wasn't sure how to respond to that. "A lot of people appreciate the sense of what I write."

"Well, it's comforting not to have to worry about things in the dark. Of course, it's not such a public service if you're telling people not to be afraid of tigers in a tiger-infested jungle." The jobbing occultist flicked through the volume. "Who would you say were the main targets you pissed off in this edition?"

"There's a whole exposé of the so-called recovered memory industry," the skeptic recounted. "Plenty of people who were convinced by dodgy psychologists to recall alien abductions while under suggestible hypnotic trances have now recanted their statements and are pursuing their former abusers – by which I mean the psychologists who write books on them."

"That's fair," Vinnie judged. "The first thing a *genuinely* otherworldly abductor would do is to shield any erased memories from hypnotic recovery. That's page one. Same with reincarnation rites." He thought deeper. "I guess you could programme in some fake recovered memories if you wanted to be extra devious."

"I also talk about the faith-healing movement, the Bible-belt conmen and the people who use Brazilian Macumba to gull people from their cash. And the harm they do when folks eschew proper medicine to try some occult nonsense."

"Are there any particular practitioners or churches or sects you really go after? I mean, Candomblé, Giro, and Mesa Blanca are all pretty different branches of Macumba. There are still animal sacrifices in Candomblé, but Giro substitutes palm tree oil, and Mesa Blanca thinks both bring evil. They only get lumped together by white Western scholars, really. Do you name names?"

Holtz listed off a string of high profile and less famous faith healers, along with his evidence against them. "And you can believe all of that has been checked by my attorneys as libel-proof," the skeptic concluded.

Vinnie really hoped he wasn't going to have to take on any of the Candomblé nations. He didn't feel any need to annoy orishas, vodun, or nkishi spirits. For starters they would have to take a number and get in line to curse or kill him.

"Who else?" he asked, flipping though the chapters of *The Occult Con Trick*. He winced as he saw a glossy picture of a skeleton wrapped in colourful Mexican robes and flowers, holding a scythe and a globe. "Nuestra Señora de la Santa Muerte? Really? You went after the cult of Our Lady of the Holy Death? That didn't seem like a dumb idea to you?"

"Speaking out against cynical exploitation of poor people in South America by criminals using alleged miracles as a weapon of control?" Holtz objected.

"Insulting a religion with ten to twenty million followers, including a lot of convicts who get tattoos of Our Lady to protect them from bullets. Offending the LGBT community and other groups who make up big components of her worshippers, along with taxi drivers, bar owners, police, soldiers, and prostitutes. And worst, annoying an entity who is probably the latest version of Mictlancihuatl, the Aztec death-goddess.[2] Why didn't you just climb onto a mountain with a lightning rod?"

Vinnie was interrupted by the sound of a key in the lock of the flat's front door.

---

[2] Santa Muerte is a feature of Mexican folk Catholicism or of its non-Christian offshoots. Variously titled the Skinny Lady (la Flaquita), the Bony Lady (la Huesuda), the White Girl (la Niña Blanca), the White Sister (la Hermana Blanca), the Pretty Girl (la Niña Bonita) the Powerful Lady (la Dama Poderosa), and the Godmother (la Madrina), her images depict a robed skeleton holding scythe and globe. Popular amongst the poor and desperate, and especially those who feel outcast from society, the Holy Death cult has been strongly linked with criminality, drugs, and violence and is especially popular in South American prisons.

"Are you expecting anybody?" he asked Holtz.

"No. Aren't I supposed to be dead according to you?"

The door opened. Vinnie hastily ducked into the kitchen, taking *The Occult Con Trick* with him. He heard the door slam wide. It almost knocked over the hall hatstand. There was giggling.

He heard Zephraim Holtz cry out, "Florence!"

There were sounds of two voices, not speaking but making little grunting sounds, the enthusiastic noises of people kissing and making sure the other knew they were enjoying it. Two bodies thumped against a wall.

"Flo!" Holtz repeated, horrified, and then, "FitzGibbis!"

Vinnie dared a peek through the slightly-open kitchen door. A middle aged man with an unfortunate beard was helping a slightly younger woman out of her silk blouse. Both were trying to maintain maximum body contact through the procedure.

Holtz had a ringside view of their enthusiastic embrace but they could not see or hear him. "What the hell is this?" he thundered. "Flo, get away from that sleaze!"

FitzGibbis pushed Flo to the opposite wall, trying to get his jacket off without shifting his hands from their vantage points.

Vinnie was dismayed to be caught as an unwilling voyeur, embarrassed for Holtz, and worried about being discovered in a dead man's apartment for no reason that would sound good to the local constabulary. Everything was going wrong.

Everything was going wrong.

Vinnie looked more closely at the volume in his hands. He shifted his focus to arcane vision, ignoring the usual spectrum in favour of examining the weft of magical currents. Now he looked carefully he could see a dark knot of twisted causality in the pages before him.

"De Soth!" Holtz hollered. "Stop them! How can Florence demean herself with this... this slimepit?"

It was a good possible motive, the jobbing occultist considered. Who would inherit the skeptic's estate? His business-manager daughter?

The front door crashed back again. There was another voice, loud, angry: "I knew it! I knew something was going on!"

"*Kenny!*" Flo squeaked. "Honey, it's not what you think...!"

"What, that you're screwing around with that walking stain? You think I was fooled with that spat at the auditorium? Well, maybe at first, but not when I had time to think it through."

"So what?" FitzGibbis sneered. "What are you going to do about it?"

"Do? I'm going to kill you!"

"Stop it!" Holtz cried out impotently. "Why won't you listen to me?"

Vinnie stared at the book again. The events in the hall were very distracting. His circumstances were very unfortunate.

"Flo got a book. Kenny got a book," he mused. "I've handled a book, too. But *I* grew up with Golgotha and the others." A de Soth who couldn't spot curses didn't live to majority.

"Get away from me!" FitzGibbis warned. "I mean it!"

"You *die*!" Kenny promised.

Florence screamed.

"Stop! Please, stop!" Holtz's ghost begged desperately.

Vinnie opened the kitchen door and stepped out. "Hold it there, everyone!" he bellowed above the furore. As they froze he added, "I'm the cliché police. What the heck do you people think you are doing?"

"The what?" FitzGibbis asked. His hands and Kenny's hands were round each others' throats. Flo was on the ground between them, clutching a bleeding nose. Holtz was flickering through them all, failing to separate them.

"Just grow up, people!" Vinnie scolded. "You, Florence, your dad died yesterday. Is this *really* the time for a nooner with his big rival? Kenny, you might want to strangle Captain Beardy, but that's not how it works these days. We have divorce courts instead of duels at dawn. So everybody chill while I check something out."

"*Who* are you?" Kenny demanded.

"Zephraim Holtz's new book," the jobbing occultist persisted, "Did you read it?"

"I flicked through my copy and took it with me to show around. I tend not to read the text. Zeph could be a bit tedious with his prose, you know what I mean?"

"He sure could," FitzGibbis sniped.

"You shut up," Florence told him, rising with her hand cupping her nose and glaring at him. She pulled her blouse hastily back into place.

"Did you read your copy?" Vinnie asked her.

"I checked the blurb. I've been a bit… busy."

"That has become very obvious," Holtz told her, trying not to show how upset he was. "How could…?"

"It's a curse," Vinnie told him. "There's a couple of books missing. One of them was stolen en route, I reckon, which is why the box was resealed. Using principles of thaumaturgy, one book in this batch is all the books for the purpose of transmitting hexes – like using someone's belongings for voodoo or something. But it wasn't enough to just kill you. You had to become a ghost and be forced to witness whatever was going to go down in this hallway scene right now. Adultery and murder maybe, while you watched and couldn't do anything."

"What are you talking about?" Kenny demanded.

"Who are you talking to?" Florence added.

"And I'm explaining thaumatugical resonance and the doctrine of sympathies to the folks running a skeptic conference," Vinnie warned himself. "Is that part of the curse or just a day in my life? Sad that it's hard to tell."

"There is no such thing as curses," Holtz lectured him.

"Like there are no ghosts. Right. I need paper towels."

"What?" FitzGibbis puzzled. "What did he say?"

"We should call the police," Flo suggested.

"And tell them I interrupted a crime of passion?" Vinnie asked from the kitchen. He emerged with a box of tissues and scooped up three fresh copies of *The Occult Con Trick*. "Right, hold these, please, all three of you. Open them to page 112. That's it. Thank you."

So unusual and unexpected was the request that the three living occupants of Holtz' hallway complied. Vinnie wasn't surprised; the curse was already half-directing their actions.

He dropped a paper tissue between the open pages of each edition and then closed the book in the hands of its reader. As the cover closed, Flo, Kenny, and FitzGibbis all stood stock still, staring at nothing.

"What did you do?" Holtz demanded. "Hypnotism?"

"No. Why bother with complicated stuff when they're already under arcane influence? I just used the curse to put them on pause for a while. Didn't you see me use the bookmarks? That means 'hold your place'."

The skeptic waved an unseen hand in front of Flo's eyes, then realised that she couldn't see him even before de Soth's conjuring trick with Kleenex.

Something small and dark skittered over the ceiling and disappeared. Holtz didn't like it.

Vinnie retrieved his copy of *The Occult Con Trick*. "Right. We need a serious talk, Zeph. I mean life and death."

The jobbing occultist's tone was grave and serious now. It frightened Holtz. "What do you mean, de Soth?"

"You were murdered. Someone cursed you. At first I suspected one or more of these three, but now its clear that they were part of the revenge, pawns not players. I can't keep them paused for too long, either. Sooner or later they'll start up again, and I think it's supposed to end in blood, right in front of you."

"That's..." The word ridiculous died on the skeptic's lips. "What if that's so? What can be done?"

"Well, if there's a thaumaturgic link channelling a hex through these books, if they're all cursed through that copy that was stolen before delivery, then there's also a link back to that volume. You can cross a bridge two ways."

"I suppose so," Holtz owned suspiciously.

"What I'd like to try is splashing back the curse through that link so it includes whoever cast it. If it works, then they'll be compelled to come here too, in front of you, and something bad will happen to them as well."

"You can do that?" Holtz winced as he realised what he was asking.

"Probably. But I'll need you to help, Mr Holtz. By which I mean I'll need you as, well, the battery for it. There has to be sympathy, you see. A connection." Vinnie hesitated. "You remember I said that transient ghost waveforms have a limited span? This will use up pretty much all of yours. And then..."

"The end," the skeptic concluded.

"I really don't know."

"But it would save Florence? And Kenny?"

"From the curse, yes. Their marriage...? No guarantees."

"I don't mind if it kills FitzGibbis. That would be an acceptable loss."

"Yeah, well we might save him too. It's not a perfect happy ending. Murder stories never are."

Zephraim Holtz rubbed his temple. "If I accept the preposterous premise then the conclusion makes sense. Not that I'm admitting the premise. But... I have to work with current data."

"Is that consent?" Vinnie asked. "You'll help?"

"I will help."

The jobbing occultist steeled himself. "Right then. I'll need a chair and screwdriver. And a metal waste-paper basket."

"Dare I ask why?" Holtz ventured.

"Chair to reach your smoke detector. Screwdriver to take the battery out. Basket to set fire to your book in, so you can get your hands on its ghost and start reading from it. I'll tweak things so that there's enough resonance from that to include your hexer in the hex."

"You make it sound simple. And a little stupid."

"I really do," sighed Vinnie de Soth.

Holtz watched as Vinnie manoeuvred around the people standing in the hall and dismantled the smoke alarm on the ceiling. After a pause to find matches, Vinnie got a copy of *The Occult Con Trick* burning. At de Soth's request the skeptic pulled the book from the fire, though it left a blackened flaky ash remnant. Holtz found he could touch the phantom text, and when he retrieved it there was no sign of burning or any other damage. It even had that new book smell.

"Start reading," Vinnie said.

Holtz opened the book. He winced at the dedication: *To my darling Flo.* "Chapter One: The Gullible and the Greedy. People want to believe comfortable myths over difficult truths..."

He read out the first chapter while Vinnie stopped himself from objecting to it. The jobbing occultist wandered round to check on the three still people, pausing to dab Flo's bloody nose and to close the flat door that Kenny had slammed open.

Holtz wondered how his throat could feel sore from reading aloud if he was supposed to be dead.

At the end of Chapter Two: Logic Over Legerdemain, Vinnie called a halt. "That should be enough. Honestly, it's quite enough." Kenny hadn't been wrong about Holtz's style, and the occultist was a bit tired of being proved wrong so often in print by a fervent skeptic.

"What now?" Holtz asked Vinnie.

"We wait for your enemy."

"And then?"

"We deal with your enemy."

"But what does that look like. What does 'deal with' mean?"

"It means..." the jobbing occultist began grimly, but stopped as he saw the phantom flinch. "What's wrong?"

"I saw something again," Holtz admitted. "I've glimpsed it before. Something dark and fast, on the periphery of my sight. Something small. Moving like a rat or a spider or a bat." He turned around unhappily, looking for the thing. "It's watching me. Stalking me. You don't see it?"

Vinnie shook his head. "Think of it like me being on a sea shore, looking out into the ocean. You're far out near the horizon, being washed with the receding tide. I can see you but I can't get to you, and eventually you'll be too far away for me to even spot you. But you can look further across the sea than I can, to things even further out over my horizon. Ships and, um, sharks."

"Sea monsters?"

"Well, it's just an analogy." The reality was far worse, but Vinnie didn't feel this was the time to brief the skeptic on it. Besides, nobody was an expert on that particular ocean.

Holtz looked about, like a man expecting to be attacked. "What can I do?"

"We've already set you as bait for whoever cursed you. If there's some other component of what was done to you, something only a ghost can perceive..." The jobbing occultist paused. There was some metaphysical mathematics that didn't add up. Curses shifted circumstance around, borrowed and distributed fortune. But this was about more than a hex.

Vinnie's thoughts were interrupted by the flat door crashing back for a third time. "What did you do?" a livid young woman in parcel delivery service jacket and cap demanded. "How did you do it?"

She was clutching a copy of *The Occult Con Trick*, but it was defaced by symbols painted on it with blood. Her hand trembled as if she would like to release the volume but could not command her fist to open.

"I added you to your hex's cc list," Vinnie told her. "The only way to get free from whatever you had set up for these three is to cancel the curse."

The woman snarled. "*Idiota*! I can't cancel it! It's not my curse!"

Vinnie gestured to the book she clutched. "Then why are you caught red-handed?"

"I just got paid to cast the hex. The money was good and the target deserved it. But the hate, the wish for destruction that makes the curse real, that's not mine. I can't revoke it."

"What's she saying?" Holtz demanded. "She's making no sense!"

"I'm making perfect sense, you ignorant Americano!" the priestess shouted at the ghost. "You know nothing – but you bray it so loudly!"

"She can see me?" the skeptic asked Vinnie.

"She might be your unfinished business, or part of it," the jobbing occultist replied. "And you, madam, shouldn't be so quick to call other people stupid and ignorant. You took money to set a lethal malediction loose. You're accessory to a murder and you were quite willing to facilitate more. What was supposed to happen here, eh? A lovers' quarrel and blood-spilling while Holtz's ghost could only watch and scream?"

"That's what I was paid for," the priestess spat. "What are you going to do about it? What can you do?"

Vinnie's affable face settled into quite a different expression, the countenance of an executioner. "I can do maths," he replied.

The bookmark pause that held Flo, Kenny, and FitzGibbis immobile failed. All three blinked and wondered what had just happened.

FitzGibbis spotted the parcel delivery agent at the door. "Ana Beatriz?" he asked, before realising that he shouldn't have acknowledged her.

"You know this woman?" Holtz demanded, unheard by his fellow skeptic.

Vinnie snapped his fingers as the missing part of the calculation dropped into place. "He knows her. Flo and Kenny are here because you gave them books. This guy never handled one. I thought maybe he just came back here because he was part of the hex on Florence, and because, well, guys go anywhere for a chance at sex. But now I'm thinking he's here because he supplied the malice that powered the curse in the first place."

Flo looked between Vinnie, FitzGibbis, and Ana Beatriz. "Huh?"

"What was supposed to happen, Beardie?" Vinnie asked FitzGibbis. "Holtz dies, you bring his daughter here to let's-call-it-date her in front of her dad's ghost, her hubby turns up and finds you, there's a struggle, maybe he has an accident too, a heart attack say – or does he accidentally kill his wife? However it works out, it's the most heartbreaking possible thing for dead Holtz to witness, right? Maybe you end up with a rich widow who inherits all Zephraim's book money. Maybe it's really about revenge. Whatever it was, you were candomblé-woman's client, weren't you?"

"I have no idea what you are talking about," FitzGibbis objected.

"What are you saying he did?" Kenny demanded. "He hired a hit on Zeph?"

"Effectively," Vinnie agreed. "But his priestess should have paid more attention to her ancestors. Candomblé teaches that evil always returns to the one who did it eventually. And there is still one copy of *The Occult Con-Trick* missing."

"Why does that matter?" Holtz wondered. Another question seemed more urgent, though. "How could FitzGibbis go to a... a witch to cast a curse on me? He's a fellow skeptic. If he believes in hexes then he's a fraud and a hypocrite!"

The skittering in the shadows was back, faster, nearer. Ana Beatriz saw it and shied back. Vinnie saw her spot it.

"You get it now?" he challenged the priestess. "You used the wrong medium to transmit the curse. You chose a book about magic not existing to send a magic curse. You picked a book in sympathy with a hard-k skeptic as your murder weapon and you didn't think that would set up an imbalance?"

"What is he talking about?" FitzGibbis demanded of Ana Beatriz. He wasn't sure why he was afraid; he only knew that he was. He could hear something like the flipping of angry pages.

"We have to leave," the priestess called out. "Break the curse. Let us go! *Rapidemente!*"

"Too late," Vinnie warned. "It's the final chapter."

The missing copy of Holtz' last book flew from the shadows like a mad bat, trailing darkness and fear. Flo and Kenny didn't see it, but they sensed it. Both flinched and ducked, though they didn't know why. Ana Beatriz tried to flee but couldn't pass the flat's threshold.

Holtz saw the descending volume clearly. It was deformed, mutated, monstrous, almost a living thing. Its spine was barbed, its pages sharp as razors, and all the pictures inside writhed and squirmed. The image that the open book displayed was Nuestra Señora de la Santa Muerte, and she had no mercy.

FitzGibbis saw it too, saw it all. He had a moment of understanding, of revelation, as he fathomed the same arcane accounting that Vinnie had concluded, as he understood the cost of his scepticism and of his sacrificing it. The skeptic book slammed into him, through his chest, the countercurse response to what had been set in motion, the denial of even life itself.

FitzGibbis clutched his heart and fell to the floor almost exactly where Holtz had died.

Ana Beatriz raised her hands in a gesture of mystic warding. Nothing happened. The power was not there.

"You live in a world where magic isn't real now," Vinnie told her. "That's your punishment. The skeptic's revenge."

The former priestess screamed, bereft as the spirits left her forever. She pelted from the flat, bounced into the wall opposite, and fled away.

Flo scrabbled over to her fallen lover, then halted, undecided. Kenny stood close. "We can't tell the police that there was a quarrel," he insisted. "He came to pay his respects and just keeled over. Right?"

"Yes," Florence agreed. "That was it. That was all."

Both of them looked at Vinnie, suddenly realising that there was another witness.

"That was all," the jobbing occultist agreed. "Call an ambulance. Maybe put on a blouse you haven't had a nosebleed on."

As Flo and Kenny retreated to their room, Vinnie turned back to Zephraim Holtz. He could barely see an outline of the ghost now. "Are you still sapient?"

"Yes. But I feel... drowsy. Dreamy." Holtz' voice was slurred and it sounded distant. "So I am dead. And I'm done."

"Your business here is finished," Vinnie agreed. "Your murder's solved. The curse is discharged. What can be fixed is fixed."

"I can't leave things like this."

"None of us gets that choice in the end. There's always more to finish."

"I don't believe in life after death, de Soth. I don't believe in ghosts."

Vinnie would have found a good reply, but he realised there was no-one and nothing left to reply to. Holtz was no longer there to deny his own existence.

Vinnie might have got the last word in then, but he preferred to stay silent.

THE EMPANATRIX OF ROOM 223

KELLY M. HUDSON

There's a particular sound a finger bone makes when it breaks. Each finger is different, and if you smashed them one at a time in quick succession, I imagine it would sound something like a xylophone.

My middle finger blurted like an out of tune bassoon, and pain shot up my arm in a single bolt of red hot, agonizing lightning.

"Why are you following the girl?" the big beefcake said. He stuck his face into mine. He wore a five o'clock shadow that was veering towards dusk and smelled like cheap cigars and eggs.

"She's beautiful," I said. Which was true. Heather Tallent was the femme fatale of every bad noir movie ever made: slim, with flared hips and jutting breasts, long blonde hair that shimmered in the dark, and ice cubes for eyes. She was trouble, alright, and I hadn't even gotten to meet her yet.

They had me tied to a chair with a small card table sitting in front of me. My one free hand was on the table and they used a hammer to break my finger. The hammer was on the floor now because the Brute, the other fellow who had been working me over initially, had set it there so he could punch me.

And he did.

The two of them loomed over me, their shadows stretching across warehouse floor. They were both big, and I mean giant, made of muscle and gristle.

"Answer the question," Cigar and Eggs said.

"What do you care? What are you two, her bodyguards?"

Cigar and Eggs smiled. He had two black teeth and a third that was as brown as a turd. I couldn't tell if they were rotten or just stained from the smoking.

"Sure we are," he said.

"Listen, I've had about enough of this," I said. "You two should cut it out or you're going to get your asses killed."

Cigar and Eggs burst out laughing. The Brute laughed, too, and his chuckle surprised me. It was high-pitched and squeaky, like he had a mouse stuck in his throat.

"No, really, guys, enough is enough. Let me go, lead me to Heather, and you might get out of this okay."

The Brute cracked his knuckles. He actually cracked his knuckles. He bent down and picked up the hammer he used to smash my finger.

"Let me smash his dick," he said.

Cigar and Eggs scratched his sandpaper face and seemed to consider it a moment.

"Nah, let's break a couple more fingers, first, then we'll get serious," he said. "Unless you want to tell me who sent you? We could get it over real quick then."

I whistled. It was loud and long, and if I had a dog it would have come running. Unfortunately, nothing happened.

"Hey!" I shouted. I looked past the two goons that were working me over. "You take too much longer and you'll get in trouble with your boss."

"Who the hell are you talking to?" Cigar and Eggs said. He looked around, stopping when his eyes fell on the Brute. "He gone crazy or something?"

All at once, the Brute let out the kind of scream you might hear if a horse got rammed up the ass with a Christmas tree. His eyes bulged and his arms flew out to his sides like he was trying to fly away. He did lift up into the air, and I thought for a moment he really was flying, until I saw the bulky shadow behind him.

"About time," I said.

Roger, who had slipped into the room in his usual way, all silent and stealthy, sneered at me. He was six and a half feet tall, with burnished skin, big green eyes, and packed with lean muscle. Roger wore a trench coat and fedora, with black slacks and a white dress shirt beneath. He was classy for what he was, I'd give him that.

He lifted the Brute over his head and threw him to the floor.

There's a particular sound a spine makes when it snaps, as well. It's kinda like a big tree when it gets struck by lightning and cracks in two. The Brute made that sound, and then he didn't make a sound ever again.

Well, okay, he farted once, but it was hard to hear over Cigar and Eggs, because he started screaming like nobody's business.

"Don't kill him yet," I said. "I need some information."

"Maybe I should kill him so you can concentrate on your real work," Roger said.

"Hey, I gotta pay the bills," I said. I looked at Cigar and Eggs. "He'll make it quick if you tell me where Heather is."

He told me, right down to the room number.

Roger did not make it quick. Roger liked causing pain.

* * *

We were in my car. I was driving. I tried to convince Roger to drive but he wouldn't do it. He said he was afraid of driving.

"I might get mad," he said. "And if I do, a lot of people will die."

"So?" I said.

"Lot of people die, that attracts the Other Side."

"Oh. I could see where that would be a problem."

So I drove, but I wasn't happy about it.

"What took you so damned long?" I said.

"I do not serve at your whim," Roger said.

"Sure, I know that. But I've got a broken finger, a busted lip, and my jaw feels fractured."

"You talk a lot for a man with a broken jaw."

"Funny. You wouldn't know what kind of pain I'm in. You've never been human."

"And you will never know the wound of the Rebellion, and how deeply it cuts into all of the hearts of my brethren."

"Oh, Jesus, here we go. You know, for a demon, you're mighty poetic."

"I have existed since the dawn of creation. I have had limitless time to learn and educate myself."

"And look what you do with all that education. You slum around with the likes of me."

"Only because it is my duty."

"Yeah, well, how about whipping up some healing shit so I can get on with my day?"

"We do not heal. If you want healing, you have to go to the Other Side."

"OK, get me an Angel, eh?"

"I am an Angel."

"But you're Fallen."

"I am still an Angel."

"Don't get your panties in a wad and start crying on me," I said. "I thought demons were supposed to be tough and mean."

"And I thought you were hired to do a job," Roger said.

I sighed. It was like this with Roger. We went round and round.

A year ago, Satan himself had hired me. There was a certain lady somewhere out there in the world who was destined to be his lover. You know, she was going to birth his son, the Antichrist. Problem was, God had done something to hide her from him. She was off his radar. So he hired me to find her. He gave me a year. One year. If I got the job done, the soul of my dear departed father would be released from the fires of Hell and set free.

"Does that mean he gets into Heaven?" I asked.

Satan smiled. He has a winning smile, that one.

"No. But he's free from suffering eternally. That's something, at least," he said.

"So you basically want me to be the guy who finds you a date," I said.

"No," he said. "You are to find my bride. I will give you her characteristics and her first name. That is all I have. She was born thirty years ago. When she was conceived, I felt her blossom into existence, and I knew at long last the prophecies were about to come true. Unfortunately, shortly after learning of her, God cut me off."

"He can do that?"

"She. And yes, She can."

He paused for a moment.

"God can be a real bitch," he said.

"Let me guess: you two had a romance and it ended bad. You got butt-hurt and stormed off, taking a tenth of the angels with you."

"Do you know who you're talking to?" Satan said.

"Sure. Old Scratch."

He shook his head. "I know of you through your reputation, Mr Marks. I have sent spirits to follow you, to study you, to find if you were worthy."

"And what did those spirits tell you?"

"Nothing. They found you but could not follow."

"Gee, I wonder why," I said.

"Your arrogance is cute, for a worm. Suffice it to say, I know you're good, very good, and you are my only hope at finding my wife."

"Future wife," I corrected him.

He grimaced. He had a hell of a grimace, did Mr Applegate.

So the deal was, I got Roger as a helper. Roger was one of the mighty Guardsmen of Hell, which meant he was the personal bodyguard to Satan. Roger was a total badass. He was with me to make sure I was doing my job and to help me in any way possible. I of course always took advantage of the situation. That money I owed a loan shark over on the East Side? Not a problem anymore. I just got the guy to lay into me, and along came Roger and took his head right off. That crazy voodoo priest who was pissed at me because I stole one of his juju dolls he was using to hex an enemy? His eyes ended up facing east while his balls were facing west. I'd never seen a man twisted into two before that. Roger really worked out for me.

The bad news was, if I didn't find the girl eventually, Satan was going to drag me to Hell and personally supervise my 'conditioning'. That's what they called it down there. Conditioning. Him and God had worked out a deal that they would stay out of each other's hair if Satan ran the prison for Heaven. He was in charge of making the sinners suffer in Hell, and this gave him the freedom to move about as he wanted, as long as none of his moves or minions threatened God or Her servants.

"Why is this other woman more important than the Bride of my King?" Roger said.

"Well, first off, I bet she's a lot prettier, so she has that going for her," I said. "And second, she made some big enemies in the Pac Con, an 'association' of the darker practitioners. You don't do that and not have some serious juice at your disposal. There's money in this."

"The Pac Con?" he said. "And she's still alive?"

I nodded. I grabbed a tube of lip gloss and put it on my lips.

"For now," I said.

* * *

For a lady on the run, she sure didn't pick a place that was nondescript. She was staying downtown, at the Riley, which is named after Joseph Riley, the richest man in San Francisco, and also reputed to be one of the council members of the Pac Con. In fact, he was the man who hired me to find Heather. It took some balls to hide out in one of his fanciest buildings. Of course, no one would ever think to look for her there.

We walked into the lobby and were met instantly by their security. These guys were no joke. They were pure muscle and stank of Bull Tart, which made them even more dangerous. It's bad enough facing high-powered adepts of magick without throwing the steroids in, too.

"Relax, guys," I said. "We're here on behalf of your boss." I held up my credentials. They looked at my papers and laughed. Thug A looked at Thug B and rolled his eyes.

"This guy," Thug A said.

"Fine," I said.

I reached up and kissed him on the lips.

He jerked back, surprised by my move. He swiped his lips with the back of his tailored shirt.

"What in the hell?" he said.

And those were his last words. The poison seized his central nervous system and he sank to the floor, curling up backwards. He looked like a burnt spider. Foam poured from his mouth.

"Alex!" Thug B cried. He bent down to help his friend.

Roger kicked his head off.

Literally.

The head hit the far wall and bounced before the stump could even spray one ounce of blood. Then it gushed and we both stepped out of the way.

"Sometimes the old-fashioned methods work best," I said. I applied another layer of gloss to my lips.

"It was certainly a surprise to him," Roger said.

"Well, these magick guys, they get so caught up in having defense spells and being acutely aware of supernatural attacks, they forget a bullet can kill them just as easily," I said.

"Or poison lipstick," Roger said.

"It wasn't lipstick."

"Sure."

"I will admit, though, that I did swipe the idea from an old spy movie, and the lady in that used the same trick, only with lipstick."

"Why didn't it poison you?"

"I've put little bits of it on my lips over the years. I've grown immune to it. I bet I could eat the whole stick and not get a tummy ache."

"I'd like to see that."

"Let's get up to Room 223 before you hurt my feelings."

* * *

We took the elevator because we're both fundamentally lazy. That's one thing I like about Roger, besides the fact he's a badass. He's just as apt to take the short cuts as I am. He sleeps a lot, too. He's like a cat. But that's how it is for demons. When they're away from Hell for too long, it's like they get tired and need to sleep a lot. I bet the bastard was probably napping while I was getting my finger broken.

The elevator dinged and the doors opened.

A small woman flew inside. She kicked me in the groin and Roger in the head before either of us could move. Blades flashed in her hands. I dove out of the elevator, and that quick action was the only thing that saved my life.

I heard Roger cry out in pain but I couldn't be concerned with him. I had my own trouble to deal with.

Two more women were waiting for me in the hall. They were tall and slender and wore gossamer dresses that glittered in the overhead light. Their faces were long, their noses flat, and they both had blonde hair and looked identical. Their eyes burned a white hot green.

The one on the left opened her mouth and the hinges of her jaws popped like the snaps on a button. Her lower jaw fell down onto the top of her chest and her teeth...wiggled. I don't know how else to describe it except they looked alive, like they had a mind of their own and in the glimmer of the hall lights, I was transfixed for a brief moment by their movement. And then the teeth flew out and zoomed towards me, little guided missiles full of death. I knew in an instant what she and her sister were.

"Tooth Fairies!" I cried, though I had no idea if Roger heard me.

I slid down to the right. The teeth whipped past my head and hit the wall behind me. They sprouted legs and scurried down towards the floor. I rolled away from them but they were coming for me, fast and furious.

I pulled my gun. I had no defense for their like. I had to shoot the Fairies and hope for the best.

The one on the right unlocked her jaw and was about to spit more teeth at me but I was too quick. I shot her right between the eyes, praying to whatever gods were out there that a bullet would do the trick. Her head whipped back and the teeth burst from her mouth. They hit the ceiling and shattered some of the lights.

Her sister screeched and spat more teeth at me. These I could not dodge. I raised my gun to shield my face and they thumped hard into the back of my hand. The top part of the molars opened up and sprouted fangs of their own. They bit deep into my flesh. Several of the other teeth scurried across my fingers and inside the barrel of the gun. Before I could pull the trigger, they ate it from the inside out.

The gun fell apart, clattering in useless pieces to the floor.

I ran for the corner of the hall, shaking my hand. I smashed it against the wall and most of the attacking teeth fell out. Some I picked with my good hand and flicked away.

I could not fight this kind of assassin, not without a lot of prior preparations. They were just a rumor, I always thought, but now I had seen them face to face. They were genetically modified women, taken captive and experimented on using a combination of computer technology and occult sciences. There were two different kinds of Tooth Fairies and these, thankfully, were the wingless kind. If they could fly...

I shook my head and tried not to think about it.

The teeth on the floor poured up my feet and nipped my ankles. I staggered and nearly fell but I grabbed the wall and righted myself. I kicked the wall to shake them loose and they fell to the floor. I crunched them under my shoe heel.

Down the hall, I heard Roger yell again.

The remaining Fairy sprinted towards me, mouth hanging open. Dozens of new teeth had sprouted in her mouth and she spit them at me. They flew like bullets.

I ducked around the corner.

There, on the wall, was a fire extinguisher. It was my only chance. I smashed the glass and yanked out it out, pulling the pin. When she came around the corner, I sprayed that bitch right in her open mouth.

She shrieked something awful.

I clanged the extinguisher against her skull. She staggered backwards and I thought I might be winning until the teeth she'd shot at me jumped off the wall and peppered my arm and face.

And started biting.

I scraped them off as quickly as I could, before they could get purchase, but two dug in deep and there was no removing them. Their stings shot through my brain and bright flashes filled my vision.

I fell to my knees and looked up. This was it.

Roger roared around the corner. He held the torn body of the woman who had attacked him in the elevator. And when I say torn, I do mean torn. She was ripped right down the middle, her face split in two. Something else I'd never seen before.

He swung both sides of the body around like pincers and crushed the Tooth Fairy's head. My enemy fell to her knees in front of me, and we faced each other for a slight moment. She pitched to the side, her crumpled head leaking blood.

The scattered teeth she had fired at me, the ones not currently eating my face, ran back to their mistress. They jumped into her mouth and resumed their normal nests in her gums I could hear them whining like puppies who'd lost their master.

Roger set down what was left of his victim and hovered over me for a minute. He glowered, breathing hard. I could tell he wasn't happy.

The world spun around and around. I blacked out again but good old Roger was right there, eager with the cure. He slapped me until my eyes opened again.

"That's the poison from the teeth," he said. His voice was slurred. I thought of salt water taffy. "You have to stay awake or you will die."

I tried to get out, "Easy for you to say," but it emerged as a jumble of nonsense.

He slapped me again.

He was a real affectionate guy, for a demon.

Roger bit his finger and sucked on it until some blood came up from the wound. He stuck the bloody finger to the teeth embedded in my right ear and my left cheek. They shrieked and hissed before falling to the floor, dead. He nodded and closed his eyes.

"I'm going to regret this," he said.

He stuck the bloody finger into my mouth.

"Suck," he said.

And I did.

* * *

Three minutes later, I was up and ready to go. The demon blood healed the wounds on my face and even made my finger and hand feel better.

"You could have done that all along?" I said.

He nodded.

"So demon blood can heal, huh? I've never heard of that," I said.

"And you won't repeat it, ever," he said. "It is a secret we hold dear."

"I get it. If people found out, it would be open season on the demon scene. And you guys have enough trouble as it is, what with all the angels."

He nodded again.

"Damn," I said. I shook my head. Everything was much clearer now. The poison from the teeth bites was almost gone from my system. Demon blood was a hell of a thing.

"Don't get any ideas," I said.

"About what?"

"The way I was sucking on your finger. I don't want you to get too excited. That was just to save my life."

Roger grinned from ear to ear.

"If you were to suck my cock, it would kill you," he said.

"Oh? You shoot some kind of poison out when you, you know...?"

"No. It's just so big, your skull would split into two."

"You know they say that when you have to brag about something, it means the opposite is probably true." I reapplied the lip gloss.

"I'm not bragging," he said. "I'm stating a fact."

* * *

Room 223 stood right there in front of us, as unguarded as could be. I found this odd but I accepted it. Heather Tallent had enough reserves to call up Tooth Fairies to protect her – I imagined she was confident in herself.

My hand fell to the small of my back where I had a gun tucked into a holster, my backup plan. I couldn't get to it quick enough to deal with the second Fairy, but now that I had some time, I decided I was going to be ready.

I didn't bother to knock. I tried the door, found it was unlocked, and stepped right on inside. The .38 was in my hand. It felt good there. After all this weirdness, something cold and lethal and decidedly mechanical was reassuring. Also, my finger wasn't hurting near as bad and my hand was steady. It was only adrenaline that had saved my life with the Tooth Fairy. It had kept my aim true. Now I wouldn't need that. I was a pretty good shot.

"There you are!" Joseph Riley said. He was holding a cocktail in one hand and a pretzel in the other. "We were beginning to think you weren't going to make it."

I stared at him as Roger filled the room behind me.

"What are you doing here?" I said.

Riley laughed. He was a skinny man with a pencil mustache and drawn-on eyebrows. Don't ask me why he did that, just know that it was weird enough looking to be totally distracting. He had an unruly mop of black hair on top of his head. He wore a pair of pajamas made of silk and bunny slippers made of polyester. He was close to fifty years old and looked absolutely ridiculous standing there like he was.

"I'm waiting for you," Riley said. He eyed Roger. "You and your friend."

"What the hell does that mean?" I said.

And she slipped around the corner. There she was, Heather Tallent herself. She was just as had been described to me, just like she looked in her picture, only there in the flesh and blood, none of those things did her justice. My God, what a beautiful woman. And how she was dressed...

She was in a dominatrix outfit, all leather, no lace, pure black from head to toe. Her breasts were exposed, big and proud, the nipples triple pierced at their tips. She was shaved down below and her privates sort of gleamed like homing beacon in the dull light of the room. It was hard not to stare down there and keep from getting mesmerized.

"No," Roger said. His voice shook me from my reverie.

"I see your friend has figured it all out," Riley said.

"What the hell is going on here?" I said.

Heather hadn't said a word. She simply stepped into the room, owned every eye, and slunk closer to me. In her right hand she held a whip, coiled and ready for use.

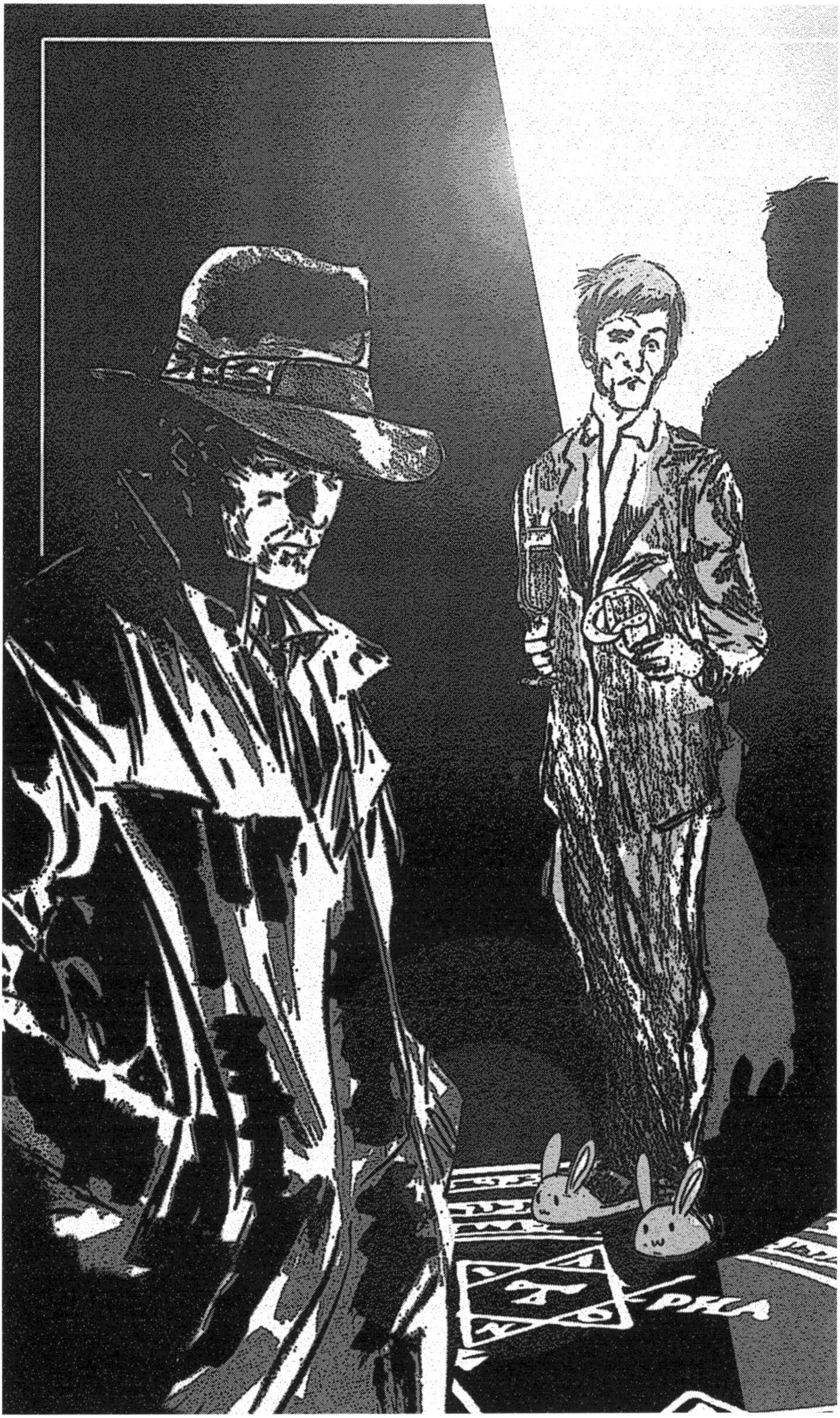

"They have trapped me," Roger said.

"Bullshit," I said. "That would take—"

"A magick circle lined with the blood of three infant girls," Riley said. "Yes, indeed."

I looked down at the floor. There was a magick circle there, all right, and it was rusty brown colored, like dried blood. I had led Roger right into the room to stand on it.

Before I could move, the whip cracked my hand and the pistol hit the floor. I staggered back and she brought the whip around again. This time it cracked by my face and if I hadn't ducked when I did, I would have lost my left eye. As it was, a long gash erupted from my temple and trailed back to behind my ear. Blood trickled from the wound.

Heather bent down and snatched up my gun. She tossed it onto the bed.

She smiled.

I still thought she looked pretty.

"Be careful with that thing," I said, pointing at the whip. "You might wreck my good looks."

"I wouldn't worry about such vanity any longer, if I were you," Riley said. He drank a bit of his cocktail and smiled at me.

"Well, shit, if I'm going to die, can I get some kind of explanation, at least?" I said.

Riley laughed. Heather grinned. She had perfect teeth, that girl. Perfect everything.

"Sure," Riley said. "Would you like a final drink?" He held up his glass.

"Nah," I said. "I don't drink."

"I insist."

"Nah."

"I cannot trust a man who doesn't share a drink with me," he said.

"Well, you'll have to send me to my grave with no trust between us then," I said.

He sighed and shrugged.

"I won't bore you with the details," he said. Heather moved in closer to me as he took a seat in a plush chair by the mini-bar.

"Talk as long as you want," I said. "I've got the time."

"No, no you don't," Riley said. "This is a simple matter, really. Amongst the Pac Con, it is rumored that you had a pet demon. These kinds of creatures are hard to come by, as you know."

"I don't think he likes being called a creature," I said.

"That's a shame."

"Or a pet."

"He will survive."

"It really does hurt his feelings," I said.

"That's not all of him that will be hurt before this evening is over," Riley said. "As you know, acquiring a demon is very hard. It's not like in the stories, where you can just simply summon one up and have it do your bidding. Things don't work like that."

"No, they sure don't," I said. Heather was really close to me now. I could feel the heat from her body. And I won't lie. Her proximity was turning me on.

"I have had some unfortunate disagreements with my colleagues in the Pac Con," Riley said. "And I determined I must split free from them."

"You can't do that. You signed a blood oath. You try to leave and—"

"I unleash a death curse upon myself," Riley said. "Yes, yes, I know that. But what they don't know and what I do know is a certain ritual that will break this oath and free me forever."

"Let me guess: you need demon blood for it," I said.

She was right in front of me now. Her breasts were almost touching my chest. My groin ached. Blood dripped down into the collar of my shirt. She smelled like cotton candy.

"Actually, I need the demon's scrotum," Riley said.

Roger groaned.

"Bad luck for you, pal," I said. But I never took my eyes off of Heather.

"So I gambled on the rumors about you being true," Riley said. "And I set the job up – led you here to this trap."

"You had Tooth Fairies to test us. Only a guy with a demon for a friend could get through such defenses."

"That's correct," Riley said. He chuckled. "For a dupe, you do have some detective skills, yet."

"So Heather was a decoy," I said.

"Exactly."

"And she doesn't speak?" I said.

"She's studying to be an Empanatrix," he said. "She had to take a vow of silence for two years."

"I get it," I said. "So she's going to kill me with her deadly assassin abilities and then you're going to cut Roger's balls off and gargle them while you jerk off in your pants?" I said.

"Such vulgarity," Riley said.

"Since I didn't take that drink, could I get a final request, anyway?" I said.

"What would that be?" Riley said. He sighed.

"I'd like a kiss," I said. I stared right into those ice blue eyes and thought I saw a twinkle of mischief there.

"It's up to her," Riley said.

"Uh, August," Roger said.

"Not now, big guy," I said.

She nodded.

"August," Roger said. "I wouldn't."

"I sure would," I said.

And I kissed her, long and hard, and even got some return tongue. She tasted just like she smelled: blue raspberry cotton candy.

I broke off the kiss and grabbed her arms, grinning.

"I'm wearing poison lipstick, bitch," I said. "You're dead meat."

She just smiled.

"August," Roger said. "I was trying to tell you. When you drank the blood, it also rendered the poison inert."

"Well, goddamn," I said. "Time for Plan B."

I threw Heather into the circle with Roger. She fell right into his arms

Riley jumped to his feet but that rich asshole was too slow. I dove on the bed, snatched up my gun, and shot him in the stomach. He gasped like he'd been punched, and dropped his drink. That pretzel he was eating hung out of the corner of his mouth, stuck there by the blood that sputtered from between his lips.

Roger squeezed Heather tight.

There's also a sound that a spine makes when it is crushed – like popcorn popping underwater, all wet and but still crunchy. Her big blue eyes turned cold and her body went limp. Roger tossed her from the circle.

I shook my head.

"It's a shame," I said. "She was one hell of a kisser."

I walked over to Riley, who was on all fours, trying to breathe. I think he was trying to speak some incantation. I kicked his teeth in to cut that nonsense out.

"August?" Roger said. "Do you mind?"

"Not at all, buddy," I said. I smeared the edges of the circle with my foot and he was able to exit. Magick circles, although powerful, can be precarious things.

I bent down and lifted Riley's head by his bloody hair. I gave him a wink.

"I think someone wants to have a word with you about the health of their scrotum," I said.

While Roger got his jollies, I rifled through Riley's belongings. I managed to put together three grand in hundred dollar bills from his stuff. I then went through Heather's things and found an odd assortment of sex toys, the kind you would use on some creature out of Lovecraft's imagination. They were all twisted and bent, some with nails driven through them and others shaped like stars. The bottom of the case where she kept her things was hollow. Inside there I found another ten grand.

Nice.

By then, Riley was through screaming.

"You ready to go?" I said.

"Yes," Roger said.

I convinced Roger to carry Riley and Heather into the bathroom and throw them into the giant tub. I sprayed them with lighter fluid and set them on fire before we left.

We strolled out the door and took the elevator down. I wasn't worried about cops or about the screaming that had been going on, or the fire. Those rooms were soundproofed, according to rumor, and the surrounding floors were probably deserted, anyhow. If Riley was going to conduct some big ceremony up there, he wouldn't want any prying eyes.

This job wasn't over yet, though. There was plenty to worry about. Once the Pac Con found out a member of theirs was dead, the city would be on high alert. I had to tread carefully. I hoped the fire would hide my trail but I couldn't be certain.

Fifteen grand would give me a nice bank for an extended vacation, though, so there was that.

"You said you put on lipstick," Roger said, smiling.

We crossed the lobby, the air thick with fire alarms.

"What?"

"Back there. You told her you were wearing poisoned lipstick. You admitted it was lipstick," he said. His grin was almost as big as his head.

"Shut up," I said.

H. P. Lovecraft's Weird Tales Reimagined As A Cosmic Horror Epic!

LOVECRAFTIAN
THE SHIPWRIGHT CIRCLE

STEVEN PHILIP JONES

"Every Lovecraftian will find something to enjoy in it."
--S. T. Joshi

Lovecraftian weaves classic H. P. Lovecraft stories and characters into a grand new single-universe contemporary series. This first novel introduces the Shipwright Circle, a gaggle of scholarly and creative friends at Miskatonic University in legend-haunted Arkham, Massachusetts.

Written by Steven Philip Jones
(*H. P. Lovecraft Worlds, Nightlinger*)

Interior Illustrations by Trey Baldwin
Cover Art by Manthos Lappas

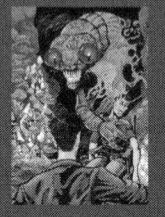

"Its scope is as dazzling as its tone is chilling."
--Matthew J. Elliott

Available from Caliber Books at *www.calibercomics.com*
and through Amazon!

CALIBER

www.stevenphilipjones.com

THE UNSUMMONING OF URB TC'LETH

BRYCE BEATTIE

I stopped the motorcycle in front of house number 435, hoping I remembered correctly. It was hard to imagine any of the abandoned houses in this neighborhood as being the right place. It was like a graveyard of murdered dreams and dead mortgages.

The sun stretched halfway across its daily finish line, and the dimming light added to the eerie vibe. I tugged off my gloves, unzipped my motorcycle jacket and pulled out my phone to double check.

"Joshua, heard you were in town. Friend of a friend in trouble. Thought you could help. Meet me at 435 Castlerock Rd. Tonight around 8:30. Dora."

I smiled just reading her name. She was the reason I had gone on my little journey of discovery. I had been smitten from the first moment I laid eyes on her. Now I'd finally get a chance to see her again. Of course, the last time I saw her, a smoke demon had exited her body via her eyes. It was my first and most visceral experience with the occult. I hadn't heard from her since that day, despite a flurry of texts sent over the ensuing week or two. She had just disappeared.

I wondered how she even knew I was in town.

A chill breeze swept down the street as if whispering an answer I wouldn't like. I couldn't see any other cars, but there was a detached garage. Maybe someone else was already there. It couldn't hurt to look around while I waited, right?

The front door had obviously been kicked in and repaired several times before. At some point the foreclosing bank had given up keeping the property secure. A yellowed paper proudly decorated the center of the door. It must have once read either "Foreclosed" or "Condemned."

I gave it a nudge and the door creaked open. The stale whiff of disuse and rot met me on the porch.

"Dora? Are you in here?"

Not really expecting an answer, I stepped inside. The smells of old urine and vomit mixed with the sick sweetness of decay intensified. Various shades of brown stained an old mattress in the corner of the front room. Someone had made an attempt to spray paint one wall black, but had run out of supplies about two-thirds down.

On the opposite wall hung the only decoration in the decrepit house – a painting of Marilyn Manson on black velvet. I raised an eyebrow and almost laughed out loud. Somewhere there existed a human being who thought this would be a good decoration for their secret hideout.

The front room emptied into a well-graffitied hallway. Disgusting bathroom on the right, filthy but mostly empty bedroom on the left, laundry closet on the right, almost closed door on the left. I nudged it open a little wider with with my shoe.

Jackpot.

My stomach rolled over once or twice. The carpet had been torn out. A stack of loose papers piled up in the far corner. A sloppy circle, drawn in chalk and perhaps six feet in diameter dominated the center of the room. The circle was split with four wavy lines, arranged similar to a giant tic-tac-toe board. In the center lay a chicken on its back, feathers intact. The bird's chest had been split wide open and a large candle placed inside.

The four corner divisions contained piles of colored sand. Dark red drip stains sprinkled the area inside and out of the circle. The scene smacked of left hand path magic.

Thankfully, the windows were open and the fowl carcass had dried out considerably since the ritual. Sure, it stank, but I'd still be able to eat something later if I wanted. Probably not chicken, though. I walked around the circle and picked up a few of the papers.

They looked like my college chemistry homework, but with bizarre and archaic symbols. At the top of several sheets was the name 'Urb Tc'leth'. A few included 'the feared' afterward.

I wondered if the doer of this spell-whatever-homework had made the name up. The more I looked, though, the more I was sure. The person who wrote these was either an insane genius, or actively receiving demonic revelation. In any case, whoever had prepared and done everything in the room had been serious. I hadn't witnessed too many actual attempted summonings, but everything jived with what I had seen and read before. More than that, the room felt wrong. It made the hair on my arms stand up.

The smell was an unearthly rot, the air thick with residual tobacco, incense, and less legal herbs. How Dora's 'friend of a friend' worked into all of this was still a mystery. Had this friend summoned something he couldn't handle? Was he obsessed with dark magic and needed an intervention?

Or was this friend simply falling in with a very bad crowd? I resumed my search but only found more papers. It was fascinating gibberish. Every page started with the same nonsense 'equation'. One of the papers had the phrase 'the feared' crossed out. Underneath, it read, 'MUST BE FEARED'. I folded that page and shoved it in my back pocket.

The unmistakable sound of a car door slamming rattled the windows. Relief washed over me and a smile crossed my lips. I tried to think of something clever to say upon seeing Dora again.

The front door creaked open, so I stood and headed for the hall. "I thought you were going to stand me up."

Apparently I was all out of clever. I turned the corner only to learn that I had perhaps assumed a little too much. Before me stood a young man, maybe early twenties, with too many piercings on his face and poorly drawn tattoos sleeving his bare arms.

We stared at each other, probably with the same open-mouthed look of idiot shock. A good ten seconds later, I spoke first.

"So, do you know Dora?"

His brow crumpled up. He looked back out the door, then again at me.

"Followup question. Is your first name Pierce? Because that would be—"

"What? No! You shut up. Who? What the hell are you doing here?"

I pointed. "Um, the door was unlocked. I was supposed to meet—"

"I said shut up!"

I raised my hands, fingers outstretched, and did the universal 'just calm down' motion.

It didn't work. The man became more jittery, eyes twitching left and right. He reached back and pulled a gun from his waistband, then pointed it at me. His hand shook and he held the gun almost sideways, like a moron. "Just stay there. And stay where I can see you."

I kept my hands up and shuffled forward until I was in the front room proper.

He sidled over to the painting of Marilyn Manson. With his free hand, he pulled it off its hook, revealing a ragged hole. I glanced around the room, searching for anything I could use as a projectile. I wasn't keen on getting shot, but I also wasn't eager to just stand around and let some jerk threaten me.

He reverently placed the painting on the ground, then thrust his hand into the hole. A moment later he worked a leather-bound book from its hiding place in the wall.

I crouched a couple of inches down, ready to dive or charge if things went further south.

"You just stay right there."

I nodded.

"I'm serious, if you try—"

The crunch of shattering glass cut him off, followed by an angry scream.

"Help!"

My new tattooed friend turned and ran for the door, keeping the gun more or less aimed behind him.

His trigger finger must have slipped, because a deafening bark filled the room.

My ears rang. I looked down at my chest. No holes there; always a good sign. The man disappeared into the front yard without checking to see if he had hit me. My nostrils flared and I set off at a sprint, stooping to scoop up the painting on my way.

I threw my body to the right of the doorway and craned my neck to look around the corner. A late 90s sedan of some sort sat backed up on the lawn a few feet away. A pair of women's boots filled with shapely legs hung out of the rear passenger's window. A spray of glass lay around the door. A frightened girl who could not have been wearing the boots stared at me through the back window.

"You stay in there, bitch." My assailant dove into the passenger's seat. "Let's go, I got it."

I stepped around and flung the painting. It was not a great missile, spinning and flopping wildly off course. It didn't even hit the car. Wheels spun on the dried, unmanaged grass and the sedan lurched forward. I couldn't make out the driver. As soon as the vehicle moved, the boots came in and a head full of long curly hair popped back up.

"Dora!"

"Joshua!"

She held up her hands, which appeared to be tied together. Who was she with? And the girl sitting next to her, was that the friend of a friend? My head filled even further with questions.

The car bounced off the curb into the street, narrowly missing my bike.

"Dora!"

I ran across the lawn, struggling to dig my gloves out of my pocket and wriggle my fingers back in. Before the fleeing car could even make it two blocks away, I grabbed the handlebars and swung my leg over the seat.

The engine of my Honda CB300F growled to life. It didn't have the deep grumbling roar of a Harley, nor the screaming acceleration of a high end Ducati sport bike. But that was okay. It had plenty of guts to catch the piece of crap beater that had stolen away Dora. I twisted the throttle and sped off toward the escaping car.

Only a sliver of sun still peeped over the horizon, but the air had cooled far more than it should have. The thought occurred to me that I might not only be feeling the night air.

In fact, I could almost feel some kind of bodiless entity chasing alongside me. Out of the corner of my eye, I could swear I saw glimpses of shades racing through shadows. It would not surprise me one bit if something followed us out of that creepy house.

I pushed the maybe-imaginary from my mind and focused on catching the definitely-real car. I'm not sure exactly when the driver realized I was following him, but his driving became more and more erratic as I closed in. He started taking curves like a wild man. Tires squealed. The car frame groaned like the whole vehicle might tear itself in half at any moment.

He must have been an idiot, as he kept doing the two things my motorcycle was way better at doing than his embarrassment of a car – turning tight corners and accelerating.

It was a challenge I couldn't resist. This kind of riding set my soul dancing. In no time I had caught up, and tailed only a car length or so behind. Dora and the other girl watched me with wide eyes. They shouted things I couldn't hear and frantically waved their bound hands.

About that time, I realized who the idiot had actually been, because now I faced the same problem that I had seen my dog confront a dozen times while growing up: I had caught up to the car I was chasing, and now I had no idea what to do with it.

Pierce leaned his head and shoulder out the passenger window as he tried to level his pistol at me. His hand bounced with the unpredictable motion of the ride.

The gun roared. I could swear I heard the bullet whiz by somewhere to my right. My heart skipped a beat then started pounding like a five-year-old waiting for the bathroom.

I instinctively swerved left. A moment later the driver did the same. As soon as he did, Pierce fired several more shots. All went wide. At least I thought they did. My adrenaline was pumping so hard I might not even notice. I made a mental note to check myself again for holes when this was over.

Pierce had wild ecstasy written all over his face. He howled what had to be some kind of profanity-laced taunt with too-wide open eyes and a menacing grin.

Before he could take another shot, a booted foot kicked through the already shattered back window and made contact with his hand. His arm flopped wide but he didn't drop his pistol.

A pit opened up in my stomach. "Dora, no!" I shouted into the wind.

His arm retracted into the car for a moment so that he could terrify the back seat captives. The bouncy road and erratic driving would make him miss me all night. But he could straight up murder Dora without a problem.

Red lights flashed and the car jerked to the right. If it wasn't for bad brakes, I would have slammed into the trunk. As it was, I leaned left and missed the back bumper by a good three millimeters.

Not able to brake fast enough, I zipped by. In the dimming evening light, I caught a glimpse of the driver. He was unnaturally pale, with horns tattooed on his bald head. I didn't want to believe it, but it looked like he was wearing a tuxedo—high collar, bow-tie and all.

There no was time for a second look. My recklessness and stupidity had now put me in front of him. And he hadn't looked like the sort to agree to a do over.

His tires squealed and his little engine screeched. I turned my full focus to the road ahead. The wind pulled against my face and jacket as I accelerated. Yes, part of me had to have known that my life was in serious danger, but the rest of me just plain didn't care. I had never raced around like this before, and it was exhilarating.

Now that I was in front I needed to pay much more attention to the surrounding area. Dilapidated and abandoned homes gave way to boarded up retail shops. The occasional car passed going the other way.

I charged straight ahead, hoping that some sort of plan to save Dora would miraculously jump into my brain. The driver behind me continued his chase, but there was no way he could hope to catch me. Not unless I did something stupid.

Up ahead loomed a larger thoroughfare. Perhaps there'd be even more cars, ones whose drivers might actually care enough to call the police and report two lunatics speeding through the twilight.

I didn't have the luxury of slowing and turning safely. I was more nimble on my bike, but if I slowed too much, he could splat me all over the pavement with the slightest of swerves.

Still, I had to chance it.

I squeezed and stomped the brakes, nearly flying over the handlebars in the process. Leaning to the right, I goosed the throttle again. My back tire spun and screamed and whirled itself around, spraying gravel in what I can only assume was a most badass wave. Somehow I stayed upright and took off like a shot down the larger road. I watched in my mirror to see if Pierce and the horned chauffeur would follow.

They did, on two wheels. As his junker crashed back to four wheels I would not have been surprised if it left a trail of broken parts.

My mind raced. How in the world was I going to be able to get back behind them? And then follow without them knowing? I had screwed up pretty bad and had no idea how I might possibly set it right. Still, there was no way I could give up now. Not with Dora tied up in the back seat of some lunatic's car.

Up ahead in the deepening twilight I saw two red lights flashing. I heard the loud 'ding, ding, dinging' before it clicked in my mind that I was coming up on a railroad crossing, and so was a train. The arms dropped toward the ground.

I couldn't stop. If I did, the horned chauffeur would run me over. Wind whipped my hair around and I poured on as much speed as possible. Street lights and signs flashed by. The striped arms slammed and wobbled at their lowest position. The train couldn't be far now.

I weaved over into the oncoming traffic lane and slowed enough to stay upright while dodging the safety arms.

The train conductor blew his horn as I crossed the tracks. It sounded like it had gone off inside my head. I cleared the intersection just as the train sped through. My heart pounded somewhere in my throat. I let out a whoop, then stopped and looked over my shoulder.

Through the gaps between train cars I saw the green piece of crap stop, back up, then turn around. Twilight darkened toward night and all I could see were brief glimpses of demon-eye-red taillights growing smaller.

I shuddered to think what they were going to do with Dora. Especially now that she had ticked them off. The pit in my stomach widened. My pride and my stupidity had condemned her. For the first time that night, I considered calling 911. But what would I tell them? "Hi, my friend's been kidnapped and she was in a greenish car whose license I don't have and I saw them on a street that I can't name but I think they've turned now..."

Yeah, at that point it wouldn't help.

As soon as the train rumbled down its steel tracks, I raced back across, then down to the street Pierce and the horned chauffeur had taken. I turned where they turned, but saw no taillights in the distance to follow—what was I expecting? They were long gone, and I didn't even know which way they were headed.

I drove slowly for two or three blocks, looking down each intersection for any type of sign.

A motion in my side mirror caught my eye. I twisted my torso and looked back over my shoulder. A woman ran down the middle of the street. She waved her left arm wildly. My eyes widened and my heart skipped a beat. Could it be? I whipped around and drove to meet her.

Dora didn't stop her mad sprint. Her dark, curly hair bounced around like crazy and she held her right arm extra close to her body.

No sooner had I stopped the motorcycle and jumped off than she threw her arms around me, nearly sending me back over my bike and down to the pavement.

"You came, thank you."

For that glorious moment, the stress-tightened muscles in my neck and forearms relaxed. The creepiness and the craziness that had screamed in my face all evening faded into fuzzy background. Neither of us spoke, neither cried. We simply held each other.

It couldn't last, however, and she winced as she pulled back. The light was bad but now up close I could see. She sported some fairly gnarly road burns on her right shoulder and elbow. The right knee of her jeans had a fresh hole behind which was probably a skinned knee.

"Dora, what happened to—"

"I can't believe you didn't see me. I was almost to the intersection. Give me your phone."

I fumbled my glove off. "Sure, but how did you—"

"I got the door open and jumped on a turn. That dick in the driver's seat took them a bit more slowly after you got stuck behind the train. Now hurry."

I dug out my phone and handed it over. "Are you okay? Do you need an ER or—"

"Hold on, Joshua." She snatched it from my hand and immediately started fiddling.

I just stood in awkward silence while she clicked and swiped and clicked some more. Every moment I half expected the kidnappers to come screaming around the corner. Standing in the middle of the street, I couldn't help but feel like a sitting duck.

"Sooo..."

"Hold on, almost got it."

The western horizon dimmed into gray blue. Somewhere off to my right, the glow above the still-living part of the city took over as the brightest part of the sky. The chill night sent a shiver down my spine.

"Do you want my jacket?"

"What for? It's still pretty warm out. Besides, my shoulder would probably stick to it."

I wondered if my experience in the abandoned house had something to do with it. Dora hadn't gone in. Paranormal sites had often left me with lingering unease, and this wasn't the first time my physical perceptions had been affected after the fact.

"Got 'em. Let's go."

"What?"

"Oh, sorry. I left my phone jammed in the crack of the seat. I have an app that shows my friends and family where I am."

"So I get to finally be a friend? Because last time you never even called me back."

"Look, I know you're not mad at me. After all, you showed up." She leaned forward and kissed me on the cheek. "Now let's go help Hayzley."

A warmth radiated from the spot where her lips touched. It drove out the cold I had been feeling. At least for a bit.

"Hayzley? Really?" I swung my leg over the bike.

It occurred to me that I didn't know who Hayzley was or why I should help her. It didn't matter anyway. Dora was going to help, and now that I'd been given the chance, I was going to be at her side. People always say that absence makes the heart grow fonder. Well, it had been about a year since I had heard from Dora, and my fondness was currently swelling toward melodrama.

Besides, it certainly felt like someone would be trying to summon a demon before sun up. This I just had to see. And then shut it down. Dora climbed on behind, wrapping her left arm around my waist. "Oh you shut up. I didn't name her."

* * *

She checked the app for directions every couple of minutes as we made our way down the unfamiliar streets. Finally, Dora's phone stopped moving in the middle of an industrial zone.

Huge sections of this once bustling city had been abandoned, but somehow this part of town was different. I mean, before, the empty neighborhood was old and broken, sure. But it had clearly once been full of flower gardens, children's toys and dreams. This graveyard of fallen industry had always been a cement sea, without personality and without pity. Now the buildings were corpses, dusty, dark and cold. Each broken window brandished teeth of glass just waiting to chew up any trespasser.

Maybe one of every twenty facilities was still open for business with lights on and a handful of cars in barbed wire-guarded parking lots. Such sparks of life did nothing to soften the deceased feel of the area. They were scavengers living off the rotting corpse of a behemoth industry.

We pulled up in the parking lot of a warehouse behind another warehouse, and were surprised to see a dozen or so other vehicles. The green beast was parked on the walkway that lead to the building's office entrance. Faint light danced through the banks of windows high up on the brick walls. Someone had graffitied a crude cartoon devil on one patch of the wall.

I turned off the motorcycle and pulled out the key. "Anything you want to tell me before we head in there?"

"I've learned some things since last time. If she summons the demon, let me handle it and you just get Hayzley out."

"Wait, if SHE summons it? I thought she was kidnapped, just like—"

"Right, but she's a conduit. I think they're going to kill her either way."

"What's a conduit? And what about all these cars? What do we do about the other people in there?"

"I don't know." She said then grabbed my hand. "Hopefully we'll figure that out soon."

As soon as we stopped talking, I noticed a 'Thoom Thoom!' throbbing from the building, like it had a heartbeat.

The front door had been forced long ago and what we saw of the office was a wreck. Cigarette butts, beer cans, and ratty old blankets littered the floor. The pounding intensified and clarified once we were inside. Someone in the actual warehouse area had to be beating a large drum. A chorus of frenzied shouts and claps joined the primal beat.

I accidentally kicked over a bag of urine-flavored garbage. "I wish we had brought a light."

"Don't worry, I've got that covered if we need it."

I didn't know what she could possibly mean by that, but I didn't have time to ask. Dora opened the back door that opened into the storage area and we slipped through.

The noise intensified and the din of echoing unhinged revelry made my eyes vibrate. This space had a bit more light. Apparently the demon-summoning club had a bonfire going somewhere near the other end. Much of the smoke left through broken windows up high, but some of it settled, leaving a cough-inducing haze in the air.

Rows of steel columns supported the roof. Stacks of broken pallets and piles of ancient metal junk dominated the vast space. I guessed at some point somebody was stripping abandoned buildings in the area to sell to a recycler.

We couldn't see the fire directly but the noise alone must have come from a fair-sized crowd.

I took the lead to the edge of the closest pile and peeked around the corner. A center aisle had been kept mostly clear, and I could see the length of the whole building. The scene occurring near the center of the colossal space filled me with fascination. If it weren't for the modern clothes, I would have thought the scene before me was happening in some uncivilized jungle during a ritual moon.

A circle of men and women danced with wild gyrations around the horned chauffeur, who made preparations on the cement. Several others stood around, clapping or dancing in place. After a while he stood erect with his arms held high and reveled in the primal display around him.

A drummer stood with his back to me and pounded on two large steel barrels mounted atop cinder blocks. On each side of him was a pile of burning wood pallets.

Beyond the drums and fires and feverish dancing stood a large chain-link dog kennel with a canvas roof. Hayzley clung to the side, shaking and shouting.

I turned back to Dora. "She's in the back corner. Come on."

We retreated to the edges of the room and hugged the deepest shadows. The crowd continued in frenzied ecstasy, reenacting a scene from humanity's primeval roots. Not a one looked away to spot Dora and I clumsily sneaking by.

When we stepped from behind the final pile, Hayzley noticed and bellowed a desperate plea. The tuxedo-clad fiend continued working on his summoning circle, now pouring colored sand from bags into the corners. I didn't stop to think. Even though there was no more cover, I ran to the back of the cage, Dora close on my heels.

It was a reckless chance taken too far.

The horned man shouted something and motioned with his thumb in front of his throat. The drums stopped. The dancing circle slowed and stopped with all eyes turning to our little rescue party.

I stepped around from the back of the enclosure. "Well, shi—"

"Get them!" shouted the horned man.

The crowd swarmed toward me.

I gritted my teeth and charged directly into their midst. One way or another this would end poorly for me, but maybe I could distract them enough to give Dora a chance to escape.

A dozen wretched revelers pressed in close around me on all sides. There was no space to lineup a good punch, so I was all elbows and knees. I connected left and right with their sweaty bodies, not doing any real damage, but keeping them from holding my arms.

In fact, the crowd had pressed in too close. No one could take a swing at me without hitting at least two of their own number first. Too hyped up to care about collateral damage, they threw the punches anyway. My arms and body were riddled with half strength strikes. I twisted to catch a glimpse of Dora and see if she had escaped.

Nope. She clutched some guy's ponytail and jerked it around like she was trying to steal it. She had charged into battle right behind me. I didn't get to see any more of the brawl, because somebody connected something hard with the back of my head.

I woke up to see Dora kneeling next to me. Her road rash arm had bled a bit more and her clothes were stretched and dirty from the fight. She gingerly ran her fingers through my hair.

"Did we win?"

She looked me in the eyes and raised an eyebrow. "Define win."

I sat up and rolled to an elbow. We were in the cage. The crowd surrounded the summoning circle, pressing closer than before. "Oh, I think this qualifies as a definite 'not yet'."

"Love that attitude, Joshua. If we get out of this, I'm making you bacon pancakes."

I rolled the rest of the way over, grabbed at the chain link and pulled myself up.

A scream tore through the air. The crowd did not helpfully part to let me see, but it had to be Hayzley.

I ran to the door. A bicycle cable lock held it to the frame. It was one of those locks with four dials of letters that spell a magic unlocking word.

The horned chauffeur raised a knife above the crowd, pointing straight upward, and began chanting in the fakest-sounding Latin I'd ever heard.

"Taste of the fear!" He roared, then returned to his Latinish mumblings.

We were running out of time. I fumbled with the lock. "I should try 'hell' or 'goth' or 'mope.' Something creative like that."

"No need. I can beat that thing." Dora nudged me aside and took the lock into her hands.

"What?"

"Didn't you have a bike when you were a kid?" She wrapped her pinkies around the cable and pulled apart. With her thumb and forefinger, she played with the first dial.

"Yeah, but I grew up in a small town. I could have left it leaned up against a storefront all night long and no one would have touched it."

"I learned real quick that if I used a lock this cheap and left for more than five minutes, then I could plan on having my bike stolen. They are almost trivial to unlock if you know what to do."

I looked around on the floor to see if there was anything around that could help. An epiphany struck.

"Hey, Dora. Save the awesome burglary skills for the next date. I don't think they anchored this cage to the floor. We can probably just lift it."

"What makes you think there'll be a second date?"

"Think of it this way." I grabbed the chain link panel low with both hands. "The second date couldn't possibly be worse than this."

She stepped beside me and grabbed the panel as well. "I don't know. I had a guy take me to a Lady Gaga concert a while back."

I looked over. "Plus, you promised me pancakes."

"Bacon pancakes even."

"Lift."

The cage would have been plenty heavy if we had to hoist the whole thing off the ground all at once. Fortunately, all we had to do was tip it.

Dora and I lifted the base about hip high. I held it up while Dora scurried under, then she held it for me. The cage clanked to the ground but the crowd was so into the ritual-in-progress that no one noticed.

The horned chauffeur raised his knife higher into the air. "I now sacrifice this conduit so that Urb Tc'leth may take form." He leered at the cowering girl.

Hayzley shrieked "No!" above the chanting of the crowd. A wave of scorching air blasted from the circle.

Most in the crowd dropped to their knees. I very nearly lost my footing. Hayzley's cowering form lifted into the air. Her head and arms flopped backwards, limp. She hovered a few inches off the ground and slowly spun like someone had attached a rope to her sternum.

A voice rumbled from the floor. "Who is most feared among you?"

The horned chauffeur wobbled on his feet and opened his mouth to speak, but all that came out was a rasping sound.

"You will do." The floor said.

A thick substance the color of old blood oozed from the chalk marks of the summoning circle.

"My master, I brought you this vessel, this conduit, so that she—"

"ENOUGH!"

The floating girl's hand lifted and pointed toward the villain in the tuxedo. The red muck formed bubbles which percolated through the air toward her hand.

I stared, transfixed by the strangeness unfolding before me.

The blobs shook and wobbled in their flight toward Hayzley's outstretched finger. The instant the first bubble actually touched her finger, it shot out and splashed against the tuxedoed man's neck.

He raised first a confused eyebrow, then a hand to his neck.

The gentle bubbling continued. Every time a blob or bubble reached her hand, it immediately changed course and flung itself across the circle. The projectiles pelted tuxedo and tattooed skin in a furious barrage. The red ooze dripped from his body in a way that resembled candle wax. He clawed at the liquid around his eyes and mouth, but could not clear it away. Underneath the thick liquid layer, his skin formed and unformed little mounds, as if something boiled underneath.

Once he was completely covered, Hayzley dropped her hand. The remaining blobs splattered to the ground. An angry hiss spat from the lines of the summoning circle followed by a geyser of deep red which shot straight up into the air. It made a crimson curtain surrounding chauffeur and conduit alike.

The eruption only lasted a second or two, then the waxy red liquid came crashing down, splashing on the worshiping revelers.

Hayzley's body now lay crumpled in a heap upon the ground.

Looming over her was a completely changed horned chauffeur. Unnatural lumps marred his face. The red liquid dried and cooled into his skin. If he hadn't still been wearing the tuxedo, I would not have recognized him at all.

A stench poured out of the summoning circle, smelling like cheap beer mixed with spoiled milk.

The transformed man-thing stood tall and looked around. "I have returned."

He lifted his hands and opened then closed his fists. As he did so, the skin cracked and blackened and took on an alligator hide appearance.

Raw energy pulsed from the summoned demon.

"I hunger. Which of you dies first?" His voice echoed into the piles of junk that surrounded us.

It occurred to me that this was no longer a person. The demon had stolen the horned chauffeur's body. This was much more than a regular old possession.

Some idiot with dyed-jet-black hair and too much mascara looked up from his knees. "Oh great Urb Tc'leth. We brought the conduit— the girl—"

"No." The demon leaped across the edge of the summoning circle, grabbed the kid by the throat, and lifted him off the ground. "Her fear is old, and too well used. But yours is new and delicious."

The demon's voice had changed, shifting from thunder and rumble to sharp and soul-piercing.

The mob who had come to summon the demon looked at each other nervously. Many rose to their feet and took a few steps back. A few remained on their knees and just gazed stupidly. A familiar face stepped from the crowd.

"Put him down." Pierce's hand shook as he tried to aim his gun at the demon. "You're supposed to stay inside the circle."

The people behind the demon dove to the side, hoping to not get hit by a stray bullet.

Urb Tc'leth made a flourish with its free hand. "It's possible he did it wrong. It's also possible I lied to the one who wrote down the instructions."

I half wanted to root for Pierce, despite the fact that he had shot at me earlier.

The black haired kid flailed and kicked at Urb Tc'leths's body. Three shots rang out. Three bullets drilled into the demon's chest and side.

Urb Tc'leth flung the hapless goth at Pierce. The two collided and rolled onto the floor in a tangle of arms and legs.

Before either could move, the demon was upon them. It crouched and flung the kid aside. "You play brave, but I taste the truth." It pulled out the knife the Chauffeur had waved around and drove it into Pierce's chest.

The once panic-paralyzed onlookers howled and shook and clawed each other in an effort to flee. The demon did not wait to act. It leaped to its feet, sprinted with inhuman speed, and snatched two running worshipers by the back of their hair.

With a fierce thrust, Urb Tc'leth drove their faces into the cement.

The demon breathed in sharply through its nose like terrified screams were the sweetest smelling thing in the world. It snapped its fingers and the resounding clang of a slamming door shook the room.

I looked around at the chaos, then shook the stupor from my head. The time for action had come.

Dora had apparently decided the same. She raised her right arm high in the air, clutching her fingers close together and making circles above her. She extended her left arm with her fingers spread and stretched.

"What are you doing?"

Her fingertips glowed. "Get Hayzley out of here."

I nodded. "Right."

Urb Tc'leth caught sight of Dora. "And what do you think you're doing?"

I ran to where Hayzley lay and crouched beside her.

The demon did something crunchy with the arm of one of the revelers he had tackled, then stood to face Dora.

Dora continued making the same motion. The glowing intensified and burst into a blinding column of light which shot from her hand into the demon's chest.

"No!" The demon shouted and raised its arms to block the bright beam.

"Go back to hell!" Dora shouted.

A thrill of tingles flashed up my spine.

Urb Tc'leth doubled over and convulsed. A deep, raspy sound spilled out of its filthy mouth. The demon strained to lift a quivering red hand into the beam of light.

It held that position for a good ten seconds before I realized that the sound was not fear or pain, but sickening giggles.

"Dora, I think—"

Urb Tc'leth sprung up straight and released the full horror of its booming laughter. "Fool! I am no weak creature of smoke and shadow. I am Urb Tc'leth, the Feared. I have form. I have taken life. I have a body."

The demon walked to Pierce's body and ripped the knife from his chest. Without even a sideways glance, Urb Tc'leth flung the blade.

Dora dropped the spell and hurtled her body backward. She cursed as she hit the cement floor.

The knife spun through the air exactly where her chest had been a half-second ago.

The frenzied pounding of terrified people echoed through the warehouse as they tried in vain to open the office door or one of the bays.

I looked down at Hayzley. Her eyes fluttered.

The demon sprung over one of the smaller garbage piles into madly dancing shadows cast by the twin bonfires. No sooner had he landed than another scream sliced through the din, then was cut short.

Was the beast getting stronger?

I turned my head. "Dora, are you all right?"

She rolled over onto her side. Her voice shook. "That was supposed to work."

I stood. "I guess that means it's my turn. Come be with Hayzley. I think she's coming around."

Dora pushed up onto one knee. "What are you going to do?"

I shrugged "Well—"

"Die!" The demon's voice stung my ears.

I pivoted.

The powerful supernatural being stepped from the shadows of a larger metal pile. He wasn't physically any bigger, but he held his posture with even more menace and assurance than before. The bizarre had come to life before my very eyes and threatened to kill me. Echoing noises hammered at my eardrums. Dora's spell had failed. In a few moments time, the beast before me could slaughter every person in the warehouse. It had already killed several. Death seemed almost certain.

I would probably end up as a messy stain on the cement, but there is no way that thing would be getting through me alive to murder Dora and Hayzley. I was going to stand and fight to the end.

So why wasn't it attacking me?

My adrenals must have been working overtime pumping all that adrenaline into my blood. My heart pounded in my chest. My hands shook. My breathing quickened through flared nostrils. A sheen of sweat formed on my body.

And then it hit me. I wasn't scared. I was excited. So excited I could taste it. Everything about the situation made me feel alive. The danger, the smoke, the noise, everything.

And then I remembered something I saw back at the abandoned house. I took the paper from my back pocket. The one with the words "MUST BE FEARED" crossed out. The right corner of my lips curled up into a smirk. I wadded it up, sauntered over to the closer bonfire, and threw it in.

"You have a problem, demon."

"Your problem is much—"

"You see, you must be feared, and I don't fear you. At all."

The hell-spawn's eyes narrowed. The warehouse shook as he spoke. "I will tear your flesh and consume your soul."

I tugged on the bottom of my left motorcycle glove, then the right, snugging them on nicely. Just for effect. "Your name's Urb Tc'leth, right? Really? Urb Tickle-eth? Like 'Behold how Urb tickleth his victims?' Yeah, you sound terrifying."

"I will crush—"

"Why don't you just call yourself Cuddles, the Snuggly?"

"I'm going to—"

"Not likely."

Chunks of wood and metal garbage littered the floor around me, but I didn't bother to pick one up as a weapon. Instead, I marched toward the unholy beast and glared into its blood red eyes.

In them swelled an insatiable lust for power. In them burned malice and unfathomable hatred. In them swirled lifetimes of pain. They were the type of eyes that would drive a coward insane.

They just make me angry.

The demon's face contorted into a mask of confusion as I approached. Like no one had ever dared to just walk up to him before. The air became palpably warmer with each step.

"You think bravado can veil your fear from me? I have… I have…" It stammered and took a half step back. "What are you?"

I shouted and charged the last three steps.

The demon raised its hand to strike, but it was too slow. I joined my hips, shoulder and arm in one full-body motion and drove my fist into its solar plexus.

It doubled over in pain, then barely managed to whisper. "Wait."

I grabbed its shoulders and brought my knee up as hard as I could.

The demon made a clumsy effort to block, but was only able to slow the strike.

I tightened my grip on the tuxedo, turned, and pulled.

Urb Tc'leth spun and flopped onto the cement.

Before it could move, I straddled its chest and began to pound its face in like an MMA champ.

Its rough skin tore holes in my gloves and then dug gashes into my knuckles. I didn't care. I was unhinged. I let fly with a flurry of punches. There was no way in hell I was going to let this abomination stand back up.

The well-dressed demon flailed and grabbed at my arms, but couldn't get a grip. I continued my onslaught.

Its counter efforts slacked and its arms fell limp. I stopped for a moment and gasped in as deep of breaths as I could manage. "Go back to wherever you came from."

"You—" *cough* "—don't have the authority to command me from this plane."

"Who said anything about authority? You know what? I'm just going to slam your skull against the floor until you leave this plane. Go ahead and stay if that appeals to you. But everyone will know that you were beaten by some poor schlub with his bare hands. You'll be lucky if anyone is ever scared of you again."

I wrapped my hands around the demon's throat and made good on my word. Three times I beat that disgusting head against the cement. Each time it made a deep and booming noise, like I was knocking on hell's door itself. With the fourth blow, its whole body just collapsed and melted into the waxy red substance that had accompanied its arrival.

All that remained was the stained, sickening tuxedo, and the leather notebook from the abandoned house stuffed in a pocket.

With the demon gone, the door locks released and were able to open. What was left of the mob bolted like cockroaches from sunlight.

* * *

I awoke on a leather couch at 2:37 PM the next day to the smell of bacon cooking. My eyes didn't want to open.

I swung my legs off and sat up with a grunt.

My neck, abs, arms and chest all complained about the effort. From the feel of things, I had a fairly bounteous crop of bruises, too.

I managed to pry my eyes open a crack then peeled the shredded gloves from my hands.

A tiny voice giggled from across the room.

I tilted my head up and winced.

A little girl, maybe 5 or 6 years old, stood over by the doorway. She covered her mouth and giggled again.

"Hey, kiddo." My voice sounded somewhat like velcro unzipping.

She turned and ran from the room.

A moment later Dora appeared in the doorway. She had showered, changed clothes, dressed the road rash on her arm and gotten her curly hair back under control.

"I was hoping the smell of bacon would roust you."

With each word the speaking got a little easier. "How's Hayzley?"

"Rattled." Dora crossed the room.

"And, uh, where are we?"

"Hayzley's folks' house. You followed us home last night, then collapsed."

I craned my neck to look her in the eye. "So, did every—"

Dora bent over and kissed me on the lips, then pushed a small box into my hands.

My mind froze and I forgot what I was going to ask. I flipped open the box's lid. Inside lay a well polished pair of brass knuckles.

"So you don't have to tear your hands and gloves apart next time you need to punch a demon."

I smiled. Even my face muscles hurt. "Thanks. I hope these don't ever need to come in handy, but somehow I think they might."

She kissed me again then pointed down the hall. "Go get cleaned up. Hayzley's dad dug out some clothes for you. If you'll excuse me, I have a bacon pancake promise to finish cooking."

I reached out and touched her hand as she backed away. "Do you want to go out tonight?"

Dora winked, tossed her hair, then walked out of the room.

MURDER, MADNESS AND THE SUPERNATURAL

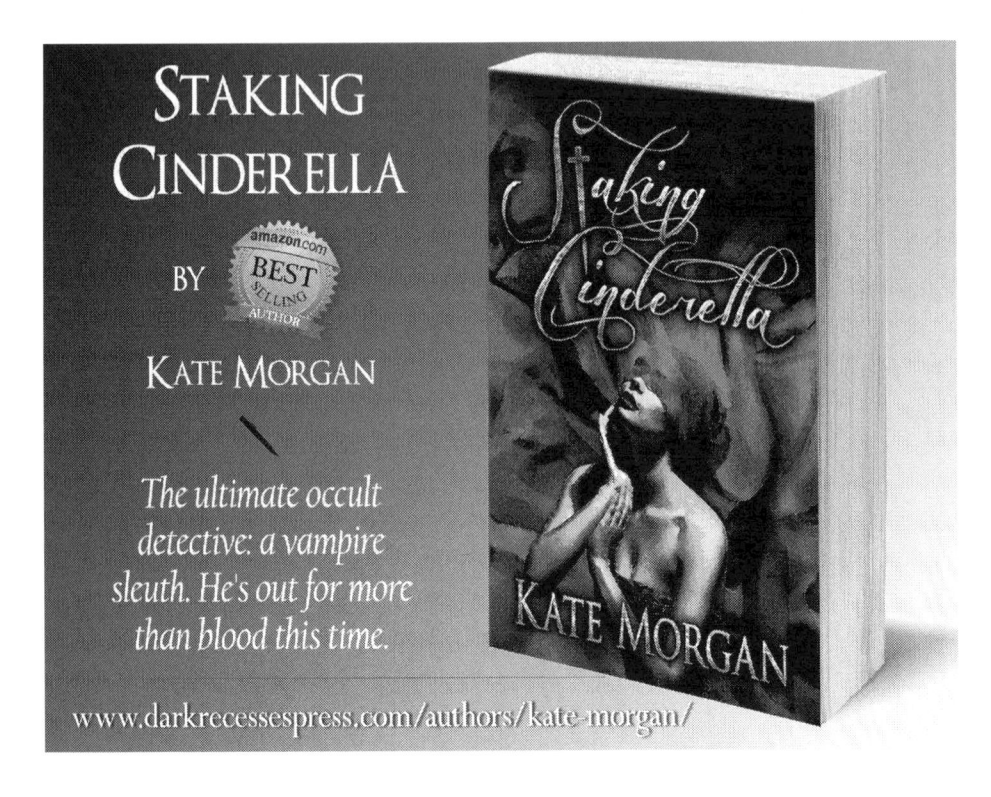

Slip into a torn overcoat, put your feet up on a street-urchin, and explore dark tales of London, the haunted Suffolk shores, the bleak North Sea, and more. Have a sherry with Great Aunt Agatha, or follow a 'bank clerk' through Whitechapel – the results may not be quite what you expected...

All three books now available in Kindle from IFD Publishing
Amazon UK and Amazon US

STAKING CINDERELLA

BY

KATE MORGAN

amazon.com BEST SELLING AUTHOR

The ultimate occult detective: a vampire sleuth. He's out for more than blood this time.

www.darkrecessespress.com/authors/kate-morgan/

IN PERPETUITY

ALEXIS AMES

Basil arrived on Phobos Station at thirteen in the morning local time, severely jet-lagged and reeling slightly from the breakneck flight from the surface. He hadn't been space-sick since he was eight years old, yet had to beg some anti-nausea and anti-vertigo tablets from the shuttle's auto-doc before he could trust himself to even set foot on the station.

When he did, an officer he could only assume was his escort saluted smartly and said, "Detective Sinclair, welcome to Phobos Station. I'm Ensign Hicks. The commander has asked to see you immediately."

"By all means." Basil adjusted his bag so the strap stopped digging into his neck. "Lead the way."

Adelaide Williamson had obviously been waiting impatiently for his arrival, for the door to her office opened before Hicks could press the chime. She dismissed him with a nod and turned to Basil.

"Commander." He grasped her outstretched hand. "Basil Sinclair. It's good to meet you."

"Thank you for coming on such short notice, Detective. Please, come in." She stepped back to allow him over the threshold. The door slid shut automatically behind him, and she waved him into a chair in front of her desk. He dropped his bag by his feet.

"Your message sounded urgent."

Not to mention the fact that an official Navy shuttle had been dispatched to bring him personally to the station, rather than wait for him to arrange for transport on a commercial ship. She nodded.

"I don't know how much you know about the research that we do here—"

"You're studying the effects of radiation and deep-space travel on various humanoid species to prepare for future extra-solar missions," he said. "Yes, I did a bit of light reading about it on the way here."

She gave him a wan smile. "Yes, essentially. Except that about two weeks ago, an experiment went awry and ripped a hole into another dimension. We were able to seal the breach, but not before a demon slipped through."

"A demon." The hairs on the back of his neck prickled. He took a deep breath. Cold flooded his body, and blood pounded in his ears. *Focus.* "How can you be sure it's a demon?"

"Absolutely sure? We can't. But there aren't many creatures that can kill a vampire, Detective." She slid a hand screen across the desk to him. "And none that kill in this manner."

Basil was glad he had foregone breakfast on the shuttle. The image of the mutilated vampire – a lieutenant, by the stripes Basil could see on the shoulders of his shredded uniform – would be burned into his eyes for a long time. He swallowed and pushed the hand screen back.

"All right," he said, conceding the point. "It's been on this station for two weeks. Has this been the only casualty?"

"There have been four other deaths: two vampires, a werewolf, and a human," she said. "We couldn't prove conclusively that any of those were the result of the demon, but they *were* suspicious. For one, we average about one death a year on this station, and there have been five now in two weeks."

"Are there plans to evacuate?"

Adelaide pulled a face. "The government doesn't want to interrupt our research if we can help it, and with two thousand civilians living here, they don't want to start a panic with mass evacuation. Plus it would be an expensive endeavor. They'd rather you look into the matter, to see if you can solve it... quietly. Discreetly."

"Demons aren't exactly known for their discretion," Basil muttered. He shook his head; it wasn't as though the government was giving him much of a choice. "I'll help, of course I will."

"What do you need?"

"I'll want to examine where the hole was ripped in reality," Basil said. "Do you have the bodies still?"

"They're in the morgue. I'll – oh, Dominic. Please, come in."

The door had opened without Basil noticing, and he turned to see another officer step over the threshold.

"Detective Basil Sinclair, this is Lieutenant Dominic Moore. I've asked him to assist you by whatever means necessary while you're on the station. He's at your disposal."

Moore turned black, pupil-less eyes on Basil and nodded once. "Yes, Commander. Detective, it's good to meet you."

"Show the detective to his cabin, please, Lieutenant," Williamson said. "Then, he will need to be taken to the site of the breach, as well as the morgue."

* * *

The lab that had sustained the breach was in ring twenty-one, a long way from the civilian population of the station, as well as most of the officers. Only the engineers and scientists lived this far away from the heart of the station. Williamson had ordered the entire ring evacuated after the incident, and anyone who ventured inside now had to do so in a stuffy contamination suit. How that would protect against a demon or a hole in reality, Basil didn't know, but he donned the clunky suit without any outward complaint.

When it came down to it, the breach wasn't much to look at – as Williamson had said, it had been sealed almost immediately. The lab where it had happened, the epicenter, had been nearly obliterated. Even the steel worktables had been reduced to ash, leaving just a warped, scorched section of flooring.

"There were three scientists in here at the time of the breach," Moore said, and didn't elaborate.

"Gone?" Basil asked, and Moore gestured *yes* with his hand. In the contamination suit, Basil wouldn't have been able to see him nod.

"Is this helpful?" Moore asked, and Basil lifted his hands in a shrug.

"I've only worked a handful of demon cases in my life. They're exceedingly rare. Most have been around for centuries, but keep a low profile." Until they don't, he thought. "I've never dealt with a demon new to this universe before. At this point, I'd say anything could be helpful, I'm just not sure how yet."

*　*　*

In the morgue, the station's medical staff had already pulled the five bodies out of cold storage and laid them on slabs for Basil to see. The mutilated lieutenant had been pieced back together, but even then, it was apparent he'd died in agony. Moore averted his eyes when Basil leaned over the body.

"You knew him?" Basil asked quietly.

"We were friends," Moore said.

"And the others?"

"Not as well. They were assigned to other departments, and we never had much reason to interact."

"Is there anything in common among them?"

"Not that we've been able to figure out. They appear to be random victims, except for the fact that they're all officers in the Navy. The demon doesn't seem to be inclined to attack civilians – yet."

Basil glanced at the doctor and nurses who stood back, silently watching the examination, and asked, "Could I have a moment, please?"

At a nod from Moore, the others left the room. Basil went over to the dead human and laid a hand on her forehead. The long journey and lack of sleep had exhausted him down to the bone, but he managed to dredge up enough power to pull her final moments from her mind. It was like trying to drag sand through water, and the images flowed away from him the more he tried to hold on to them, but it was enough. All he'd needed was an impression, and the implication of it made him stagger.

Well, that and the lack of food, probably.

"Your file says you're human." Moore grabbed him by the shoulders to steady him, the chill from his death-cold hands seeping through Basil's shirt. After the oppressive heat of the containment suit, it felt wonderful.

"I am," Basil said. He leaned against a nearby wall, and allowed himself only a moment of disappointment when Moore withdrew his hands. "There's a wizard or two in the family tree, but so far back that it hardly matters. I'm... sensitive to energy, I suppose. I can channel it and use it in certain ways, but it's not always reliable and only works on living things. Er, no offense."

Moore's lips quirked briefly. "None taken. What did you see?"

"Her final moments. The last thing she saw was a person. Human, vampire, or werewolf, I have no idea, but it was definitely a person. *Not* a demon."

Moore frowned. "What does that mean?"

"It means," Basil said, "that it was no accident that rift was created, and that something came through. Someone on this station brought it into this universe, and someone is controlling it. It's walking around in human form as we speak."

"So what do we do?"

"We lay a trap," Basil said grimly, "and hope like hell it takes the bait."

* * *

What the textbooks said about catching a demon was that you needed power, single-minded focus, and a hell of a lot of negative energy. What they *wouldn't* say is that, even with all the right elements, it came down mostly to luck.

Basil figured that, of all the places on the station, the cabin of the first murdered lieutenant would probably contain the most negative energy. Not that there was a way to accurately quantify that, of course. One person's agony was another's walk in the park, but he figured that being dismembered while still alive was probably high on no one's list.

Fire on a space station was strictly prohibited by Mars Authority, even on a station like this where the atmosphere wasn't overcharged with oxygen, so he had to improvise. They gathered every spare lantern on the station and a few Moore bartered for from fellow officers. They set them on every available surface and on the floor, blanketing the room until there was almost nowhere left to stand.

"Demons are attracted to energy. The fact that this one hasn't taken up residence in the station's power core is further proof that someone's controlling it," Basil said. "But I wouldn't be surprised if it has made several visits to this cabin since killing that lieutenant, and right now we're lighting the place up like a beacon. It's bound to have caught its interest."

"You hope." But Moore said it matter-of-factly, not like he doubted Basil's expertise. He took his blaster out of its holster and adjusted the setting. "This will incinerate any werewolf or human that walks through that door, and severely inconvenience any vampire. But if they've been possessed by a demon, willingly or otherwise, I can't say for certain how effective it'll be."

"We just need them in this room. Leave the rest to me, Lieutenant." Basil went to each corner of the room, sketching symbols in the air the way his grandmother had taught him, drawing on the energy from the lanterns to maximize his powers. The wards were an added layer of protection, to keep the demon confined once they'd caught it – and to serve as an additional weapon, should Basil need it.

"Comforting as that is," Moore said dryly, "I'd like to have a Plan B in mind. Preferably a Plan C and D as well, but I'll take what I can get. Suppose this demon takes you out the first chance it gets. What then?"

Now probably wasn't the best time to mention that, while he might have been human, he'd taken a few shots to the heart from demons before and lived to tell the tale – something no normal human could do, he knew that much.

"Take up position there," Basil said instead. He gestured at the far corner, the only part of the room that couldn't be seen immediately from the door. "Vampires don't show up on sensors, right? They won't have any idea you're here, so you'll have the element of surprise."

"Where will you be?"

Basil shrugged. "Might as well stand right here. I show up on sensors; no use in hiding."

"What, you can't magic yourself away or something?"

"Good to know you can joke in the face of near-certain death, Moore."

"Since we're going to die here, you might as well call me Dominic."

Basil snorted. "Buy me dinner first, and we'll see."

"Just to get you to call me by my given name? You drive a hard bargain, Detective." There was a smile in Dominic's voice. "But you've got yourself a deal."

Basil glanced at him in surprise, then shook himself. Now was precisely the wrong time to get distracted.

"How long have you been in the Navy, Lieutenant?"

"The Martian Navy, or any Navy?" Now *that* definitely sounded like a smirk. "I joined the Royal Navy in 1736."

"So I assume that means you know how to shoot that thing without hitting me? Blasters make me nervous in tight quarters like this."

"Oh, yes." Suddenly, Dominic's voice was steel. "I'm quite good with a weapon."

"You'll get your chance to prove that very soon, I'm certain." The hairs on the back of Basil's neck prickled, and cold trickled down his spine. The air had an electric taste to it, and all at once, he smelled sulfur. "Don't shoot until you absolutely have to. Let me do what I need to."

"Aye," Dominic said quietly, melting back into the shadows.

Basil closed his eyes and reached out, *reached out*, until he felt each lantern in the room, all one hundred and eight of them, bright points of white-hot power that he drew on, absorbing and absorbing and *absorbing*, soaking himself in raw energy until it filled him to the brim.

The door opened.

Ensign Hicks stepped through.

The moment it shut behind him, Basil twitched his fingers and the first ward activated, sealing the room. As long as he was alive, nothing could get out – or get in.

"You're smarter than you look, Detective." Hicks cocked his head, considering him. His eyes should have been black, pupil and iris combined, but instead they glowed yellow. "But not smart enough, I'm afraid. Lieutenant Moore, you can stop hiding in the corner, I know you're there."

Dominic appeared silently at Basil's side. He still held his weapon trained on Hicks.

"Ephram," he said quietly, "don't do this."

"It's already been done, Lieutenant. If you don't put up too much of a fight, I'll even make your death a merciful one."

"Do you have any idea of the damage you could have caused," Basil said, "ripping a hole in reality like that? The dimensions are separated from each other for a *reason*—"

"Yes," Hicks interrupted, "and I intend to remove those barriers."

"*Why?*"

Hicks cocked his head, considering Dominic.

"You're very young, aren't you?" he said quietly. "I can *smell* it. Six hundred years, is that all? Try six *thousand*, and then ask me why I would dare do something like this. Vampirism isn't a gift, it's a curse, and I'm so *very* tired of it. Aren't you? The same thing, generation after generation. The food changes, the clothes go in and out of style, the music improves, but essentially it's all the same. Variations on a common theme. Haven't you realized that yet?"

"That doesn't give you the right—" Dominic started forward. Hicks put out a hand, and Dominic froze, completely immobilized.

"It gives me *every* right," Hicks said in a low, unnatural voice. "I have a demonic link bound within me; the demons will purge our kind from the universe, releasing our souls from this hellish existence, and all they ask in return is to rule over everything that's left. I find that's a fair bargain, don't you?"

He flexed his fingers, a barely-perceptible movement, and red energy engulfed Dominic. He began to glow, pulsating like the last glowing ember of a dying fire. Hicks raised his hand, and Dominic's body went along with it, until he was hovering two feet off the deck. Basil could see the thin strand of energy connecting them, yellow and sparkling. Hicks murmured something in a language Basil didn't recognise. White-hot energy seared through the link, slamming into Dominic's chest and throwing him across the room. His body hit the wall with such force that the metal bowed, and Dominic crumpled to the ground.

Basil started toward him. Hicks stopped him with a flick of his hand, freezing him in place.

"Now that it's just us, Detective," he said, lowering his hand, "I have a proposal for you. Use your powers to help me manipulate the station's core, so that I may expedite my mission, and I'll ensure you a quick death. You'll never have to submit to the coming demonic invasion."

"Like hell," Basil spat and, drawing upon the power that he'd sucked into himself, he raised a hand and blasted Hicks in the chest with a ball of pure energy.

The vampire-demon staggered, and the room filled quickly with the acrid scent of burning flesh. Hicks touched his chest, brushing his fingers against the charred skin, and then looked at Basil.

"Cute," he said, and tossed Basil against the window with a twitch of his fingers. Basil heard the two-foot-thick window crack, and starbursts exploded behind his eyelids. He crashed to the ground, rolled over, and spat a mouthful of blood on the deck. The room swam. He tried to focus on Hicks, but the other man kept slipping away from him as the room tilted.

Hicks grabbed the front of his shirt and hauled him to his feet.

"And these pretty little *wards* of yours," he snarled. He snapped his fingers, and Basil felt his protections cleave neatly in half. He cried out as pain seared through his head, drowning out all other thought. "Did you really think they could withstand me? I have existed for six *millennia*. The wizard in your bloodline was an infant when I was already three thousand years old. What hope do they have of defeating *me*? What hope do *you* have?"

He tossed Basil against a nearby wall and pinned him there with an unseen hand on his chest. He then grasped Basil's head, hands pressed to either side of his face, and closed his eyes.

Basil's back arched, his spine cracking. Energy coursed through him. He was nothing more than a glorified conduit, something that Hicks could control – something that he could use.

One corner of Hicks' mouth lifted in a smirk.

"Ah, little human," he murmured, delighted. "You have no idea how *fortuitous* your presence is, and how little you know about yourself and your powers. I had yet to find an efficient way to employ the core, to make a permanent breach. But you will do, my little channeler... you will do quite nicely indeed."

"*No.*" Basil tried to struggle, but the force on his chest pressed down harder, squeezing the air from his lungs. "No, don't do this, you can't—"

"I can do as I like," Hicks said icily, and he began to pour energy into the detective, using Basil to form a link with the core. Basil felt the power start to pulse through him, a thin trickle at first, then a great rush. He couldn't withstand this, his body wasn't built for it. His organs would boil, his bones would turn to ash, his brain – his brain was on *fire—*

"I can't," he gasped. "I can't, this body is too fragile, you *know* that—"

"Then *burn*, little human," Hicks snarled. "Burn, burn, *burn.*"

Sweat trickled between his shoulder blades. His insides were on fire. Energy flooded him, pure *power,* more than he had ever tried to absorb in his lifetime. Hicks gritted his teeth, pouring even more of that white-hot energy into him, faster and faster and faster—

Power flows both ways.

Basil sucked a breath into burning lungs. The mere act of lifting his arm felt like picking up lead. He caught a scream behind clenched teeth and, with a growl, brought his hand to the side of Hicks' face. He closed his eyes, and *thrust back.*

At first it was like an ant trying to withstand a gale. For all the power that Hicks was pouring into him, Basil could send only a trickle of it back.

But Basil still had his own will, his identity, whatever Hicks was doing with his body. He thought of every incantation he had ever been taught, everything passed to him by his grandmother, every spell and cantrip and ward. He reached out with all of his senses, pulling on every bit of light and life he could grasp for himself. All the lanterns and the light fittings on the station, every living being – yes, even Dominic, thready though his life force was. Basil pulled these forces together to bolster not Hick's efforts but Basil's own willpower. He pulled, and he *pulled*—

"What..." Hicks gasped. "What are you doing?"

Basil's eyes flew open. Their gazes locked, Hicks' wide yellow-gold eyes boring into his own.

"You wanted power," he hissed. "You can damn well *have* it."

Power slammed through him and into the thing which held him. He screamed, head cracking off the wall as his spine arched. Hicks howled, his hands burning against the sides of Basil's head as every bit of energy he had poured into Basil was returned to him ten-fold, cascading through their bond, burning him up from the inside out.

It went on for a lifetime. Agony, searing *agony*, reduced Basil's world to nothing more than a white roar. Wave after wave of power coursed through him. Hicks' screams became unearthly, and he started to glow as Dominic had. Yellow at first, then orange, then a vibrant red that Basil saw even through his closed eyelids. When he forced them open again, Hicks was incandescent, a glowing orb, no longer even vaguely human-shaped.

And then, he exploded.

Basil crashed to the floor. The shockwave slammed into his chest, followed seconds later by the deafening roar. Every light in the room went out, the lanterns drained, and the smell of smoke was acrid in his nostrils.

Then it was still, and silent, except for the persistent ringing in his ears. Digging his fingers into the pitted deck, he dragged himself over to where Dominic lay and grasped his unnaturally-cold hand.

"Dominic," he whispered. "Dominic, come on, come *on*, don't do this to me now—"

He dug a scanner out of Dominic's pocket. Its fuel cells had nearly been depleted, but it functioned long enough to tell him that Dominic didn't have long. Even with his supernatural strength, his inhuman healing abilities – even all of that wouldn't be enough.

Eyes deeper than the night flew open and fixed on his own.

"Can you move?" Basil nudged his shoulder uselessly. "Come on, we have to get moving. We need to get out of here, and you need blood—"

"Can't." Dominic's eyes were on his, his gaze unfocused. He was beyond weak. Drained of everything – of strength, of power, almost of life.

Basil yanked up his sleeve and held out his wrist. Dominic stared at him, uncomprehending.

"Here," Basil said. "Drink. It's all right. I give you my permission."

Dominic's lip curled, revealing one fang, and he looked away. He hissed, "You *stupid* human."

"You have *minutes*, Dominic, for Christ's sake. The nearest medical team won't be able to reach us for hours, not with the damage I just did to the station."

"You're too weak—"

"*Drink*, damn you!"

Dominic reached out a shaking hand and brushed his fingers lightly over the blue veins – and then he surged forward, sinking his fangs into the delicate flesh, and Basil's world narrowed to those two bright points of pain. He gasped, the blood rushing from his head and leaving him dizzy. Dominic's free arm clamped around his waist, holding him close, his other hand holding Basil's wrist pressed to his mouth.

And then he pulled back abruptly, wrenching himself from the pulsing veins, and Basil sagged. Dominic caught him, and they lay on the deck in a crumpled heap. Basil's head swam, and he could feel Dominic's chest heaving under his.

"Are you...? did it...?" he gasped.

"I'm fine." Dominic's voice sounded stronger already. He added quietly, "Thank you, Basil."

"Don't thank me, I did it for purely selfish reasons," Basil murmured. The world swam less when he closed his eyes, and as soon as darkness washed over him, he spiraled down into unconsciousness.

* * *

Between his injuries and depleted reserves, Basil slept for forty-eight hours straight. He woke long enough to inhale about five thousand calories in rations packets, answer a series of questions from the doctor on duty, and then fell back asleep. When he woke for the second time, Williamson was at his bedside.

"Detective, I don't know how we can thank you," she said when she saw him awake.

"Paying me in full, even though I destroyed almost an entire ring of the station, would be a nice start?" he said, and was relieved when she laughed.

"No lives were lost and the demon is gone, which is more than I could have hoped for. You'll get your payment and then some. I believe we can mark these days you've had to spend in the infirmary as a potential loss of income and have the government give you a bonus."

"I knew there was a reason I liked you, Commander." Basil grinned. "How's Moore?"

"He fared better than you. It took three blood bags to get him on his feet again, but he returned to duty two days ago. I'm told he spends all of his off-duty hours here."

Basil flushed, but could have sworn he saw a glint in Williamson's coal-dark eyes. She patted his shoulder.

"Get well soon, Detective. For his sake as much as yours."

* * *

By the time Basil was allowed out of the infirmary, life on the station seemed to have returned mostly to normal. Ring twenty-one was still sealed off until Mars Authority could send an inspections team to clear it, and ring fourteen would be undergoing repairs for the next six months, but the tension had dissipated and the station was bustling once again.

The twenty minute walk to Dominic's cabin shouldn't have tired him out as much as it did; when Dominic answered the door, he took one look at Basil and said, "Sit down, for pity's sake, before you fall over."

He gripped Basil by the elbow and steered him into a chair. He then stood there, arms crossed, glaring down at Basil.

"Why?" he demanded.

"Why'd I save your life? Sorry, I didn't realize you had a death wish."

A muscle pulsed in Dominic's jaw. "We are bound now. Do you have any idea what you have done?"

"I gave you my permission. I knew what I was getting into. Believe it or not, I know how this all works. And we're not *bound*, we're simply connected. Is that really such a bad thing?"

"What if it doesn't work out?"

"What if it does?" Basil countered.

Dominic looked away. "You've never been with a vampire before. You have no idea—"

"Then let me find out." Basil pushed himself to his feet, ignoring the ache in his muscles. "The connection isn't binding. If it doesn't work out, then it doesn't work out, and we'll never have to see each other again. You fed from me, which means I'll always feel a bit of you here—" He tapped his temple. "—but it's not a promise. It's simply a new normal."

Dominic sighed, but he met Basil's gaze.

"What was it I promised you? Dinner?"

Basil stepped into the circle of Dominic's arms and tilted his head up. Cool lips touched his own, and he was lost.

NURY VITTACHI'S THE FENG SHUI DETECTIVE AND THE SINGAPORE UNION OF INDUSTRIAL MYSTICS

AN APPRECIATION BY CRAIG STANTON

The Occult Detective comes in many and various shapes and sizes. There are however, a few stereotypical avatars which recur throughout the literature – the hoodoo-wielding American gumshoe; the bookish late-Victorian ghost-hunter; the haunted Nineteenth-Century medic on the trail of the supernatural – which have become the comfortable mainstays and 'go to' tropes of the sub-genre. Over many years, the standard, non-supernatural, literary detective has intensively diversified and now comes in a variety of iterations and sub-types, from bounty hunters, substance-abusers, people with disabilities – even cats! How good then to discover something completely out of left field in terms of the occult sub-class, a version that works with the supernatural, solves fiendishly-clever crimes, and which is hilarious to boot. I give you Hong Kong-based author Nury Vittachi and his feng shui crime-buster, C.F. Wong.

Vittachi was born in Sri Lanka in 1958 and now lives in Hong Kong with his English wife and three adopted Chinese children. He has been a columnist and social commentator in various news organs and holds positions of eminence on many Southeast Asian literary boards including the Man Asian Literary Prize (an offshoot of the Man Booker Prize). He rose to eminence through the writing of regular columns highlighting humorous cross-cultural clashes in the colony, before being politically silenced after the return of Hong Kong to Chinese control. He won his way back into the spotlight however and today is known for his amusing observations of the modern Pan-Asian society, both in print and on-line. He writes children's books as well as non-fiction and has submitted to academic journals on the nature and style of Asian English, but he is best known for his feng shui detective books.

There are five books in the series, kicking-off in 2000 with *The Feng Shui Detective*. They mainly consist of a series of interlinked short stories wherein our detective – Chinese geomancer C.F. Wong – discovers and solves crimes while correcting the flow of energies at a given location (usually the scene of said crime). With him are a bunch of colourful characters who round out the humour and move the story along. His secretary Miss Winnie Lim occupies his office, painting her nails, talking on the telephone and doing little else, secure in the knowledge that her Byzantine filing system will ensure her place on the company payroll. A passing parade of Chinese, Malay, Indian and other Southeast Asian types in the form of police detectives, shady businessmen and other mystic individuals, facilitates the delivery of juicy enigmas to Wong's attention.

Rounding out the personnel is Joyce 'Jo' McQuinnie, an Australian student and the daughter of one of Wong's patron's Perth-based business associates: she intrudes upon Wong's activities by becoming his intern during her semester-break holidays and she stays on to become his apprentice. Initially, Wong grudgingly endures her presence because refusing to take her on would result in an extreme loss of face; later, she proves to be a quick study in the art of Chinese geomancy and of enormous use when bridging the cross-cultural and interpersonal hurdles that daily imperil Wong's success.

The two of them – Wong and Jo – are established in a well-known dynamic, feeding off the works of Sir Arthur Conan Doyle: Joyce is the 'Watson' to Wong's 'Holmes', but adherence to this format is by no means dogmatic. In many ways Wong's facility with feng shui is treated much like Holmes's application of observation and logic, and – in that sense – Joyce is much like Watson being newly exposed to the regimen and by turns bewildered and delighted by the results. Sherlock is not a figure of fun, however, and unlike Wong, is never allowed to appear foolish, which Wong does every time he steps out to face the modern world around him. Wong's bumbling with contemporary society is leavened by Jo's youthful dynamism, revealing that, in some ways, she is just as much the master – in her own areas of expertise – as he is. The homage to the Sherlock Holmes oeuvre is clear in the title of the very first feng shui detective tale entitled *'Scarlet in a Study'*.

In this story, Wong is called-upon by a property development company to examine a building in a remote village on the Malaysian mainland. The building is a moderately-aged Dutch construction which an enterprising couple (the last residents) outfitted as a private funeral parlour. Both owners became ill and the husband died, leaving the widow to sell up and move on, but not before Wong and Jo get an opportunity to work their mojo in the place and minimise the impact of its having been a 'yin' (that is, negative-energy) building for a period of time, something that would definitely impact upon its future saleability, or the profitability of later businesses setting up there. Of chief concern to Wong is the former study in the building – now tricked out as a mortuary laboratory – and decorated in flocked scarlet wallpaper. "Anyone who can have a red-colour study," he observes, "they can do any evil, I think." Over the course of a long, working weekend, Wong and Jo uncover a nefarious plot and reveal the presence of an ingenious killer.

Vittachi talks at length about feng shui (pronounced 'foong soy') in his narratives and oftentimes the novice (ie: the reader) has no option but to coast along with the discussion of influences, energy flows and quadrants until the resolution makes everything clear. That being said, Vittachi's insights are to the point and are very revealing of the cultural mindset behind the practise. Often, the mystery is resolved not by Wong's and Jo's facility with the lo pan (the geomantic compass) but by their attunement to the people around them – and their intimate knowledge of the crime-scene's floor plan. In one story, Wong is duped into entering a supermarket where – unbeknownst to him – a white tiger, escaped from a nearby circus, has taken up residence. By getting a policeman outside the now cordoned-off building to describe via mobile telephone the geomantic rectifiers placed around the supermarket – put there by another feng shui practitioner when the business was first established – Wong escapes a hideous death by mauling after locating a covered-over exit doorway that was disturbing the flow of energy in the store, saving not only himself but a mother and child who had also walked blithely into the building.

At times, Vittachi seems to be making fun of the whole feng shui rigmarole as, often, it's not so much the 'energies' at play which uncover the crime, but Wong's familiarity with the building structure which solves the issue. Having previously worked in an environment sometimes gives Wong insights to which other investigators don't have access, like being the only one in the room who knows that there's a walled-up dumb waiter in one corner. Still, Wong always has his eye on the money and he knows that downplaying, or undermining, the mystic aspects of his activities is bad for business.

Wong is a clear nexus of Asian proclivities and he highlights many aspects of the Singaporean/Chinese Malay character. He is a traditional, old Chinese man from Guangdong, obsessed with money and always seeking to maximise profit – at one point when a client tells him that he is desperate for a miracle, Wong instantly tells him that miracles attract a 15% surcharge. Wong's other obsession is food: much of his travelling is predicated upon the opportunities to visit certain street food markets or restaurants and, in the full-length novel *The Shanghai Union of Industrial Mystics*, he is confronted by the (to him) inexplicable horror of militant vegan terrorists who threaten to ruin his gustatory working holiday in that city. During a stay in the West Australian capital of Perth, his inability to find anything remotely praiseworthy in the way of comestibles is a recurring theme. Throughout the stories, descriptions of Wong's intake offer alternate moments of delight and disgust, from flash-fried, 'show dish' banquet offerings seen during Jo's first visit to a Singapore street-food market, to the steamed colon breakfast that he is forced to forego one morning at work when an emergency descends.

As the tales progress, we become aware that Wong is not alone in helping the police forces of the city uncover crimes. We are introduced to The Singapore Union of Industrial Mystics, a loose but elite gathering of supernatural practitioners, each with their own specialities, who advise local detectives whenever they run into dead ends in their investigations. On one occasion, we are told, membership numbered up to around 40 experts; now it consists of C.F. Wong, Dilip Kenneth Sinha – a garrulous Indian practitioner of that country's form of astrological-geomancy called vaastu shastra – and Madam Xu, a fortune-teller, adept with cards, numerology and tea-leaves and who runs a thriving prognostication business empire. Together, across the length of an exciting dinner in *'A Kitchen God's Life'*, they resolve the closed-room murder of an internationally-renowned hotel-chef, by about the sixth course.

The fourth book – which is a full-length novel rather than a series of connected short stories – sees the Union of Industrial Mystics take a jaunt to

Shanghai. For Wong the trip involves his two main priorities – money and food – and the renovation of his Singapore office is his excuse to take off to his homeland and explore the possibilities of re-locating there on a permanent basis. There are some issues: Joyce has become vegetarian for no clear reason that Wong can define and there is a massive political summit taking place in the city between the leaders of two world superpowers. The city winds up in lockdown as an escaped rare white elephant, a gang of militant vegan terrorists and an enormous bomb converge to ruin Wong's holiday. This novel demonstrates that Vittachi is not above walking a line between the fantastic and the absurd, and the masterful thing about this story is that he manages expertly to never fall across into the realm of complete farce.

Vittachi has a natural 'ear' for the local melting-pot version of English which predominates in Singapore and he captures it marvellously in the course of his stories. The local propensity to add "-ah" or "-lah" to various words, seemingly at random, is showcased, along with the rhetorical "is it?" at the end of an interrogative statement, as in this announcement by Winnie Lim of Jo's imminent arrival into Wong's world:

"One of Mr Pun's contack, he wan' a favour. M.C. Queeny or something. He wan' you to fine a job for his son, you know already, is it?"

From this, Wong learns that his quiet and contemplative world is to become occupied by the 'son' (Jo) of Mr. Pun's business associate.

Jo McQuinnie's language is another source of amusement for everyone involved. Initially, Wong decides that having her around would be good for developing his own language skills – having written two previous books about feng shui in Chinese, he sees the production of a third book in English as a new potential highlight in his career. We learn that he has been taking lessons in colloquial English at a nearby school, but he bemoans the expense of these classes and decides that working with Jo will be a good short-cut to honing his skills (and will also allow him to show-off in front of the other students). To his horror, her style of communication is almost completely impenetrable to him:

"I'm like, 'So how am I going to become an instant feng shooee master, then?' And my dad's like, 'My mate Mr Pun's got a real feng shooee master and you can work with him for three months.' And I'm like, 'Wow.'"

There are many humorous moments along the road of their growing relationship as he tries to understand why things 'suck', why things are 'rad', and – at one point – to try and fathom the British expression 'not a sausage'. Jo heroically tries to guide him through the minefields of colloquial English idiom; however, her own understanding as to why certain colourful expressions exist and from where they originate, is limited and, generally, her efforts only serve to underscore Wong's growing sense that English-speakers do not function with anything akin to logic.

Vittachi's characters are all endearing and instantly recognisable to anyone who's ever dealt with the Southeast Asian milieu. Wong is greedy and self-important, with his eye on the money, the food and the nearest exit when chaos ensues; Jo is warm-hearted but facile, mired in her fascination for pop-culture and brash in her youthfulness. As much as we cheer them on as they solve crime across the western Pacific and Sub-continent, Vittachi is not above knocking the shine off them, making them not only forces for good, but decidedly human ones as well. Thus, Wong may muse at length on the writings of Lao Tze only to be distracted by thoughts of noodles, while Jo can dramatically launch into action, sweeping the contents of her desk into her hand-bag, only to remember after the fact that there was a polystyrene cup of coffee sitting on her blotter.

An inescapable element in dealing with Chinese geomantic principles, as they apply to modern urban development, is that architecture is discussed not infrequently throughout Wong's and Jo's adventures. We travel from rural plantation settlements established by mid-Twentieth Century Dutch occupants, to ultra-modern Hong Kong business skyscrapers; even to the sci-fi, city-skyline confections of Shanghai. Whether the crime has taken place in a run-down Chinese supermarket, a sleek Singaporean Secondary school, or the kitchens of a ritzy Raffles-era hotel, all of these rollicking tales are effectively grounded in real locales and Vittachi's finely-honed eye for novelty, local colour and the humorous, works overtime.

The crimes showcased are not simply murders, for the most part. Many of the stories revolve around corrupt business practise, often revealed when Wong tries to get to the bottom of why an otherwise healthy company is steadily failing to turn a profit. In understanding the energy flows at a company's headquarters, Wong inevitably comes to an understanding of the processes and individuals involved and quickly spots where the corruption has crept in. Is it supernatural? Maybe not, but the occult, Taoist roots of C.F. Wong's procedures certainly are and – along with Joyce McQuinnie's finessing of his stuffy Confucian ways though a modern environment – are what gets them to the correct solution in the end.

Whenever C.F. is called into action, the first thing he does is to cast the horoscopes of everyone involved, in order to ascertain who had negative – possibly even murderous – influences affecting them. In several cases, it transpires that the person who has been killed had no such aspect in their chart and Wong starts to worry that he's losing his knack. In one particular case set in Manila – *'The Case of the Late News Columnist'* – both C.F. Wong and Madam Xu face economic ruin when the subject of their readings, whom they had just determined would enjoy long life and success, was found to have leapt from a building to her death. Worried that, if word got out about how badly they'd misread things they would lose clients at a rapid rate, they pitch in to resolve the issue. It transpires that they were given someone else's birth details to work with: their services coming at an exorbitant rate, the dead columnist, for whom a free reading was owed by Wong's patron, switched details with her best friend and business partner as a treat. Once the switcheroo is identified (and the logical flaw in the police department's investigation exposed) the two Industrial Mystics find themselves back on track and on the way to resolving matters. By the end of the tale, Wong and Xu are vindicated, their reputations restored, and the killer is unearthed.

There are several occasions where Sherlock Holmes encounters the supposed supernatural – *'The Sussex Vampire'*; *The Hound of the Baskervilles* – and, using his processes of deduction, is able to reveal that the ghostly and the ghoulish are anything but. Thomas Carnacki too, falls into situations where an occult pretext gives way before a well-deployed range of investigative apparatus. For both detectives, there are decided 'Scooby-Doo' moments where the ghostly pirates attacking the waterfront amusement park are actually disguised property developers, or contraband smugglers. In the case of C.F. Wong, all of his cases are ones where the bad guys "would have gotten away with it too, if not for—" the little old Chinese guy and his bratty Aussie sidekick. In these stories it's not the cases themselves that are occult; it's the method which our detective uses in order to solve them. Some people might think that feng shui is just 'better living through interior decorating', but in the hands of C.F. Wong it's a little dose of Chinese magic.

* * *

This is the complete list of titles in the Feng Shui Detective series:

The Feng Shui Detective (2000)
The Feng Shui Detective Goes South (2002)
The Feng Shui Detective's Casebook (2003)
The Shanghai Union of Industrial Mystics (2006)
Mr Wong Goes West (2008)

THE WAY THINGS WERE

S.L. EDWARDS

The 'Great Savini' was a man shivering with delight, his confidence endowed by a power he shouldn't have. From the back of the auditorium his face seemed indistinct, a mustached blur with brown eyes and a wide, white smile. He turned his tall stovepipe hat toward the crowd and released a flock of shimmering doves that glowed white on the dark stage. Pounding their wings against the air, they burst into blue flames; the crowd screamed first with panic and then with delight as the ashes morphed into cool, crisp snow.

The Great Savini beamed, his smile pulling aging skin across his face into a tight, brown leather mask. He wore a campy magician's suit, complete with a glittering purple tuxedo vest and tailored, gray-striped slacks. He laughed with his audience and waved his arms theatrically. Infected with his own stage presence, Savini took wide, gangling steps across the stage front, clapping himself and sending the audience into thunderous applause.

He stopped abruptly, summoning one white gloved hand to his mouth to shush the audience. He raised the other to the side of the stage, beckoning forth a beautiful woman dressed in a tight black leotard and leggings who reminded Joe Bartred of a playboy bunny. She beamed in mock shyness to the audience, long black hair shining in silken cascades under the stage lights.

Savini smiled as he took a gloved hand and rubbed it against his lovely assistant's cheek. He moved in slowly, as if to kiss her lips. Suddenly, a knife came from his gloved hand and slammed into the woman's stomach. She buckled forward, holding the knife blade and coughing up blood onto the stage in long, hacking wet cries.

"Vulgar." Johann Koenig remarked in a contemptuous, growling whisper.

Johann and Joe stood towards the back, leaning against the wall to survey the audience and performance on stage. Joe leaned against the wall, hands cradling his long hair and posture matching his casual flannel shirt and too-loose jeans. He chewed a piece of dying mint gum, periodically scratching his beard and blinking to keep himself awake.

Johann stood with his feet planted apart in shining, leather shoes. His olive-green jacket fell to just above his knees, shirt tucked in neatly by a black belt. His face was sharp, alert, with burning gray-blue eyes and thick blonde hair combed to the left. He grimaced and thrummed his fingers against his elbows.

"Yeah," Joe answered, "But it's getting the reaction they want."

The audience was crying out in fear, and as the lovely assistant's leg twitched in a death-spasm some of the bolder men shouted threats towards the Great Savini. For his part, Savini seemed shocked, reaching down onto his partner's shoulders and whispering her name in unheard syllables.

The assistant raised her head, blinking. Then, she slowly raised herself to her knees, offering Savini her arm and letting him pull her slowly up. With one hand she held a bloody knife, with her other she motioned to her ripped leotard, a gashing hole in her outfit revealing unmarred and unbroken skin.

The crowd erupted into applause once more.

Savini took her hand and the two bowed, dipping their heads and smiling. The magician raised something above his head and threw it against the floor.

When the smoke settled, the stage was empty. The crowd went wild with applause, a contagious joy spurred on by something which even the most skeptical among them were straining to explain. Savini had levitated, his assistant had changed from a beautiful young woman to a snake and back to a woman again. She had even winked towards the audience as she pulled a wide flake of reptile skin from her delicate human face.

That was enough for Joe. Enough to convince him that the Great Savini was dangerous, if for no other reason than the undue attention it would draw from the wider world. The best slights of hand were kept out of sight, and the most potent spells were those which the cursed were unaware of.

The world was a better place when the masses didn't believe in magic, and though Savini may only be a marginal threat to this secrecy, he was a threat nonetheless

* * *

Joe had trouble sleeping since he got back from Nicaragua.

He wasn't particularly afraid of monsters, of demons or witches. His life had been in greater danger before. He didn't know why he kept seeing mutilated, inhuman corpses when he closed his eyes; or why every white light reminded him of the beautiful glinting smile and sharp stone knife.

He knew Seattle was too quiet for him, that the city – for all of its cloudy calm – was not a good place to be alone with his thoughts. Elyria, his original reason for coming to the city, was gone. Now there was nothing there for him and he didn't know why he stayed. He needed a new case, something to take his mind away from the recent past and bind it firmly to the present.

But that was only one reason Joe was relieved when Johann called him.

Joe's mother was fond of telling him that he could be 'smart' but not 'wise'. With a wry, knowing smile Haley Blackwell would gently remind her son that he was a young man, that no one in their early twenties could have anything resembling true wisdom, no matter how much of a prodigy they were. Wisdom would come naturally to him, she claimed, and aspiring to some deliberate heroism would be a catastrophic waste of time that could be better spent discovering the world rather than mastering it.

But despite his youth, Joe felt that calling Johann his 'oldest friend' was meaningful. The Bartred and Koenig families had been allies in World War II, Joe's parents had settled Johann's mother in the United States with her young son when it became clear that Europe would no longer be safe for them. Johann had been Joe's friend for his entire life. They were taught the same secrets, the same tricks from monks at the top of the world and the serpent men in the dark cavern temples deep beneath the earth. They were both prodigies, whose exploits and talents had sent ripple-gossip through the webs of the occult world.

They had both been twenty-four when Pan sought them out, when they ventured behind the Iron Curtain and almost lost their lives.

The man who walked through his office door was weighed down by his recent past. Johann was getting old faster and more irreversibly than Joe, his eyes getting paler and peering out from darker sockets each time Joe saw him. Johann moved formally, spine straight, eyes forward, and always seeming a step away from a military march.

The way he sat down, sighing and gripping onto the handle of his cup with white knuckles made it hard to believe that Johann had ever been capable of smiling. But his habit of dressing sharp, keeping his appearance clean, allowed him to be extroverted and charming when he needed to be. Amongst the few close friends he counted though, Johann Koenig was perpetually grim, focused and never at ease.

"Thanks for seeing me." He spoke quickly.

"Sure."

Johann wasted no time with small talk.

"I need your help."

"Okay?" Joe made sure to draw out his syllables, perhaps forcing Johann to slow down.

It didn't work.

"Camilo Figueroa is dead, killed by two attendants who I believe he cursed and enslaved."

Figueroa. Joe recalled the old man, a crane-spined shaking thing full of *pomposity and self-importance. A beard that fell to the floor and an old house filled to brim with magical artifacts from all over the world. A man Joe had met on several unhappy occasions, often with the referral of someone like his mother or Pan. Figueroa collected more than cursed masks and portal paintings, going so far as to buy and lock away haunted objects to keep ghosts as servants. The legion of trapped spirits had served as his alarm system, his housekeepers and his protectors, bound to him until he died.*

Joe never hid his contempt for the old slave owner, and Figueroa for his own part would spit on the ground that Joe stepped on, laughing as some forlorn spirit was forced to clean it up with nothing but their ethereal skin.

"Good riddance." Joe spat.

"Yes, the world would have been all the better if Doctor Salazar had killed him when he had the chance." Johann spoke quickly, keeping his hands and body still as his steely eyes moved slowly across Joe's sparse office, "The death of one fascist by the hands of another... hardly the tragedy our parents thought it would have been.

"More to the point," Johann continued, "Figueroa died with no children and left nothing resembling a will. I have the distinct impression that he never intended to die at all, if you can imagine such a thing."

Joe kept silent.

"With his death," Johann continued, "The wards around his house fell fast. Even though it was nearly impossible to move around that house, the old man was a pretty thorough record keeper. I found a complete inventory of artifacts in a safe in the master bedroom, and had some help in cataloging and locking up some of the more potent charms and weapons."

"Where are they now?"

"Some are in a vault in Washington, others are too potent to move. I plan to contract a specialized exorcist to undertake a thorough cleansing."

Joe grimaced. That didn't make him feel any better.

"However, there was one thing missing. A trunk." Johann shifted in his seat, gritting his teeth and readjusting his posture, "I looked over Figueroa's notes, trying to figure out what might be in it and... I found it."

"What was it?" Joe asked.

"Mostly a few charms, scrolls for flying, for conjuring smoke and fire, a book of healing spells. But there was something else missing from the house, something he bought from an Iraqi source during the fall of King Faisal. And the same source sold him something from the king's private collection. A lamp, Joe."

Joe was overtaken by vertigo. He felt clammy, the cold rushing over him and carrying him away to somewhere dark and roaring.

"I believe the attendants who murdered him took it."

"Do they know what they have?" Joe heard his own voice as if it was a distant, faraway whisper.

"I don't think so." Fear bled into Johann's voice. "But you know just as well as I do what someone could do with a d'jinn, or what an ifrit could do to them."

"Why would he keep such a dangerous thing!?" Joe needed to vent his panic and anger, even if he knew the answer to his question.

"He was obsessed with having power, even if he could never use it. The same reason he enslaved these 'attendants' – novice stage magicians who Figueroa probably found easy to manipulate until one of the poor souls took a candle holder to the back of his head."

Johann slid a manila folder across Joe's desk. Carl Fields and Delia Dawson, a traveling pair of magicians who came into Figueroa's orbit and were bound to him just like everything else he could ensnare. The two were novices kept in the dark, unaware of the world they were dipping their toes into and knowing just enough of the truth to be a danger to themselves and others.

"Where are they now?" Joe asked.

Johann slid him a playbill. 'Statehouse Theater, Buffalo New York. "The Great Savini." '

"Joe, I need your help because you might be able to convince them to hand it over, without a fight. Without anyone having to die. I'm hoping we can do things your way instead of mine."

"Of course," was all Joe said. He picked up a jean jacket from his coat rack and followed Johann out into the Seattle rain.

* * *

Out of the guise of 'Great Savini', Carl Fields was a tired man. His dressing room was meager, a few chocolates from some local store and a bottle of wine sat in front of the mirror as a gift from the theater manager. His exaggerated mustache was pointed and gray, his eyes resting behind dark shadows and bright red veins. Without his tall hat Joe could see his hair was thinning, long black strands ending in gray streaks that gave him the appearance of an ill-kept mop.

Fields didn't seem that surprised to open the door of his dressing room to find Joe and Johann standing there, arms folded and waiting.

"So..." Fields spoke with the resignation of a man facing the firing squad, "You the Devil's friends, then?"

"No." Joe tried to speak compassionately, patiently. "No, Camilo Figueroa was a sick bastard who got lucky by falling on the right side of history. He got protection and status that he never deserved. I'm guessing you and Delia found that out the hard way?"

Fields looked confused, planting a foot behind him and turning towards the door.

"Mr Fields," Johann's voice was glacial, "Running won't do you any good. Even if a man your age *could* outrun us you wouldn't make it through that door again." He pointed above the door, where a dry piece of paper with a twelve-pointed star pulsed with burning orange light.

"No one is going through that door until I end the spell. Try anything else and you'll come out the other side a pile of ash."

Fields was shivering, his mouth hanging open wide and low.

"Carl," Joe called to get his attention away from the death-trap door, "We just need to know where the *lamp* is. Tell us where the lamp is, hand it over, and we'll let you and Delia keep everything else."

Fields shook his head. "What lamp?"

"Carl," Joe let his voice ebb and flow with pity, "That's not the right way to go about this. That thing doesn't belong in *anyone's* hands. It doesn't matter if they're good or bad. You shouldn't have it. You don't need it."

"He threatened to use it on us," Fields' eyes were far away now. "Figueroa took us on as apprentices because he was obsessed with Delia. That evil, perverted old man." His hands were shaking now, his resignation boiling over to growling anger, "He would leer at her, lick his fat lips and laugh. We didn't know what we were doing when we found him, we just thought this was an old wizard who could teach us a few things. Well... turns out he did.

"I'm twenty-seven. I look like I'm fucking seventy and it's because that greedy bastard poisoned me every chance he could get. By the time I found out, we couldn't leave his house. He was just going to keep me there, accelerating my death so he could have Delia locked up there like some sort of..."

His voice was fluttering, hand coming up to his eyebrows so he could lean his forehead into it. Joe let him cry, shifting his eyes to Johann. Johann was strumming his fingers against his crossed elbows, tapping his foot against the hardwood floor. Though his mouth was closed, Joe could see the slow, deliberate grinding of his jaw.

He lifted a hand in Johann's direction as Fields turned away to compose himself, motioning to be patient.

Johann tightened his frown in response.

"He said he was going to use it on *her*. He was going to summon that thing and wished that Delia would always have 'unmarred beauty'. He said he was going to make her his 'thrall'." Fields spat the word, shuddering as it left her lips, "He was going to take her control away from her, and because of that that

I beat him to death with a candle holder."

Carl Field's tone had changed, void of any emotion and echoing the emptiness of his eyes.

"I took the candle holder to the back of his head."

"Understandable," Joe whispered. "But then you know what it can do. You know that the lamp has magic without normal rules. You know that you need to hand it over to us."

"Why?" Fields shifted a glance towards Johann. "What are you going to do with it?"

"Lock it away. Make sure no one else is able to get to it."

"Lock it away for *who*?" Fields pressed on.

"For *everyone*," Johann coldly added.

"Look, Carl," Joe stepped between them, "I'm—"

"No, stop." Fields waved his hands and stepped forward, coming close enough to Joe that he could smell bitter, acrid smoke on the man. "Are you really going to leave us alone if we hand it over?"

"Yes."

"Then I don't want to know your names, I just—"

Fields stopped. He gasped, reaching for his throat as his eyes widened. He wobbled briefly before falling to the floor with a loud crack, screaming through closed lips as he clawed his throat ferociously until it bled. Joe tried to pin down his arms, but Fields swatted them away and continued to tear at his neck. His lips became paler and paler, and there was a wet, sizzling sound like burning sausages as smoke rose from his face, leaving only a patch of new skin where his lips had been.

He clawed at where his mouth had been, trying to dig deep into flesh that would not break. His eyes exploded into white terror, his arms seizing in erratic, dying spasms. Joe climbed on top of him, trying to administer CPR before he realized the man had no mouth to breath into.

Joe was panting, blinking through adrenaline tears and trying to dim the electric whine in his ears.

He turned to Johann, who had not moved once while Fields was dying.

"I tried," Joe began to speak.

"You did your best, Joe. But we need to move," Johann cut him short. Johann moved around him, grasping the shoulders of Carl Fields' corpse and dragging it to the threshold of the open door. He stood the corpse up and thrust it forward, covering his mouth with his sleeve as the body fell through, burning for just a moment before turning to a cloud of ash.

He muttered a few syllables under his breath, reaching up for the sigil and pocketing it as the burning orange light became dull, red ink.

"Dawson has the lamp, Joe. She just used it."

That snapped Joe back to reality, and with a leap he was back on two feet, running past Johann through the dark backstage corridors of the theater and bursting through the exit door. The wet, hot upstate New York night was full of rain that blotted out the sky. Through the haze he saw Dawson, black lamp in her hands. She was surrounded by pulsing, swirling embers – things that fluttered like fireflies before dying in the all-consuming torrent of rain.

Across the parking lot she noticed Joe and Johann bursting through the door. She stood there swaying in a thick coat, the coat open enough to reveal her shimmering leotard reflecting the dim, muddled orange light of the parking lot. She paused, caught by a moment that offered several competing choices.

She turned fast, her coat swaying behind her as Joe heard the click of Johann's pistol behind him.

CRACK.

The bullet hit the car in a brief spark of orange and yellow. Dawson screamed sharply over the rain, cursing as she fumbled for her keys. Johann shot again, this time shattering the passenger window before it peeled away in a long, scraping screech.

* * *

It was pure luck that they spotted her car on the road, good guesswork that led them down the same route Delia Dawson took.

The rain was coming down harder, making the road sleek and dangerous beneath the thrumming wheels of the 1970 Ford Maverick. Joe's knuckles were white on the steering wheel, lip bitten so tight that blood was lapping at the back of his tongue. The red lights of Dawson's car pulsed through the curtain of rain, the only thing in the whole world that Joe could focus on.

Johann leaned out of the passenger window and fired his first shot.

The first bullet pierced the trunk. Dawson panicked, swerving wildly before she regained control and accelerated down faster. The second bullet went through the back window. Suddenly the red lights were dancing in front of them, swirling as Dawson tried too quickly to correct her course – and sent her car into a spinning wreck. It howled as it burned and crashed, hitting a ditch at the side of the road and splintering apart into metal shards.

"SHIT!" Joe screamed, slamming on the breaks and turning the wheel of his car in a continuous smooth loop. The Maverick swung around, only narrowly staying on the road as it stopped just short of the edge of cracked asphalt and the wreck.

Through the light of the rain-defying fire, Dawson's shadow limped onward, something long and narrow in her hand.

"STOP!"

Johann planted his feet apart, protected from the rain by some hastily drawn sigil in his pocket.

Dawson had no reason to stop, but she was limping. Joe ran forward, feet weighed down by the mud and the wet grass as he overtook her stumbling, short strides.

"Hey! Delia!"

She screamed, falling to the earth and cradling the lamp in her hands. Her eyes shook with the rest of her body, bitter sobs sending her body into quaking throws.

"S-stop!" She cried out between hissing breaths.

"Delia..." Joe tried to calm her. He bent down to touch a bare shoulder, noticing the wounds of her body sealing themselves up as she recoiled further into the grass.

"Delia... please, give me the lamp."

Joe could feel Johann's stare before he heard footsteps on the grass behind him. He prayed silently that Johann had put his gun away, or that the rain would hide his figure from Delia. She was scared, panicked. There was still a chance though, that she could be persuaded to hand it over. Still a chance that they could save her.

Her face trembled, unable to move her mouth. Thunder broke and by the lightning's glare he saw a wounded, panicked face looking up at him.

"I've been where you are." Joe held out his hand, hoping she would take it. "I've been scared. I've been caught up in things I don't understand and can't control. But I also knew when I had no other option than to take the help that I was offered."

"W-w-where is Carl?" Her voice was nearly empty, meek and desperate against the storm around them.

"Delia..."

"Tell me where he is!"

"Dead, Delia. He's dead."

She fixated her bright, brown eyes on Joe for a moment before looking down to her chest, defeated and ruined by the news. She tucked her knees into her, cradling herself but never letting go of the black lamp she now cradled next to her stomach. The rain hissed against the fire of her burning car and washed away the blood on her forehead.

Joe walked up to her, waiting patiently and lifting a hand to Johann to follow suit. The rain slowed, and the sound of her whimpering rose above the gentle pattering of the puddles beneath them.

"Why... why did you have to kill him?" She finally asked.

"We didn't," Joe reached out to touch her shoulder. This time, she didn't pull away. "His mouth sealed shut, he panicked. Probably a heart attack, maybe something else."

She looked up from her knees at him.

"What? No. I..." She opened her arms, motioning wildly, "I only wished that he wouldn't say anything about the lamp, I thought it would be a way to protect us I—"

"The thing in that lamp isn't a cartoon, Delia. It isn't a storybook problem solver. It's a trickster, something so dangerous that the old kings sealed them away and locked them up forever. It's a power that ruins people. It won't help *anyone*."

"But Figueroa, he—"

"Shouldn't have had it. It was stupid, but he wasn't a novice. He knew what he was doing."

She nodded, understanding what little she could grasp from the conversation.

"We just wanted to learn... that was all. We just wanted to be part of this world"

"I know," the pity in his voice was genuine. "But there's still time, you can still make this right."

Her face went blank for a moment, muscles slackening until the fell into a smile. She stood up, lamp still in her hand.

"I can still make this right," she echoed.

She dropped to her knees, huffing frantically as she rubbed the lamp.

"DELIA, NO!"

The bullet engulfed the competing sounds. Delia Dawson's back was against the ground, a rose-blossom wound pouring from her forehead as her eyes gleamed with wild, desperate happiness.

Before he could yell out, Joe felt a tugging at his shirt as Johann jerked him back.

Around them the already black sky drifted into total darkness. The grass around them was swallowed whole, the rain ceased entirely and soon the only sound was a low rumbling which shook the earth. The lamp burned bright red, illuminating Delia's corpse as a small tongue of flame flickered in a testing, snake-tongue motion.

The rumbling became a bemused, crawling laugh.

"MOVE!" Johann was lifting Joe now, pulling him back as a tower of white lightning shot from the lamp into the sky.

The lightning became a web, sprouting off in cracking branches that intersected into a blinding white mass. Fire lined the ground beneath it, towers of flame shooting up to meet their source as they interwove into burning pillars. The mass of light wove together, linking to form legs that rose twenty feet into the air; it coalesced and grew, making long arms and a swiveling neck atop of which two red eyes peered down.

The ifrit first turned to Delia, issuing an electric hiss that might have been a "Tsk tsk."

Then it turned to Joe, the weight of its stare was unlike any pressure he had ever faced before. Joe saw the eyes immediately before him, as if the lighting were only inches from his face.

"I am al-Marid. He of countless names. He who broke the planets. He the unbounded fury, the cosmic chaos. Spiller of stars and father of gods and demons. Speak your desires, that I may return to my restful imprisonment."

Joe, still silent, gasping and struggling to congeal his thoughts into a single word. Somewhere far away Johann was screaming at him, words and pleas from a long forgotten friend.

"The mortal who summoned me is gone, and yet I must grant one wish before I may return. I see into you," Joe felt an intrusion into his being, as if something warm and soothing was coursing through his veins and massaging him from the inside. "There are so many foolish things you want, little wizard, things of which even you yourself are not aware. You want to be great. You want to be good. I am al-Marid, and I can give you these desires if only you speak them..."

Behind him a small, irrelevant person cried out for his attention. In front of him was an opportunity, an opportunity he would never have again. He could make the world a safer place, he could make his mother safe. He could bring his father back to life. He could heal the relationship with his brother, and make it to where he never wronged Elyria. All that separated him from everything he could ever want were a few words."

Impatient, the eyes of al-Marid vanished from his face.

"And what of you, warlock? What is it that *you* desire?"

Johann was standing firm, his hand in his coat ready to reach for the countless charms he had prepared for such an encounter. He gritted his teeth, scowling at the tower of lightning and not giving it any sign of his fear.

"I don't want anything."

Al-Marid laughed, and behind it stars exploded and died in fluid color.

"You *lie*, you want *everything*. I can see it written on your face, I can hear it beneath the beating of your heart."

"I don't want anything *given* to me."

The ifrit considered his for a moment, a long blue claw of lightning scraping against what might be a crackling, shifting outline of a chin.

"I wish," Johann began.

Joe lunged at him. He brought a fist to his face, connecting to Johann's nose with a wet crack as blood flooded out from bent nostrils. But Johann called out, over Joe's protests and screams:

"I wish you to be freed after my final wish."

The tower cackled, lowly and loudly over the now swaying grass.

"Clever warlock... clever *master*."

The lightning fizzled out abruptly, leaving a thin stream of white smoke which wove its way down from the cloudy sky and back into the lamp.

Beneath it Delia Dawson was a small corpse in a growing puddle of blood.

* * *

The lamp rested on the dashboard of the Maverick.

Upstate New York folded beneath the blue sky, green hills and stray white-gray clouds shining brilliantly through the car windows. Joe glanced at Johann, who despite all his composure would not take his now glimmering eyes off of the lamp. The highway hummed beneath them, and the drive to New York would be a long one.

Plenty of time for Joe to ask Johann his questions.

He'd start with an apology.

"Look, Johann—"

"It wasn't your fault," Johann answered, making sure his eyes fell on the lamp at all times. "There aren't any spells to combat these things. The drawing of desires, it's why the old kings trapped them, locked them up and threw away the keys."

Joe couldn't bring himself to point out that Johann hadn't been tempted, that the old kings hadn't been tempted either. True certainty, a command and discipline of even the subconscious mind, was necessary to guard yourself from an ifrit. Johann had that, it seemed. But Joe did not.

And this begged another question:

"Johann... what are you going to use the ifrit for?"

Johann didn't respond, his expression was placid and immovable.

"You're not turning it in, are you?"

Johann sighed, shaking his head and breaking his gaze from the lamp. He turned to Joe, the gleaming in his eye now alive with the smile beneath them.

"Who would I even turn it in to, Joe?

"You know things have been different since we began detonating atomic bombs. All these gods, these demons, they're scared that mankind can finally hit back. And we can, Joe. We're getting so close. It's why they're more active now than ever before, and why they're trying just as hard as we are to keep all of this out of the public eye. Could you imagine the public outcry if the public found out that earth was right in the crossfires of an inter-dimensional war? Imagine if they found out that we could fight back..."

Joe kept silent. This side of Johann was strange, alive and darkly animated. His friend was abandoning his pretense of reserve, that cool façade that he had used for so long to carefully build his reputation.

"And humans are getting more dangerous too. They're latching onto sides in wars that they have no part of, roping the human race into conflicts far beyond its interest or control. The Soviets have Volkov, but he isn't the only one; that witch you fought down in Nicaragua—"

"How do you know about that?"

Johann blinked. He had overplayed his hand and his face said he knew it. He tightened, turning away from Joe and back to the car window. He strummed his fingers against the door, letting his eyes rest on the crest of some distant hill.

"Johann," Joe's voice was venomous now, "I didn't tell you I was in Nicaragua. I didn't tell my mother, I didn't tell Elyria."

"You told the CIA. You wrote them a report. I read it."

"*How?*"

Johann closed his eyes and frowned. He had no out, no other choice than to lie. But they'd known each other for too long for Johann to be able to get away with that. There was nowhere to go, and in exhaustion Johann threw his hands in the air and sighed.

"I've been approached to build something. He wanted to approach you too, but I asked him to let me talk to you first."

"*Who?*"

"Come *on* Joe, who do you *think*? Who do you think had this car for us, waiting at the airport? Who do you think reached out to me when Figueroa died? Who do you think had those files about Fields and Dawson written up?"

"I'm not working for the CIA," Joe spat, furious at Johann. "It's not fucking happening."

"I'm not here to ask you to work for them. I'm asking you to work *with me*."

The air hissed through slightly open windows. Another car passed them, its blaring radio a garbled mess of guitars and voices as it sped past them. The sun became covered in clouds, and the world was gray again.

"I'm building something new, Joe. A new agency, independent of existing intelligence networks. I think this is going to protect us. You're my oldest friend. You're better at this than I am. I could use your help."

Joe was still angry, biting his lip and keeping his eyes on the road in front of them.

"Why wouldn't you just tell me that you read that file? Why'd you have to do your typical 'man of mystery' bullshit? I'm not someone you need to fool, Johann. I'm your *friend*!"

Johann turned his gaze to the floorboards before lifting it back to Joe.

"I'm sorry. I really am, if you can believe me. I know I'm... difficult to be around, Joe."

The wheels turned on the asphalt beneath them.

"Do you... want to talk about what you saw down there?" Johann ventured.

Joe laughed dryly, "Not right now. Not anymore."

"Then... will you think about what I'm asking you?"

Joe kept silent.

"You don't need to answer now. Give it a few weeks, I'm going to do this with or without you. But I could use someone who knows me, a friend who can stop me when I'm wrong."

"What are you going to use the ifrit for, Johann?"

He couldn't help himself as the smile cracked back across his face.

"I don't know, but now I *have* it. The Soviets could launch all their nukes at once and I could turn them back with a sentence. I could make their satellites rain from the sky, I could knock their planes out of the air. I could bend demons to my will without ever setting foot in Hell... I have something greater than any nuke. And when I'm dead, it's gone."

"Life insurance? Global blackmail?" Joe asked.

Johann shook his head, "Call it what you want. But things aren't going back to the way they were. The world is a more dangerous place, and the only way we're going to get by is by being more dangerous ourselves. And with that," Johann pointed to the lamp. It shook gently with the rhythm of the asphalt beneath them. Even inside its prison al-Marid was probably keenly listening to its new and last master, learning and scheming for what it could get by any means necessary.

"I'll be more dangerous than anyone."

ANGELUS

JOHN PAUL FITCH

Anna felt it before she heard it. Her charm tattoos burned white hot, pain plunging its tendrils through her soft flesh and down to the bone, ripping her from the velvet comfort of sleep into agonising reality. Her moan rose to a pain-flecked scream and she threw the sheets off the bed, her right-hand grabbing at her left wrist, where the tattoo shone bright blue in the darkness. She realised what it meant a second before it happened, and there was no time to warn Rachel, the brunette stripper who snoozed beside her...

Anna squeezed her eyes shut and covered her ears a moment before the angel appeared in a blast of fiery light and the deafening trumpeting sound that accompanied it. Rachel, startled awake, didn't have the wit to look away, staring at the glorious being before her as the membranes of her eyes haemorrhaged, and as the sound ruptured her ear-drums. The windows in Anna's bedroom blew out into the night air, shattered to glitter.

Anna opened her eyes a crack, just enough for the light to sear her corneas, but also to let her catch a glimpse of the monstrous being, which was stooped over in the corner of her bedroom to stop from pushing its head through the ceiling. The hermaphroditic angel, its body taut and sinewy and woven from beatific light, clutched a spear and sword in its massive hands, glaring around the room with eyes of golden fire. Anna yelled in pain and screwed her eyes shut again, but as she did the being winked out of reality just as suddenly as it arrived. She was left with the imprint of the figure bouncing around the inside of her eyeballs and the loud, high pitched ringing in her ears.

"What the shit?" she squealed, falling back onto the bed, rubbing her eyes. "Bloody angels!"

***

Anna closed the taxi door gently and leaned in through the window to kiss Rachel on the mouth. Rachel stared at her dumbly. She held the blood spotted bedsheet wrapped around her like a shroud. Red streaks crusted on her face, crimson tracks ran from her eyes and nose down over her mouth and chin and neck. Thick red blood clotted in her ears.

Anna mouthed 'I'll call you' and made a phone gesture with her hand. The taxi pulled away. She watched it go. Shards of glass on the pavement caught her eye and she glanced up at her now non-existent bedroom window.

"Bastard."

Shivering from the cool night air and barefoot in her vest and pyjama bottoms, Anna made her way quickly back up the steps to her flat, careful not to step on any shards of glass.

Turk sat on the couch with his legs crossed watching the news when Anna plonked herself down beside him, rubbing the side of her head. A serious looking news anchor was busy describing the spate of angel sightings across the country and the report kept cutting to show grainy camera footage of streaks of light in the night sky. Hysterical crowds of people milled in the streets; panicked masses were flocking to churches, who welcomed them with open arms and smiles. The camera focused on a placard that read "THE SECOND COMING IS NIGH." The reporter pushed his way through the crowd. The camera panned across the gathering fanatics and settled on a minister who implored the crowd to remain calm. The congregation responded to his every gesture, like a seething ball of cobras hypnotised to submission by a snake charmer.

"Look at this idiot." Turk motioned towards the television, "out preaching in his best Christmas jumper and it's only September. I bet his gran knitted it during the war."

Anna lifted the remote and turned the TV off. She rubbed her temples. The minister looked familiar but she couldn't place him.

"How's the hearing?"

"Coming back. Still rings a bit."

"And Rachel?"

Anna sighed. "I put her in a taxi home. She was pretty shaken, but what do you expect when a screaming angel busts into your bedroom in the middle of the night unannounced, trumpets blaring and shooting fire out of his arse?"

"Do I even have to ask?" said Turk.

"For a ghost with supposed connections to the underworld, you really are useless at times, Turk. No. I have no idea why an angel appeared in my bedroom and melted all of my mirrors."

"I don't appreciate your tone, young lady. And what do you mean *supposed*?" Turk said.

Anna ran a hand through her shoulder length black hair. "Never mind."

"So," Turk continued, leaning back on the couch, "a spate of angel sightings. Mass panic. Religious nutters in horrible jumpers holding sermons in the streets. We have to do something, right?"

Anna nodded. "I know a few people who dabble in Enochian magick. I'd say that's a good place to start as any. Well, one person."

"The occult is your job, Anna. You know chants and spells and stuff. Why can't you evoke an angel or something and find out what's happening?"

Anna shook her head. "It's not as simple as that, Turk. Enochian magic is dangerous. If it's not done properly it can... dissolve your mind. And besides, you saw what that thing did to my bedroom, and to my girlfriend. I don't plan on a re-run." She lifted her leather bomber jacket from the arm of the couch. "It's almost morning. We have work to do."

"Hi-ho," said Turk.

* * *

The streets were quiet, save for the odd bus and car, early risers and tradespeople off to their jobs. Anna and Turk walked briskly in the fresh morning air. They headed south towards the river, passing out of the labyrinthine apartment complexes and into the industrial part of town where factories were awakening, their lights flickering, the cough of cold machinery on the air.

"Are you going to tell me where we are headed?" asked Turk.

"The river. He usually hangs about there, down by the bridge."

"Who? He must be homeless if he hangs about under a bridge. Or a troll? Is he a homeless troll?"

A large, noisy truck belched black smoke as it careened past. Anna watched it go, then checking the road was clear, crossed to the other side. They were standing at the opening of a bridge which squatted low over a fast-moving river. On the other side, under the bridge, the faint yellow glow of a fire flickered and the echo of a singing voice carried clear across the water.

"For a ghost, you ask a lot of dumb questions." Anna pointed. "There. That's who we're here to see. Christ on a bike." She huffed and walked away across the bridge. Turk looked at her incredulously.

"Oh come on... old mental Tom Foolery? The Singing Vagrant?"

Anna took the steps down the embankment. The singing was much clearer now, a deep vibrato, belting out the old Sinatra standard, 'Witchcraft'.

"It's strictly tabooooo..."

Anna chuckled. "Tom."

The singing stopped abruptly and a wizened, bearded face peered out from the underpass, green woollen hat on his head, barely keeping a lid on a tangle of long white hair. The old man beamed as he recognised his visitor.

"Annie, my girl! How are ye?" He came shuffling out of the underpass, arms held wide, almost empty bottle of Grant's in one hand, and gathered Anna up in a warm embrace, lifting her off the ground as he did so.

"I'm good, Tom. How you keeping?"

"Aye, fine. Who's yer big pal?"

Turk stopped in his tracks. "You can see me?"

Anna chuckled. "Yes, Turk. He can see you. And hear you."

Tom looked Turk up and down. "Nice threads, my man. A bit out of season, but nice all the same."

Turk shot Anna a look. "Imagine our luck finding Tom-fucking-Ford under a bridge. Don't you have some goats to terrorise?"

Tom sucked in some air and glanced at Anna sideways. "Oh. He's salty, isn't he?"

"Turk, leave off. Tom's just having a laugh."

"Come on, young Turk," said Tom, "step into my *casa de tutti casa*. What's mine is mine and what's yours is yours."

"Charming." Said Turk, sneering.

Under the arch, Tom swigged from the whisky bottle before passing it to Anna. Turk watched her sup from the bottle and grimaced. Tom took the bottle back and slugged it hard.

"Mother's milk! So, what can I do for you this fine mornin'?" He splayed himself out in a grotty camping chair and leaned back against the concrete underpass wall. Everything Tom owned, or had stolen, was here. A small table sat to his right, decorated ornately with hexagrams and strange looking letters. Several small pieces of metal, which looked like they'd been cut from tin cans, lay on the table top next to a small wooden stick. A shopping trolley sat off behind the chair, piled high with plastic bags stuffed with clothes and assorted knick-knacks. Anna stared at the flickering glow from the small fire Tom had going in a rusty bin.

"Don't know if you saw anything out here," said Anna, "but a couple of hours ago the windows in my flat were blown out by an uninvited angelic visitor."

Tom nodded slowly.

Anna continued. "My tattoos woke me up just before it appeared. I was lucky. It glared around the room and then... disappeared." She clicked her fingers.

"I seen them, aye. They burned arcs through the sky like it was Guy Fawkes night. Dozens of them, shooting like sparks." Tom looked serious. "Never seen anything like it in my puff."

"What do they want?"

"I don't know, Annie." Tom paused. "but I suppose you want me to find out?"

"It'd really help, Tom."

"I haven't spoken the Keys in a long time, Annie."

"I know."

Tom nodded to himself sadly, then stood and moved to his shopping trolley. He began to rummage in the plastic bags.

"It's... dangerous."

Anna nodded. Tom pulled a red velvet cloth from one of the bags and turned, placing it carefully on the table. Then he pulled five little wax figures from his pockets, holding each of them up and examining them before placing them on the cloth. He caught Turk looking and winked. "My talismans. They keep me safe."

"And here was me wondering if you still played with action figures."

Tom snickered. "Most ghosts are dour, all wrapped up in the melancholy of being dead. You? You're funny." He lifted the bottle and drained the last of the whisky from it before tossing it over his shoulder. It bounced twice before shattering, the sound reverberating off the concrete. "Alright. Okay, I'll do it for you. You might want to stand back though, Annie. I don't know what will happen."

Tom arranged the table just so, fixing the positions of the talismans, and lay the cloth over the biggest of the charms. Then he rummaged in his coat and produced a large piece of round glass, which he placed on top of the red cloth so that it was elevated above the table. Tom shuffled so that the crystal was between him and the river and got down on his knees. He took several deep lungfuls of air. Then he leaned forward and peered through the round glass stone. He muttered to himself under his breath, his voice rising and falling and rising again, shaking his head slowly from side to side.

"What's he doing?" asked Turk.

"He's whispering the Calls of the Thirty Aethers. He's beginning to work his mind through the visionary states, from Tex through to Lil in order to be able to communicate with—"

"Angels and that. I get it. But why is he leaning over the river?" Tom had shifted from his place behind the table and moved to the river. He knelt at the edge, leaning over to the point of toppling. His eyes were wide open and fixed upon the swirling black eddies.

"He's scrying?" Anna said.

"Aren't you supposed to do that in a bowl or something?"

"Why use a bowl when you can use an entire river?"

Tom was rocking back and forward now, chanting like a shaman. His voice reached a crescendo; he pitched himself backwards till his head almost touched the ground behind him, and then flung his body forward, eyes wide.

"The Great Table of the Earth!" he screamed and raised his arms over his head. Tom's eyes rolled backwards till only the whites showed. His face turned a deep shade of red going on purple. He tilted sideward and then forwards.

"He's going to topple into the water." Said Turk.

"Shit." Anna darted forward and grabbed Tom by the back of his jacket just before he lost his balance. It was like touching a bare wire. Anna felt the electric jolt of Tom's power shoot fire up her arm and into her head. The world flashed grey. Everything drained of colour except for the black swirling river, but it wasn't a river any more. Where once was water was now a sky full of fire and light; four pyramids, structures so large and complex that Anna could not begin to comprehend them, rose up out of the light, and between them a monstrous black iron cross jutted up and towered out of sight above her and somehow around her. She heard Tom yell to her through the divine wind that battered them. He was there with her, beside her. The wind tore at them, threatening to strip the hair and skin from their bodies.

"Do you see them, Annie? The four watchtowers of the elements?"

She turned her gaze back to the pyramids. They spun slowly in unison. They were patterned with arched windows inside which were the faces of angels. From the towers came a phalanx of winged beings, sixteen at Anna's count, who swooped down quickly towards them. They landed heavily, muscles straining. The nearest angel turned its gaze on Anna. Such terrible beauty, such fire in its eyes and heart. Anna couldn't bear to look at. She heard it converse with Tom with a voice that sounded like the rumble of thunder. Her eardrums felt like they'd burst any moment. She turned her eyes towards the four pyramids but now there were twenty... no... now there were more, hundreds, all moving, all turning eternally. They were all around her. Anna screamed and covered her face, and somewhere far off she heard old Tom yell her name just as the light swallowed her and it faded to black and the sound of the wind fell away...

When her wits started to return, Anna could hear Turk arguing feverishly with Old Tom.

"She could have died."

"She wasn't supposed to get involved."

"She was trying to save you from drowning!"

Her head felt like it was made from tissue paper and the pain in her temples was from a fat child poking a saliva-slicked finger through the tissue and into her brain. Anna lay with her eyes closed, knowing that if she opened them, then the light would burn its way into her eye sockets and she'd probably throw up. So instead she kept them closed and in the slightly more comfortable dark whispered.

"Please. Keep it down. I'm actually dying here."

She heard a gasp, then "Shh! Keep it down, you silly old fool. Anna?"

"Hey, lassie. You alright?"

Anna tried to shake her head from side to side. Her insides tilted. That's when the rush of saliva filled her mouth, followed by a bellyful of warm whisky.

* * *

Tom stuffed the hot, fat-dripping chips into his mouth. He began to pant as they scalded his tongue, but didn't stop eating them. He even started talking with a full mouth.

"... so, he... it... it was a lesser angel, not one of the big boys. From what I could gather he said they'd lost something and couldn't find it." Tom turned to the spotty teenager behind the counter. "Got any tomato sauce, my love?"

Anna held a cold can of cola against her temples, rubbing it into the skin. The smell of the chip shop, the grease, the scent of pickle juice, made her want to vomit again. Tom had convinced her that food was the thing to make her feel better. They'd waited till the chip shop opened at 10am, Anna nursing the worst hangover she'd ever felt the whole time.

She squinted at Tom. "Lost something?"

"What on earth could an angel lose?" Turk leaned against the chip shop wall.

The girl handed Tom the ketchup bottle. "Ta much, m'dear." He slathered sauce all over the chips.

"Actually, not 'lost'. It was more like *hidden*. They're definitely looking for something."

"And while they do so, they're causing a ton of trouble and whatnot. Not to mention the hysteria." Anna nodded towards the road where several dozen people were gathered and more were joining the crowd with every passing minute. A man stood on top of a milk crate and, using a megaphone, preached salvation. Several signs alluding to the immanent "Rapture" were bouncing above the heads of the people, held aloft by fevered arms. Anna recognised the man on the milk crate.

"That's the guy from the telly."

"Maximus something-or-other. He's the minister at St John's out in the west end." Tom mumbled between mouthfuls.

"Since when does a tramp become an expert on local religious figures?" Turk sniffed.

"Well, I do sleep under a lot of newspapers, Turk, my man. Sometimes I even read them."

Turk shook his head. "Look at the state of that jumper. It's like something Noel Edmonds would wear."

Anna stepped out of the chip shop and onto the pavement. She instinctively rubbed her arm. Her tattoos had begun to tickle. Something was off here; magic was afoot. Anna scanned the crowd for the source, for something that stood out, but her eyes were drawn towards Maximus the Minister. He pontificated with such vigour, with such passion that she felt herself swept along with the emotion. He held his hands out to the crowd and a man in a yellow jacket reached up and grabbed Maximus' hand and pulled him from his makeshift mount. Maximus lost his balance and tipped forward into the crowd, who surged to catch him. As he tumbled into the tangle of arms, Anna's eyes fell on a girl in a white dress who had been standing directly behind Maximus. She had deep red hair pulled into a ponytail and a white blouse buttoned up to the neck. Anna's breath caught in her throat.

"Holy shit."

Turk looked at her. "You know your mouth is hanging open? You'll catch flies. Especially with breath like yours."

"Turk. The girl. It's Jane."

"Jane..." Turk stared at the girl. "Oh yeah! Jane the Pain. She was into kinky shit, wasn't she? Found God and became pure and that. Strange, considering the stuff she was into before."

Anna frowned. "Maximus is her dad. That's why he looked familiar. What are the odds, Turk?"

"Of an angel appearing and setting fire to your room and deafening your girlfriend, and then you seeing your *ex*-girlfriend at what amounts to an evangelical rally? If I were you, I'd be buying lottery tickets."

The crowd lifted Maximus back up onto the milk crate and a huge cheer went up. Jane stepped from behind him and handed him a bible which he took and held aloft to the crowd.

The chanting and the placards went up once again, a wave of energy washing over them. Anna was in amongst the congregation before she had even realised what was happening, and found herself encircled by the arms of an overweight woman and her equally overweight daughter. The woman wiped tears from her cheeks and hugged Anna and began to sing. Without knowing the words, lost in the atmosphere of the crowd, Anna began to sing along with them. She looked to Maximus, his arms held aloft, bible clasped in his right hand. There, in the bible, like some extravagant bookmark, was a large golden feather, as long as Maximus' arm. The energy of the crowd washed over Anna. It felt so good that she forgot about the feather. The hymn felt so right and the arms around her, the embrace of others in rapture. Anna swam in profound love, drifting on currents of ecstasy.

* * *

"I still can't believe it." Turk could barely speak for laughing.

Anna tried to curl into a ball on the cushions of the couch. Turk stood in front of her, unable to contain himself. Tom sat off to the side in the corner of Anna's living room.

"Psalms. Hymns. You were even rejoicing."

"It was glorious, Annie," piped Tom from the corner. He was rolling a cigarette and licked it, smacking his lips.

"Piss off the pair of you." Her head still thumped.

"You should have seen your face. Angelic!" Turk bent double at the waist with laughter.

Anna groaned and hauled herself up off the couch and stormed out of the living room.

"There's got to be some booze in here."

Turk called after her. "Come back, I haven't even got to the best bit."

"A minute of your time, Turk, my man?" said Tom.

Anna rattled around in the kitchen cupboards for anything drinkable and found a bottle of Smirnoff half full. She tossed the lid across the kitchen and slugged the vodka down. It seared her gullet down to her stomach. Her head felt lighter almost instantly. She wasn't drinking to calm her nerves, or to stave off the embarrassment. She drank because she could feel the remnants of something on her, some psychic afterbirth that clung to her very being. Anna ran through the events again, remembering what she could before her mind clouded over with rapturous contentment. She recalled the swaying crowd, Jane, still gorgeous, fully immersed in her minister's daughter get up, and Maximus with his bible held aloft, beaming with righteousness.

Then it hit her.

* * *

"An angel feather?" said Turk, again.

"I'm telling you. It was in the bible. When he held it up to the crowd, that's when I lost track of myself." Anna spun the wheel and the car sharked around the corner and headed down the hill out of town. Tom had 'borrowed' the car from a house several streets away.

"Are you sure it wasn't just you... you know... getting into the holiness of it all?"

Anna shot Turk a look. "I've seen a feather like that once before. It was on the wings of a flippin' angel."

Tom grunted and frowned. "Makes as much sense as anything else."

"How would they get themselves an angel's feather?"

"I don't know, Turk. Where do you think?"

"From... an angel?"

They hit the bottom of the hill and turned left onto a narrow road that cut through an industrial estate, the buildings and factories long since shuttered, their doors marked with graffiti, their windows smashed to pieces. Turk leaned on the window as the light pattering of rain began to dot the glass. He spied their destination in the distance. The approach to St John's was littered with abandoned cars, doors open, some with lights still on. They crowded the small road like a roadblock. Unable to go any further, Anna, Turk, and Tom disembarked and began to trudge towards the church. Anna could see caravans and tents pitched on the road sides. As they neared the church they could make out the people in their hundreds, all cramming together, crushing against the stone walls as they all pushed in to catch the sermon. Anna gasped. There were people with the life squeezed from them, kept standing by the others around them. Squashed. Ribs broken and popped. Lungs pulped by the weight of the crowd around them. Some people had fallen to the ground and been trampled as others walked over them, jostling for position. Women, children, elderly.

Anna covered her mouth with both hands. Tom pressed his lips together and set his jaw.

"This... this..." Anna started, but trailed off. Tom finished for her.

"It's ungodly is what it is."

Anna's tattoos fired up again, burning with an intensity she hadn't felt in a long time. "We won't be able to get in through the front. We'll have to look for another way in."

They skirted the edge of the church, rounding the corner and pushing through the hedges that separated the front entrance from the back courtyard. No sooner had they begun to brush the leaves from their clothes than Tom spotted a red wooden door set into the brickwork. Turk approached the door and bent to study the lock.

"I'm sure you know how to pick one of these, Tom? Being a homeless thief and that."

Tom snorted. "You're pretty funny for a dead man. And stupid." He reached for the handle and turned it. The door swung open easily. Tom tutted and breezed into the church with Anna close behind.

They stood in a modern looking kitchen, all chrome cupboards and work tops and a checked linoleum floor. A door stood open on the right of the kitchen which led into a hallway. Another door was set into the wall opposite. The muffled sound of Maximus pontificating rumbled through the walls. Anna slinked up to the door on the left and cracked it open. Beyond was a small chamber with a coat rack and a small cabinet, with another door which she presumed led into the main church hall. Anna let the door close. She looked at the other door and the dark hallway beyond.

At the end of the hallway were two empty bedrooms, a small bathroom, and one other door which led down a flight of stone steps to a basement. They descended the steps, illuminated only by a bare bulb, and came to a thick metal door, held in place with a bar across the front. Anna and Turk locked eyes. He nodded to her and she slid the bar back across the door. The instant it opened her tattoos came alive, sending tendrils of pain and energy through her body. She fell forwards as she heard a familiar voice. "I knew you'd come," said Jane.

Jane stood in the centre of the windowless brick room. It was bare, empty of any furniture, except for a pile of blankets bundled up in the centre of the room directly behind Jane. She smiled serenely, one hand on her hip, her head tilted to the side. In her other hand she held a long shimmering feather. For a moment it looked like it was made of gold, then silver, then diamond. The light from the halogen bulb in the room fractured when it hit the gossamer surface of the feather, breaking into fractals of multi-coloured light. Anna felt herself awash with joyful emotions again. Love surged in her chest, love for Turk, and for Tom, but most of all for Jane. The feather's reflections lit Jane up in such a way that she looked like an angel herself. Her hair fell over her shoulders, her white dress hung off the shoulder exposing her porcelain skin. Anna felt tears prick the corners of her eyes.

"I saw you earlier at my father's sermon in the street. I knew you'd figure it out eventually." Anna drew a breath to answer, but it fled her lips before she could form words in her mouth. Tom and Turk stumbled into the room as people, faithful worshippers, bloodied and pale, began to spill down the stairs, gathering like a mob at the threshold. Jane glanced at Tom then back to Anna.

"I don't think she can see me," whispered Turk.

Tom glanced at him and whispered. "Let's keep it that way. Remember what I told you back at the flat." Turk nodded and turned away from Tom. It looked like he stepped behind something that only he could see and then he was gone. Tom turned his attention back to Anna and Jane.

"That's an angel's feather, isn't it?" He eyed Jane intently, recognising the madness in her now.

"Quite right. And you are?"

"The Singing Vagrant, at your service. There's only one place you could have gotten a thing like that, and that's off the wings of a bloody angel."

Jane smiled approvingly and nodded. "Correct again." She turned to Anna, who had sunk to her knees, tears cascading down her cheeks. Jane knelt beside her and took Anna's face in her hands. "Would you like to see it?"

Anna reeled from the power of the feather. Her tattoos were going batshit crazy; she felt surges of power through her body, overloading her mind. The feelings, the warm swell of joy in her chest. She knew it was false but could not help herself. She reached for Jane, longing to feel her arms around her, to hear Jane's heart beat in her chest, to feel the love they once had.

Jane slipped her hand into Anna's and pulled her to her feet. She turned and took a took a fistful of the blanket off the floor behind her. She tossed it away to the side. Anna looked down and blinked. There were shapes gouged into the concrete floor, a geometric pattern, two concentric circles, between which were scrawled words, invocations in Latin and Hebrew, and inside the circles a seven-pointed star and inside that, encircled in more magickal words, was a Jewish star. And in the centre of this, lying on its side with two bare claw-like and featherless wings wrapped about its thin body, was a being so emaciated it looked near death.

Anna panted. "That's a bloody angel."

"Yes."

"You caught it in a Grand Pentacle—"

"In an Angel Trap. Then I stripped it of its feathers. It can't leave here, ever. I have what I wanted."

"You're just going to leave it here to... wither away?" said Tom.

"If that's what happens." Jane held up the feather again. Anna felt woozy and stumbled. Tom caught her just before she fell. "The feathers. They hold such power. It's your fault, you know." She pointed the feather towards Anna, who sagged and leaned into Tom. "You're the one who got me into magick in the first place. Those long nights we spent working, summoning, casting. I learned from you, from the best magickian I've ever met. But I've gone further than you ever did. Enochian magick, I learned the Keys, and I summoned this thing." She motioned towards the angel, lying still in the centre of the pentacle.

"Why?"

"This is a godless world, filled with non-believers. We were running out of money. This church is my father's life, it's all he has, and it was failing. We needed a miracle, and we got way more than one. Angels have *thousands* of feathers on each wing."

Anna managed to find the strength to stand on her own. "You want to know the reason I never messed with Enochian magick? It makes people crazy, it scrambles your brain. You should have known better." Anna glanced at the angel, its skin pallid and grey.

"Crazy?" Jane's voice rose. "Look upon my people, ready to die at my command. Do you know what that makes me? I'm a god, Anna." The crowd began to bristle. "Real power!"

Anna saw Turk materialise inside the room. He looked at Tom and nodded. There was a rumble, like deep thunder, then the entire building shook. A crack opened in the ceiling dropping pieces of plaster and dust into the air.

Then came the deafening sound of trumpets. The mob in the doorway looked at each other, panicked expressions on their faces as intense light rose in the stairway above them. Anna saw Tom mouth the word 'Drop.' She pushed Jane away from her and dived behind the metal door.

The blast of holy fire shot through the doorway, throwing Tom clear across the room. Anna was shielded from it by the metal door. She kept her eyes open just enough to see a phalanx of angels swarm into the room – and to see Jane scream as their fire and fury enveloped her and burned her to ashes. She blew apart like a pile of dried leaves, even her bones crumbling to dust in the whirlwind. The concrete of the floor began to melt, scorched by the intense heat of holy fire. Anna screamed and covered her head with her leather jacket. The wind shrieked, or maybe it was Anna, and then before she knew it the light dissipated and the wind died and the room turned back to darkness again.

* * *

Turk's face swam into view. He was smiling down at her. "Can you hear me alright?"

"What?" Anna could hear nothing but high-pitched ringing.

Turk smiled. "Bloody angels."

When her head stopped ringing, Anna hauled herself to her feet, feeling more battered than she'd ever felt before. Turk was crouched in the corner over a crumpled body. Tom had been burned black, turned almost to charcoal. He lay curled up like a foetus, his arms up under his chin and his legs tucked under his body.

"Poor Tom. The fire caught him as it came through the door. He never stood a chance."

Anna stood behind Turk.

"Back in the flat..." murmured Turk. "He told me what to say. To make them come. He knew we'd need them."

"It's okay, Turk. He knew what he was doing."

"I can't feel him any more, Anna."

"Me neither. He's gone completely."

Turk spun and stalked towards the door. "Stupid old bastard. The hell was he thinking?"

Anna watched him storm up the stairs, mumbling to himself.

The floor had been scoured by the wave of angel fire, a wide strip of blackened concrete where the angel trap had been gouged was now wiped clean. Jane had been vaporised completely, nothing, not even dust, remained of her. The swarm of angels had wiped the world clean of her very existence.

On the stairs, those members of the congregation who had followed them down to the basement lay burned to a crisp. Anna navigated their bodies and made her way outside. Crowds still milled around confused, placards and banners, discarded and tossed to the ground, lay strewn like litter. Jane's father, Max, sat on the steps of his church, his head in his hands. He looked up at Anna as she passed him, his eyes red with tears.

"Did you see them? They were glorious. Like shooting stars."

Anna nodded. "I saw them."

"Jane. She missed them. She'll be so upset she missed them."

"She saw them, Max. I promise you." Max beamed up at her, and for a moment, he looked like a small child. Anna left him there and moved down the steps, heading through the milling people and trekked up the road. As she drew near the car she could make out Turk sitting in the passenger seat, staring out the window at the grey sky above.

"What now?" Turk asked as she settled into the driver's seat.

Anna closed her eyes for a minute and took in a breath. The feeling of the feather's power still clung to her; she felt ribbons of it ripple through her.

"Now? I'm hungry."

"The Greasy Egg Cafe?"

"Sounds like a plan, Stan."

The engine kicked over on the third try. Anna reversed till she found a part of the road wide enough to turn around and they headed up the hill.

"How's Rachel?" asked Turk.

"She won't answer my calls."

"Maybe she can't hear the phone?"

"Shut up, Turk."

THE LAST PERFORMANCE OF VICTORIA MIRABELLI

IAN HUNTER

If you had been there...
You would have heard the screaming, pleading, shrieking of spirits in torment.
Would have heard the insane cackle of a shrivelled old woman.
Would have seen the flash of a sharp silver razor catching the stage lights.
And the shocked faces of those who were splattered with blood, who were sitting too close to the stage.
So much blood.
If you had been there...

* * *

He got the idea from his undead friend, Alex Harper, about the need for another resting place.

"The world is closing in on us," Harper told him, leaning forward out of the shadows in a corner booth of a dingy waterfront bar. "We live in an age of global terrorism, and all the constraints that brings."

"We don't live," Roam said dryly.

"You know what I mean. It's alright for me. I just bum around from bad motel to bad motel, righting wrongs that occur on the dark side of life."

Roam chuckled and leaned forward, batting his white eye lashes. "My hero."

"I mean it, I'm not a jet-setter like you."

Roam smiled. Harper did look like a down and out. Unkempt hair, broken nose, handsome, but still a down and out, an undead crusader, even if he was in love with a woman who might pass for a goddess, while Roam in his present incarnation was a renowned historian and historical novelist, making the occasional book signing, the odd, restricted lecture tour, no pictures please. There were none on the jackets of any of his books, not even pictures taken during the psychic phase of his existence, when the lens could capture his image and he wasn't a mist, a smudge, a nothing, an empty space when the bloodlust ruled his world.

He watched as Harper tugged on some gloves and slowly began to load silver bullets into his Colt Python. Roam reached out and picked up a bullet, weaving it around and around between his fingers like a coin in one of his tricks, then pretended to pop it into his mouth. He held out his empty hand.

Harper sighed as Roam stretched forward and produced the bullet from behind his ear. "I wish I could handle silver like that."

"It takes a lot of practice," Roam muttered, trying not to recall the years he had spent languishing in an English dungeon – because that only brought back memories of Madeleine de Fernier, whom he had lost to the Knights Templar, and he tried to keep her in the deepest recesses of his mind. Out of sight. Out of mind. Out of heart. Almost. Still, all those years being bound by silver meant he had gradually grown immune to it.

"Anyway, we ain't like old Dracula," Harper muttered. "We can't charter a ship and jump off as a dog at the other end."

"After murdering all the crew," Roam added.

"Dracula wasn't real," said Harper. "At least not that version, but what are you going to do when you don't show up on some airport security camera?"

"Blame the camera, of course."

"And you can't keep travelling around with that beat up magic cabinet."

"It's home."

"You don't really need that thing. It's only a habit, despite all that resting place mumbo jumbo."

"It's not a resting place, it's a cabinet, not a coffin; besides I toured for years as a magician, so what better place to sleep in? In a way it's almost expected."

Harper chortled. "Yeah, expected by readers of bad novels or watchers of old black and white movies – and what happens if it goes missing in transit? You need a spare."

Roam could feel his eyebrows rising, tugged by the idea. "A spare?"

"Yes," said Harper, spinning the chamber of silver bullets around before aiming it at his albino friend. He would never dream of pulling the trigger, and knew he would miss if he tried, even from this close. "Why don't you get yourself another box to lie in?"

"Another box?" Roam said hesitantly, clearly thinking about it.

"Yeah," said Harper. "Or another magic cabinet, so you can have the pair, the set."

"Well, there is one I would like to have," Roam said, nodding slowly, convincing himself that after all these years this might actually be the time to acquire it.

* * *

The mobile phone shook into life beside him like a rattlesnake in a box. Without looking — and there was no point since he lay in complete darkness — his long slim fingers pressed the correct buttons. This was just another form of magic trick, after all.

"HI, MR B. GOT IT, RGRDS E (OF S OF H)

Roam snorted. E (OF S OF H)? Who else could it be? He pressed some more buttons and his call was answered immediately.

"Sleight of Hand."

"Eddie," Roam breathed.

"Mr B! How are you?"

"I'm resting."

"Did I wake you?"

"No," He tried to work out the time difference between them. "Isn't it very late over there?"

"I'm on nights, or early mornings," the magick club's Mr Fixer told him. "All this week, then I go home and sleep like the dead."

"You must tell me what that's like sometime."

Eddie laughed. "So you got my text?"

"I did, and you've been successful, as always. What would I do without you?"

"Wasn't that difficult, Mr B, I just made a few enquiries on Google, then delved into a few more obscure websites."

"Ah, the glories of the internet, I must get one sometime, after I've mastered the mobile phone."

Eddie laughed. "The last known owner of your cabinet is in America."

"Well, that's handy, given my present location, but it's not my cabinet yet."

"I have an address and a phone number."

"The address will be fine, Eddie," Roam said, smiling in the dark. "I find the personal touch a lot more persuasive."

* * *

He rang the door bell again.

And waited.

He sighed and made a fist to pound the door.

Look, I know you are in there, he wanted to say. I heard you scurrying about. It's late, and the dark will run out eventually and I'll leave a really gooey mess on your porch when the sun comes up.

He stepped back, night eyes looking at the windows. Locked as far as he could see. Some of his kind would give up at this point, believing they needed an invitation to cross any threshold. Some of his kind believed in a whole lot of things, almost all of them wrong. He looked down at his hand, willing it to become sharp, and his fingers obeyed his shape-shifting powers, stretching, becoming pointed.

Then a key turned. Whoever was inside had been waiting behind the door.

"I dreamed an angel would come and rescue me," the painfully thin young woman with wild orange hair told him, her voice high, almost singing. "He had a head of fire, but your head looks cold, like snow. Are you an angel?"

"Hardly," Roam said, as she opened the door, and grimaced at the sight of what she had done to herself.

* * *

He made her – Lucee Andrews, Eddie had said – lie down on the sofa, then covered her with his long coat.

"Don't you have any food?" he shouted, opening and closing doors in the kitchen.

"She won't let me go out any more," Lucee whispered.

He came through with a cup of water, and put his hand behind her head. She sipped, then gulped. Water trickled down from the side of her mouth.

"I'm almost used up."

He nodded. Every part of him was sensing, smelling, tasting the festering wounds on her arms. He could practically lick minute quantities of blood out of the air. He stepped back a few paces, taking his rising bloodlust with him.

"Sleep," he soothed, and her eyelids began to flutter. "Sleep."

She astonished him by shaking her head and trying to get up. "It's dark, she'll call me soon."

"Who is she?"

Her trembling hand pointed to the large cabinet in the corner. He had intended waiting until she was asleep before he examined it. At first, it looked like a badly made wardrobe without feet, a big coffin, perhaps. There were cuts on one side of it, about waist high. Roam's eyes narrowed. They were also slashes, deep gouges, done in a hurry, he thought and all of them were smeared with blood. Smear after smear, down through the years, like endless coats of paint on top of each other. He raised his head, and sniffed, eyes widening in surprise. He turned to Lucee.

"Some of this is your blood?"

Now it was her turn to look surprised. "How do you know that?"

Roam smiled and shook his head slightly. "It's hardly great detective work considering the state of your arms."

"My blood keeps them here."

"What?"

"My blood, it holds the spirits."

"Ah," Roam said, nodding as he turned to stare back at the cabinet. He closed his eyes, focusing, ignoring the smell of her blood and the rest wiped across the cabinet. "Witchcraft, a binding spell."

Her eyes looked far away. "I suppose you could call it that. I never thought of it that way."

"How did you get the cabinet?"

She sipped some water. "From my father, with this other..." She shrugged, and giggled, an embarrassed look on her face. " 'Stuff'."

Roam looked around taking in masks and statues and paintings and stones and photographs and posters, all to do with the occult. "So he worshipped Santa, huh?"

Lucee laughed. "Far from it. He was a ghost breaker, ghost buster, ghost debunker, or whatever you want to call it. He didn't believe in the supernatural and spent his whole life trying to disprove it. Scams, crimes, you name it. He tried to solve them all, a bit like Scooby Doo before it went Buffy."

"Buffy?"

"Yes, the TV series. Surely you must have seen it?"

Roam gave an apologetic shrug.

"Well, anyway, before her, the monsters were fake and they were just a bunch of pesky kids. After Buffy all the monsters were real, there were no masks any more."

Roam nodded. "No more masks, I like the sound of that. So where is your father now?"

"In the box, of course. She killed him – Victoria Mirabelli."

He nodded more slowly this time.

"She died there too."

"So I heard," Roam said. "I always meant to catch her show, but our paths never crossed, probably because I specialised in more exclusive venues with my act"

She frowned at him. "What are you talking about? That happened decades ago. Longer than that, probably, you can't be that old."

"Forget it, I'm rambling, that's all," Roam said, waving his hand.

Lucee moved closer to him, eyes filled with excitement. "She cut her throat when the cancer became too much, then stumbled backwards to die in the cabinet. Can you believe that?"

"I can believe anything," he told her.

* * *

Lucee was finally asleep. Roam glanced towards her as she muttered something, her face contorted. Bad dreams, but they would fade eventually, once he took the cabinet away from here. His hand hovered over the gouges in the wood, splattered with crimson. Layers upon layer of blood, all from different owners, smeared there over the years. Suddenly he gasped and touched his ear, hearing a yell which disappeared as suddenly as it had started. Then something seemed to chatter beside him, giggle madly. Whisper. Shout. Scream, and above it all there was laughter.

Laughter.

And static.

Like a radio searching the wavelengths, catching nothing.

He cocked his head to the side.

Something...

He opened the scarred door of cabinet, and the buzzing static noise faded as he stepped inside.

No noises, just cold. Roam exhaled and watched the cloud of his breath ribbon across his shoulder, sucked back into the room.

He looked down. The bottom of the cabinet was stained too. Blood had been spilled here. Too much blood, if there ever could be such a thing to one of his kind. Her blood, he knew. Where she had killed herself. He turned and stepped backwards until he was pressed against the rear of the cabinet. Then he closed his eyes.

An icy hand dragged across his cheek. Something tugged at his hand, pulling him, trying to turn him round. He exhaled, took a deep breath, then followed the hand when it tugged him again, spirit leaving his body behind. He was still in the cabinet, but now it had no back panel, and seemed to stretch on forever, a dark rectangular tunnel.

And he was not alone.

Arms emerged from the wooden sides in front of him as he passed. Gesturing, pulling, pleading like the arms of forgotten prisoners protruding through bars in a cell door.

Wanting.

Help us.

Help us please.

"Who are you?"
The ones who would wander.
If we could.
Trapped here.
Forbidden to go across.
Don't talk to him, he's worse than her.
Shush, Andrews, better him than her, better him than anything.

Andrews, he thought. That would be Lucee's father. Roam walked on down the dark tunnel, hands clawing at him, then falling like chopped limbs, devoid of hope and energy, of purpose. He looked at them as he walked past. Phantom though they were, each had something wrong with it. Running sores, lumps, growths, skin hard like a reptile's, or red raw, peeled, flayed.

The wooden tunnel didn't go on forever after all.

There was someone waiting for him.

An old woman, small and thin, with translucent skin and dark, beady eyes that shone with a dark malevolence. There was a bloody wound across her throat, like a red, wet, glistening grin.

Roam bowed. "Madame Mirabelli."

The old face cracked open to reveal blackened stumps of teeth. Roam could feel hands at his back, pushing him on.

"Who are you who enters my realm?"

"Someone who desires this cabinet."

She smiled. "You can have it. I always encourage new owners, but be warned, it comes with a price."

Roam smiled back. "I know. You died here, didn't you? Bound yourself to the cabinet as you have bound others, but the difference was that they were wandering spirits drawn here by your powers."

The old woman nodded. "I have them all, even the man who did not believe, who only collected, but I showed him. I bound the rest when I was alive and they remain here even in death. My will is too strong. My body was weak, cancer of the bowels eating me up inside, but I knew I could live on if I died in my cabinet."

"As your cancer has lived on," Roam said. "It infested your will and your soul. You died too quickly, and it made the jump with you. That's why you have possessed the weak like Lucee so you could use them up, and use them to draw other spirits here."

"Like you." Victoria Mirabelli chuckled, a rasping sound that almost made Roam squirm. "This is my world beyond life and death, beyond the physical and the mental." She moved closer, walking awkwardly, almost rocking from side to side. Her mouth opened impossibly wide, teeth growing, sharpening from every angle. "I will eat part of your soul," she told him, holding up a gnarled hand to rub her thumb and forefinger together. "Just a smidgen, although more than enough to imprison you here forever."

Roam stepped forward, grabbed her arms by the wrists as she tried to reach for him. Her head jutted out, teeth snapping at him.

"This is my world," she hissed, rising up, drawing strength from her surroundings, and the walls of the cabinet began to change, the mask of wood dropping away to reveal the true corruption beneath.

She was powerful, perhaps too powerful, he realised as his legs started to buckle and she forced him down to his knees. Something sloughed across the side of his face, and he was aware of wavering faces on the edge of vision, coming closer, whispering in his ear.

Save us.

Kill her.

Free us.

A face was staring at him, cold and impassive. Lucee's father, he knew, before it moved away out of sight.

* * *

"Lucee, wake up!"

"What?" she mumbled, hands weaving through the air above her. "Go away! Get away from me!"

"Lucee!"

She sat up sharply, almost fell off the sofa. "D-ad?"

"Yes, it's me, I don't know how long I have, how long that creature can distract her."

"The ice angel? I like him."

"Oh, Lucee, he's no angel. Go and get the bleach and a scrubbing brush from under the sink and I'll tell you what to do."

* * *

Madame Mirabelli was weakening. He didn't know why, but he was glad of it. Her grip was less forceful and she gasped, almost doubled up in pain, but still he dared not let her go.

"Die, you old harpy, die!" a spirit shouted.

"That's right, pale one, kill her!"

"What's happening?" she asked. "What have you done to me?"

Roam didn't want to admit that he wasn't doing anything; instead, he let the bloodlust rise within him as his face transformed into something ancient, a cross between himself and the restless thing which lived in his blood. Then he smiled, opening his fingers, raising his head.

The old woman didn't hesitate, weakened though she was, she was still driven by her own form of bloodlust, her own hunger. Her mouth clamped shut on his throat, tearing out a clump of his flesh.

Is this how my victims feel, Roam wondered, aware of some of his psychic essence being drained away.

Victoria Mirabelli shrieked, rearing back, dragging her hand across her mouth, then clawed at her tongue with her fingers. She made a face and tried to spit.

"What is this?" she asked, "What are you?"

"Neither dead, nor alive," he told her, watching as she collapsed to her knees. "I too died before my time, and live on with something inside me. A piece of what drives me dwells within you now, trying to take control of you and the cancer that still eats away inside you."

Victoria Mirabelli did not reply — she simply crumpled as her knees buckled and hugged herself, shaking uncontrollably, black beady eyes rolling back to reveal empty white. Roam turned and walked back the way he had come. Around him the decaying walls melted back to wood, the desperate arms cast off their wounds, but still they clawed, pleading.

* * *

He paid over the odds for the cabinet, but it had been worth it, even with the bleach stains on the bottom and around the cuts and gouges where Lucee had attacked the blood of the binding spells with a scrubbing brush. If she used the money wisely she could have a fresh start, and he got Eddie to throw in some free flights, give her an incentive to get away from the house of occult objects for a while. Besides, her father was still there, haunting the place. Roam owed him something, he supposed, and had released him.

As for the others...

Please, Roam, please.

You defeated her.

Let us go.

Please.

Please.

Roam opened his eyes. He lay in darkness in his new home, pining slightly for the many stories he had etched inside his old magic cabinet, The holes he thrust swords through. The little devices which aided his tricks. But in his new home there were none of these things, just the smell of old spilled blood, and it felt cold. It would always feel cold, he supposed.

Please.

"No," he said, smiling. "I like the company. After all, we are going to be here for a long, long time."

That's when the wailing stared, and the pleading. Whispering entreaties, shouting protests, all asking for release, but he would get used to them, he supposed.

Over the long years he had found he could get used to almost anything.

Ghostly Clients & Demonic Culprits
The Roots of Occult Detective Fiction
Edited by TIM PRASIL
Phantom Traditions Library

Before Carl Kolchak, Agents Mulder and Scully, and Buffy the Vampire Slayer...

Before John Silence, Jules de Grandin, and Carnacki the Ghost Finder...

Visit BromBonesBooks.com

COLD CASES

An Occasional series of reviews of older, perhaps lesser known material.

MICHAEL KELLAR

SUPERNATURAL SLEUTHS: STORIES OF OCCULT INVESTIGATORS
EDITED BY PETER HAINING
William Kimber & Co. Limited, London, 1986
ISBN #0718305973

I have been collecting books by Peter Haining for over fifty years and while I own nearly sixty volumes of his work, my efforts are far from complete. A bibliography of his anthologies alone exceeds a hundred and thirty books (mostly related to horror and the supernatural), while his nonfiction writing is also considerable and covers such diverse topics as bullfighting to Elvis. Indeed, his complete output may never be known as some of his works at the New English Library in the '60s and early '70s were uncredited. [1]

While some of the early books were rather undistinguished – they mostly collected well-known tales in the public domain – it was about 1967, with his *Gentlewomen of Evil: An Anthology of Rare Supernatural Stories from the Pens of Victorian Ladies* that he began to hit his stride (and was allowed a budget for more ambitious books).

---

[1] See *'From Beyond the Grave'*, an interview with Peter Haining, which appeared in issue number six of *The Paperback Fanatic*, February 2008.

Many themed anthologies were to follow, but the 1986 *Supernatural Sleuths: Stories of Occult Investigators* seems to have been his only attempt to assemble a collection of occult detective stories.

A brief introduction suggests the reason for the timing of the book – it was released to capitalize on the popularity of the *Ghostbusters* film. The following twelve tales were included (along with a short introduction to each as well as a notation as to which detective is featured in the story):

'*The Ghost Detective*' by Mark Lemon
'*Selecting a Ghost*' by Sir Arthur Conan Doyle
'*The Story of the Moor Road*' by E. and H. Heron
'*A Victim of Higher Space*' by Algernon Blackwood
'*Case of the Haunting of Grange*' by Sax Rohmer
'*The Telepather*' by Henry A. Hering
'*The Poltergeist*' by Seabury Quinn
'*The Sinister Shape*' by Gordon MacCreagh
'*Panic in Wild Harbor*' by Gordon Hillman
'*The Case of the Bronze Door*' by Margery Lawrence
'*The Case of the Red-Headed Women*' by Dennis Wheatley
'*Apparition in the Sun*' by Joseph Payne Brennan

At the time I purchased this anthology, six of the twelve stories were completely unknown to me, which illustrates one of Haining's greatest strengths: in the course of his career, he unearthed hundreds of little known tales and saved them from complete obscurity – his greatest weakness was sloppy and sometimes (admittedly) dishonest scholarship.[2] At times it seems as though he felt compelled to produce backgrounds where he had none, and many of his anthologies are best appreciated for their contents rather than his supplementary information, unless the latter is independently confirmed.

James Loxley, the sleuth appearing in '*The Ghost Detective*' tells of a man who was accused of embezzlement and attempts to prove his innocence through occult methods. Writing over thirty years ago, Haining mistakenly calls this – written in 1866 – the "earliest short story which has been traced featuring spirit detection," although recent scholarship gives examples dating as far back as 1817.[3] This story first appeared in a Christmas issue of *Once a Week*, in 1865, and was later reprinted in *Victorian Ghost Stories* edited by

---

[2] See *Wormwoodiana*: Thursday, August 30, 2012 – '*Another Peter Haining Fraud*'.
http://wormwoodiana.blogspot.com/2012/08/another-peter-haining-fraud.html?m=1

Montague Summers who suggested that it "might well be a relation of actual fact." This suggestion was confirmed by Mike Ashley in his *'Fighters of Fear'* article[4] where he informs us that the story may have been based on an adventure of the crime-solving spiritualist Charles Foster of Salem, Massachusetts. So this volume's first ghost hunter tale may be a fictionalized version of an actual case.

Sir Arthur Conan Doyle's *'Selecting a Ghost'* is a quite amusing tale, which demonstrates that while Doyle was serious in his spiritualist beliefs, he was not lacking in a sense of humor.

Our main character, Argentine D'Odd, is a grocer who has worked himself up to a state of independent wealth. He purchases a feudal mansion which has everything that could be desired except, he decides, a ghost. He is uncertain as to how to acquire a suitable apparition, and his initial theories are misdirected. "My reading taught me that such phenomena are usually the outcome of crime. What crime was to be done then, and who was to do it? A wild idea entered my head that Watkins, the house-steward, might be prevailed upon – for a consideration – to immolate himself or someone else in the interests of the establishment. I put the matter to him in a half-jesting manner; but it did not seem to strike him in a favorable light." He was later put in touch with a Mr Abrahams who is considered to have some knowledge in such matters. Haining notes that this might be "the first story in which the ghost hunter is employed to find a spirit for a house rather than get rid of one!"

After certain preparations, there's a delightful scene in which Argentine begins to interview prospective spirits, and all explain their strong points. (For example: "I am the embodiment of Edgar Allan Poe. I am circumstantial and horrible. I am a low-caste, spirit-subduing specter. Observe my blood and my bones. I am grisly and nauseous. No depending upon artificial aid. Work with grave clothes, a coffin-lid, and a galvanic battery. Turn hair white in a night.")

In order for this piece to remain spoiler-free, I will not indicate whether or not our hero ends up acquiring his ghost, but I did find the story highly entertaining.

Our next two sleuths – Flaxman Low and John Silence – are probably well enough known to regular readers of this publication that they do not need to

---

[3] See Tim Prasil's *'The Legacy of Ghost Hunter Fiction: A Chronological Bibliography'* https://brombonesbooks.com/occult-detectives-ghost-hunters-in-fact-and-fiction/the-legacy-of-ghost-hunter-fiction-a-chronological-bibliography/

[4] See Occult Detective Quarterly Presents, Ulthar Press, 2018

be discussed in any great detail. In 'The Story of the Moor Road' we are presented with an entity that apparently takes the form of a coughing man. Low usually gives us the sense that there is a mystery that is actually being solved; in this instance we are presented with a certain amount of occult lore and it is combined with a physical event in a way that allows the detective to examine clues and deduce a solution in a manner in which "my own theories and observations and those of the old occultists overlap."

'A Victim of Higher Space' concerns Mr Racine Mudge who has discovered the existence of another dimension and has begun to interact with it. This terrifies him and thus he considers himself to be a 'victim' and consults Silence for assistance. Interacting on this plane is quite familiar to John Silence, of course, and he takes on the case. This was a later tale that Blackwood did not include in the original collection of stories, and I consider it one of the least satisfactory. However, it still is considered among the classics of occult detective fiction. (I have wondered how this tale was originally presented/received since its first appearance was in the pages of The Occult Review in December 1914.) Complete collections of the Flaxman Low and John Silence stories are readily available in fairly inexpensive editions.[5]

'The Case of the Haunting of Grange' features Sax Rohmer's Morris Klaw, the 'Dream Detective'.

Haining's introduction encourages the rumor that Rohmer was a member of the Hermetic Order of the Golden Dawn, which has largely been disproven. (For one thing, Rohmer would have only been about 17 years old when the Order was beginning to crumble, making membership quite unlikely.) His one non-fiction book, The Romance of Sorcery, was a quite superficial survey of the field. Unlike Blackwood and Machen, whose membership in that organization was well-documented, Rohmer was more than a bit of a poser and most of the occultism in his tales was quite fictitious.

In the present story, Klaw is called upon to investigate a haunted house called The Grange. His particular talent is to go to sleep and allow his third eye to open and receive psychic impressions. It is interesting that his talent works even if – and again I want to avoid spoilers – the nature of the haunting is far different than we have been led to believe.

I consider this to be the least substantial story in the anthology. (I've

---

[5] Experiences of Flaxman Low by E. and H. Heron is collected in Supernatural Detectives, Volume 3, Coachwhip Publications, 2011, ISBN #1616460997 (which also collects Arabella Kenealy's Some Experiences of Lord Syfret), and The Complete John Silence Stories by Algernon Blackwood (edited and with an introduction by S.T. Joshi, Dover Horror Classics, 2011, ISBN# 0486299422

always wondered how he pitched the idea of this series to his editors – "Well, you see I have this detective who takes a nap and solves mysteries in his sleep" – and made it sound at all exciting!) There is also in this case a collected edition available. [6]

'*The Telepather*', Henry H. Hering's tale of Mr Psyche, the occultist, may well be Haining's most obscure find of this anthology. It is certainly a humorous and entertaining piece.

A bookseller named Banwell was owed a great deal of money by the artist Alymer Lupton, recently deceased. Banwell wants Mr Psyche to contact Lupton and compel him to find a means of fulfilling his debt. Psyche deems his regular mediums (who are best suited to emotional affairs) inappropriate for what is basically a business matter, and instead he resorts to using his Telepather "a machine invented by an adept in Thibet (sic) for establishing communication with the spirits of the departed."

The experiment proves to be a success – at first.

'*The Poltergeist*' features Seabury Quinn's Jules de Grandin, who also does not need an introduction here. This is a straightforward case of de Grandin's attempt to cure a young woman from the title affliction, although the patient's symptoms exceed Poltergeist phenomena and extend to the area of possession and vampirism to a certain extent.

At one point de Grandin does make a curious statement: "There is nothing in the world, or out of it, which is supernatural, my friend; the wisest man today cannot say where the power and possibilities of nature begin or end [...] I do declare we have never yet seen that which I would call supernatural."

If de Grandin maintained this opinion later in his career, this would seem to remove all the ghosts, werewolves, vampires, foreign deities, curses, and so forth he has encountered from the realm of religion, the occult, or the paranormal, and redefine them as merely little-known aspects of nature! (I prefer to view this attitude as a momentary lapse.) Out of print for decades, all of the de Grandin stories have now been recently released. [7]

Gordon MacCreagh's '*The Sinister Shape*' marks the second time Peter Haining included a tale of Dr Muncing [8] in an anthology. In the present story,

---

[6] *The Dream-Detective* by Sax Rohmer, Dover Publications, 1977, ISBN #0486235041

[7] *The Complete Tales of Jules de Grandin* are available in hardcover editions by Night Shade Books. These are not particularly inexpensive books, but they may later be released in trade paper editions as was done with their Collected Fiction of William Hope Hodgson.

[8] Ten years earlier the story '*Dr Muncing, Exorcist*' appeared in his anthology *The Black Magic Omnibus*. Taplinger, Co., New York, 1976, ISBN#0800808096

Muncing feels compelled to travel to an unknown hotel where a man has been horrifically murdered and witnesses report seeing the appearance of a dark shape. He comes to determine that the shape is an elemental spirit with which he has a past history, and feels that it has grown in power enough to feel comfortable challenging him. Through the device of explaining himself to a police detective, the reader is informed of the nature of the entity as well as of the doctor's occult theories.

As with the de Grandin story, an effort is put forth to explain things in natural terms: "But listen now again. You've got to know this. It is the lot of the universe that to every natural ill Nature has provided an antidote. We don't know all the antidotes; but science is continually finding more of them. There are repellents as well as attractions for all spirit forms. The old-timers practiced a mumbo-jumbo and call it magic. Rubbish. There is no such thing as magic. They knew some of the rules, that's all."

Presenting events in this type of framework seems to allow the occult detective to put things forth in such a manner that they seem to be solved like a conventional mystery. (As noted earlier, dealing with supernatural occurrences specifically as a puzzle to be solved was usually an aspect of the adventures of Flaxman Low. Far too often, I feel, we encounter occult detective stories that are really not all that much concerned with the detecting aspect, and I particularly appreciate it when a writer extends an effort in that direction.)

Gordon Hillman's *'Panic in Wild Harbor'* seems rather out of place in this volume. While his sleuth, Crenshaw, is indeed called to a seaside town to investigate a haunting, his role seems primarily to be to report the town's history and current manifestations to the story's narrator. The haunting is acted out to completion and at the end our detective proclaims the matter resolved, although throughout the adventure he takes an essentially passive role and does not actually influence its outcome to any substantial degree. What we end up with is an admittedly atmospheric nautical ghost story, but that is all.

As the anthology is approaching its conclusion, Haining notes that "Curiously, fictional supernatural sleuths have been in rather short supply in recent times..." (Remember, this was written in 1986.) "Still, though, there have been a trio of writers who have kept the tradition alive and they contribute my last three selections."

Margery Lawrence gives us Miles Pennoyer in *'The Case of the Bronze Door'* and Haining tells us that the author admitted that his cases had been "partly inspired by those of John Silence and Dr Taverner." However, it seems to me that he actually had more in common with Carnacki as the detective comes with elements of his own fabricated mythology such as the 'Min Yu process', the 'Yimghaz test', and the 'Ritual of Hloh'. He also receives assistance from a vaguely described 'Them' who occasionally leave Pennoyer messages on "the blank pad of writing-paper I always keep beside my bed."

The current adventure concerns a man who acquires (and becomes obsessed with) a Bronze Door, to the dismay of his wife who is repulsed by it (as well as with what may possibly lie behind it). In addition to having to solve this mystery, Pennoyer also has to contend with overtones of reincarnation. Not a bad story, once we realize the author is basing it upon rules from her own imagination.

In *'The Case of the Red-Headed Women'*, Dennis Wheatley's Neils Olsen must unravel the supernatural connection to the pattern behind a series of suicides.

Haining and Wheatley were friends and the author told Haining that this story was "based on actual events", and the character of Neils Olsen was based on one Henry Dewhirst, an acquaintance of Wheatley.

In the final tale, Joseph Payne Brennan's Lucius Leffing must deal with an *'Apparition in the Sun'*. This rather brief piece has many of the trappings of a traditional ghost story, the only real difference being that the spirit in question makes its appearances in bright daylight.

All things considered, this anthology combined a few classic tales – I have indicated collected editions of the more well-known detectives – along with some unexpected and interesting discoveries in a very satisfying mixture, and I believe it still deserves a wider readership. (Even the couple which are not strong on detection are interesting in and of themselves.) As of the time I am writing this piece – while some sellers have an asking price exceeding a couple hundred dollars – very good copies can often by bought on Amazon for as little as $10.00 to $11.00.

The Arkham Detective Collection

The Devil Came to Arkham — Byron Craft

The Innsmouth Look — Byron Craft

The Dunwich Dungeon — Byron Craft

Cthulhu's Minions — Byron Craft

Latest Arkham Detective Release:
Death on the Arkham Express

Byron Craft

"Byron Craft writes cinematic, action-packed science fiction horror with panache: smart plotting, engaging characters and attention to detail put him a cut above the field. If you like your aliens slavering and carnivorous, your heroes rugged and your action explosive, you're going to love his work." David Hambling, Author of the Harry Stubbs series

ByronCraftBooks.com   Available at **Amazon.com**

The OCCULT LEGION

BIGGERS   FREEMAN   GAFFORD   MEIKLE   MOORE   REYNOLDS   RUTLEDGE

THE OCCULT LEGION is a multi-chapter serial story written by some of the best writers of Occult Detective fiction today. ODM is proud to present the final part of this landmark tale.

CHAPTER SIX:
HE IS THE GATE

JAMES A. MOORE AND CHARLES R. RUTLEDGE

Police Constable Suzy McNabb went to see the castle. The castle wasn't there. A call had come in a little after midnight to the Saltcoats Police Office. A pensioner named Simson, in the nearby village of West Kilbride, had called to tell them the well-known landmark, Law Castle, had disappeared. No one had given much credence to the story, but the man had seemed very upset and Sergeant Ferguson had decided someone should make the quarter hour drive north to West Kilbride and have a look see.

Being the newest PC, that duty had, of course, fallen to Suzy. A driving rain made the trip at least twice as long as usual. It also made navigating the narrow streets of West Kilbride slow going. A few years back, West Kilbride would have had their own Police Office to call, but it had closed during the restructuring of the Police Scotland organization. Saltcoats was the closest office now.

Suzy found the street she was looking for, Law Brae, and went up a steep incline toward the site of Law Castle. She remembered reading that the castle had been built in the fifteenth century. It had changed hands many times in the ensuing centuries, and was now privately owned and could apparently be rented out as a holiday home or a wedding venue.

Law Brae narrowed to a single lane as Suzy reached the top of the hill. She had seen Law Castle before, a big, white, boxy structure. She couldn't see it now, but Suzy figured the dark and the rain would account for that. She parked her car beside the low, gated wall that surrounded the castle. Suzy grabbed her torch and her hat and stepped out of the car into the rain.

Law Castle was gone. The light from her torch should have shown the looming white bulk of the castle. It simply wasn't there. Her first thought was that someone had bombed the place. But there was no rubble. Suzy shone the beam of her torch around the area. Something was definitely amiss. There should have been a hole or some sign of the building's ancient foundation, but there was nothing. No water lines or hookups for the electrics. Just nothing.

Suzy fought down a wave of panic. She was looking at something impossible. She leaned forward, resting her hands on the short gate. That at least was real and solid. She sought to control her breathing, remembering her police training. There had to be an explanation for this. Had to be.

Suzy jumped as a voice close to her ear said, "You didn't believe me, did you?"

She turned to find an ancient looking man standing there. He had appeared out of the dark and the rain, making no more sound than a phantom. He had to be at least ninety and maybe older. He wore a shiny black rain slicker that was too big for him and carried an umbrella, but his hairless head was bare to the elements. His face was so gaunt that it was almost skull-like and his eyes were a clear china blue.

Suzy said, "Mr Simson?"

"That's me. Couldn't they find a man to send?"

"I'm afraid I was the best they could do, sir."

Simson didn't look like he thought much of their best. With one claw-like hand he pointed at the empty space. "You see I wasn't crazy like you thought. The castle's gone."

"I can see that. I don't know how that could happen."

"Magic," Simson said. "Black magic. That's the only way."

A nutter, Suzy thought. But then she didn't have a better explanation. She said, "When did you first notice that the castle was gone, sir?"

"I came out for my walk about eleven. Not many people about then. I like to walk when the town is quiet. Got to the top of the hill and saw that the castle was gone. Strange place. Always weird things going on around it."

"What do you mean, weird?"

"Like I told you. Black magic. Ghosts and bogies and drums in the depths of the earth."

Yep. A proper nutter. "You haven't seen anyone around recently who seemed out of place, have you?"

"What? You mean like a bloody terrorist or something? Look at the ground, lassie. The bleeding castle is gone as if it had never been there."

"I'm sorry, Mr Simson but I can't call my governor and tell him that Law Castle was spirited away by black magic."

Simson seemed like he was about to say something but then those china blue eyes widened at something behind Suzy. She turned, shining her torch behind her, just in time to see a huge, amorphous thing come lurching out of the darkness.

It had no discernible head, and only something resembling arms and legs. It looked more like a bipedal starfish than anything else. It raised its arm-like appendages, showing that the undersides were covered with barnacle encrusted sucker discs and what looked like the beaks of squids. The thing's torso was covered with similar orifices, all working and making obscene sucking noises.

Suzy screamed and hurled herself to one side. The thing enveloped Simson, closing its appendages around him until he almost disappeared in its grasp, and bearing him to the ground. He screamed, first in a long cry of pain and then in a series of desperate high pitched wails.

Suzy looked around for a weapon. There was nothing, and so she ran up and started kicking the back of creature. Her brain was telling her to run away as quickly as possible, but she gritted her teeth and kept kicking. She heard the sound of something heavy moving through the grass and turning, she saw another of the things shambling toward her.

"Oh God, oh God," Suzy said, leaving Mr Simson to his fate. She was shaking so badly that her legs would barely support her at the thought of the other creature catching her and doing to her what the first had done to Simson.

The light from Suzy's torch played about wildly as she stumbled through the rain, throwing flickering shadows all around. The beam fell on the figure of a tall, slender man standing in her path.

"Run!" Suzy said. "There's some sort of thing chasing me."

The man said, "Yes, I know. Step aside, please."

That's when Suzy saw the shotgun. The man raised the weapon and fired. Suzy spun and looked at the pursuing creature in time to see a large chunk blown from its mass. The shotgun boomed twice more and the thing fell to the ground.

The man stepped past Suzy and walked over to where the first creature was still devouring Simson. Suzy didn't want to see but she followed. The rain-slicked hide of the thing, formerly dull gray in color, was infused with red as the horror drained the lifeblood from Simson. Some blood had escaped and made a dark pool under the creature. Terrible sucking, rasping sounds still came from the entwined pair.

The tall man pointed the shotgun at the creature's back and Suzy said,

"Wait! What about Mr Simson?"

"I'm afraid it's far too late for him," the man said. He shot the thing twice and more blood stained the ground as the creature seemed to deflate like some great tick. The rain mixed with the blood and the scarlet water ran toward Suzy's feet. Suzy felt another scream coming on and she jammed the heel of her hand into her mouth.

Suzy shook herself, trying to calm down. She looked at the man and said, "What... what were those things?"

"Creatures from outside," the man said. "Are you all right, Constable?"

"I'm not injured, but I'm sure as Hell not all right. Thank you for stopping those things, but who are you? And what do you mean by outside?"

"My name is Carter Decamp, and you really should leave this area. There are more of those things around. And worse."

"I can't just leave. I'm the police."

"And you're not equipped to handle this situation. Trust me."

Suzy jerked her head around as she heard more gunfire in the distance. She said, "Someone else is in trouble."

Decamp said, "That would be my associate, Mr Crowley, and I doubt that he's the one in trouble."

"You said there were more of those monsters. Where are they coming from?"

Decamp pointed at the empty space beyond the walkway. "From Law Castle."

"The castle is gone."

"No it isn't. It's still there, but most of it is standing in another dimension. It's always stood on the borderland, but now it's shifted more to the other side, leaving a wound in our reality that things from outside can slip through."

"You're talking crazy."

"I probably am. It's true none the less."

"Carter," a voice said from Suzy's right. She turned to see a man walking toward them. He was of average height and average build, plain to the point of seeming nearly unidentifiable; brown eyes regarded her past rimless eyeglasses. Despite his mundane appearance there was something unsettling about him. He was smiling, and it wasn't a pleasant smile. "Things are going bad quickly. We need to get into the castle."

"The castle isn't there!" Suzy insisted.

The second man looked at her and she suddenly wanted to hide. She took a deep breath and squared her shoulders. She would not be intimidated. She already felt like she was losing it and she wasn't going to let these strangers make it worse.

The man said, "Who's your friend, Carter?"

"I'm Constable McNabb, sir," Suzy said. "And just who are you?"

The man grinned. "My name is Jonathan Crowley."

"I've got to call this in to the office."

"Feel free," said Crowley. "Anyone who comes here will probably die horribly, but knock yourself out."

Suzy caught movement out of the corner of her eye. She turned and saw a worm the size of a small bus squirming out of the emptiness where the castle had stood.

"Jesus Christ!" Suzy said. Her heart was hammering so hard she was afraid she might keel over dead right there. The gigantic worm slithered and lurched away from the castle grounds and was heading toward the town center. "What is that thing doing?"

"Looking for a meal," Crowley said.

"We have to stop it."

"Not us. We've got bigger fish to fry."

Suzy looked at Decamp. He shook his head. "Jonathan is right. He and I have to close the threshold before more horrors slip through. All of these void spawn will be pulled back when we do that. But we can't wait. The wound is doubtless growing larger."

With that, Carter Decamp turned and started toward the empty plot of land. Crowley fell in beside him. Suzy followed.

Suzy said, "If those things are in the castle, they'll kill you."

Decamp said, "It's a chance we have to take. The creatures are coming through the void between this dimension and the next. You aren't seeing where the castle stands, but what was there before it was built."

"Then how will you get into the castle?"

"He knows a way," Crowley said.

Decamp stopped at the end of the walkway, where the front door of the castle would have been. He held his shotgun in one hand and unbuttoned his raincoat. He reached inside and drew a long, glittering blade from a sheath at his waist.

Decamp held the slender blade in the space the door should have occupied and Suzy heard him say something that sounded like, but wasn't quite, Latin. He moved the sword about, as if drawing something in the air.

Suzy felt her ears pop as there was a sudden change in atmospheric pressure. As she watched, a hazy, indistinct shape began to appear in front of Carter Decamp. It was Law Castle, but an insubstantial Law Castle, like a phantom building.

Decamp reached out and turned the latch on the front door and swung the door inward. Then he stepped through the portal. Even as Crowley followed, the castle began to grow hazy and indistinct. Apparently whatever Decamp had done didn't last long.

Suzy knew she should go and call Saltcoats, but instead she sprinted toward the shimmering castle. It was fading from view as she launched herself through the door.

Suzy experienced a moment of disorientation, as if she were falling, and then she found herself on hands and knees inside the front door of Law Castle. Not unexpectedly, there was no electricity, yet she found that she could see. The very walls seemed to glow with a faint luminescence.

Suzy said, "Now will someone tell me what the hell is going on?"

"Not very bright, are you?" Crowley looked down at her, a sour expression on his face.

Decamp turned to find Suzy sitting on the floor beside Jonathan Crowley. He said, "You shouldn't have followed us, Constable. It isn't safe."

"It isn't bleeding safe out there either," Suzy said, pointing at the door. "That starfish thing ate Mr Simson alive and you said that worm was going to eat the people in the village!"

Crowley said, "If it makes you feel better there are probably things in here that will eat us too."

Suzy glared at Crowley. He smiled at her as he got to his feet. Decamp crouched and ran his hand along the floor.

Decamp said, "There's no seam, Jonathan. If there's a way down it isn't physical."

Suzy said, "Seriously, Mr Decamp. Can't you give me some idea of what's happening here?"

Decamp stood up and looked at her. To Suzy's surprise he smiled in an almost kindly way. He said, "We appear to have a quiet moment while I'm trying to think of what to do next. I'll give you the Reader's Digest version. You probably know that Law Castle was built in the fifteenth century."

"Yes, I read about that part."

"Well what you didn't read was when the master mason, a man named Douglas, dug a foundation for the castle he found another structure already there. A tomb or a vault of some sort."

"That's not in any of the history books," said Suzy.

"No, I got that information sitting up drinking with a man named Seton. That incident set something in motion that has been going on for centuries. You see, Constable, there are other universes very close to ours. Some are similar to our own. Others are vastly different. There are beings in some of those alien dimensions that once were part of this one. They were banished centuries or even eons ago from our plane of reality. Some of them want to come back."

Crowley said, "And other things that live in the outer darkness want to visit for the first time. We're a popular spot."

"Indeed," said Decamp. "For the last several centuries, something has been trying to enter our reality through Law Castle. There are places in our world where the walls between this dimension and others are thinner than normal. We call these places thresholds. Someone built a structure over one of those thresholds in the distant past, perhaps seeking to block something from entering, or perhaps to help it. In any case, Law Castle stands upon that threshold."

Crowley said, "Over the centuries others like Decamp and me, specialists in the occult, have dealt with different manifestations caused by this thing's presence."

Suzy said, "But none of the others who came here ever stopped this thing?"

"They stopped it from coming through," said Crowley. "The vault below has been sealed off more than once, and warded by powerful adepts. But whatever it is that's trying to cross over has always managed to find a way to try again. This is the worst it's gotten, actually drawing the castle into the outer dark."

Suzy said, "I won't say I believe all of this, but given what I've seen in the past hour, I can't ignore what you're saying. But why are you two here? Shouldn't we call the army or something?"

Decamp said, "There isn't time, even if we could get to the right people. Jonathan and I have both been keeping an eye on Law Castle for... well, for a long time. The descendants of John Douglas have kept watch over this town for centuries. They contacted me when the eldritch energy began to build up here and I asked Jonathan to come along."

"I always help when people ask nicely," said Crowley.

Suzy felt a tingling at the base of her neck, an almost overwhelming feeling of being watched. She turned her head to find that there were three people, a man, a woman, and a young girl, standing at the foot of a spiral staircase in one corner of the ground floor. The girl bore enough resemblance to the man and the woman that it was obvious she was their daughter.

Crowley noticed them too. "What have we here?"

Suzy said, "People rent the castle for holidays. These people must have been trapped inside." She turned to the newcomers. "Are you three all right?

I'm Constable McNabb."

"He is the Gate," all three people said in unison. The combined three voices sounded louder than they should have and had a strange echoing resonance. "He is the Gate!"

Suzy stared, unsettled by the voices as they boomed across the chamber.

Decamp stared at the three with sorrow etched into his features. Crowley's grin got two notches wider.

"Work on the opening down under, Carter. I'll try to take care of these three."

Suzy looked his way and couldn't stop the scowl that crossed her features. "They're lost. That's a little girl."

"Don't bet on it, cupcake."

"He is the Gate!" The family spoke together again. The little girl took a step forward and her parents on either side shuddered, their facial muscles twitching spasmodically. The man's left eye expanded with all the finesse of a novelty toy, bulging to a preposterous level, even as his face sagged on that side.

Suzy stared on, fascinated and horrified. As she continued to stare the man's face continued its metamorphosis. His eye grew, pushing beyond the physical limits of his skull, cracking bone and shoving flesh aside. The face around that eye rippled and split and bled. The mouth below it slid sideways and opened wide, wider, impossibly wider, showing too many teeth, none of them at all symmetrical.

Suzy couldn't look away. She knew she should, knew that what she was seeing was likely to leave her with nightmares for the rest of her life but she couldn't make herself stop staring.

In front of her, to the right, the family stayed in the same place and the father became an abomination. Wet, viscous things popped from skin and split through his clothes. That one eye ballooned across the top of his head, where the top of his head should have been, and as she looked on, horrified, the eye grew what at first looked like black freckles and soon became recognizable as additional pupils in its wet, quivering mass. There was no symmetry to what happened to his body. It simply became something else, something almost spidery and horridly wet.

"Carter," Crowley said, "Try to be quick about it."

Crowley sounded casual but he moved in a crouch, circling slowly between Suzy and the family, his arms held slightly away from his body. More than anything else he made Suzy think of a wolf preparing to pounce.

Carter Decamp nodded his head. "I can only go so fast, Jonathan. You know that."

"I do, but Suzy-Q being here is sort of putting a damper on my plans."

Suzy-Q? She turned her attention to the grinning bastard. She'd always hated that nickname.

"See here. I'll not have you—"

Crowley moved as the thing that had been a man a moment before lunged toward her, a low, moaning noise coming from the bleeding wound that had been a mouth once upon a time.

Suzy looked at the thing, shocked that she'd ever managed to look away. It came on fast, multiple stalk-like limbs propelling it forward. The eyes on the top of the thing swirled and moved at a dizzying speed and three of those limbs rose into the air and came down like hammers, slashing at the air and at her.

Crowley was there, shoving her backward, his lean body moving between her and the hellspawn. One of the limbs drove into his shoulder and through it, bursting out the other side. Crowley let out a scream and reached with his hand, moving past the stabbing limbs and grabbing at the mass of eyes swelling from the top of the thing.

His fingers sank into tender, wet flesh and drove in deep, breaking the surface of that organ and driving deep into the thing.

An instant later Crowley was sailing backward, still grinning despite the horrid wound in his arm. The father-thing shrieked in outrage and charged after him, ignoring Suzy completely.

"He is the Gate!" The mother and child still screamed together but the daughter's look of fury was overshadowed by the seizures that knocked her mom sprawling. Legs kicked frantically, arms seized and fingers dug at the hard stone floor, tearing away nails and bleeding as they sought to dig into the rock.

The girl screamed something else in a gibberish that made Suzy's ears ring with a fine, clear note.

She might have paid more attention but the change in the mother was even worse than what had happened to the father.

Skin split in an explosive wave that shredded the woman's jeans and blouse and coat. Waves of red, cancerous meat expanded outward, slopping across the stone even as they hardened into something different. The skin and muscles and blood calcified, solidifying into an uneven shell. Somewhere in that mass of dark hair that had once adorned the top of her head, thin tendrils of raw meat rose up, vibrated and let out a keening scream.

Suzy backed up, shaking her head. Madness. It was madness to think about what she was watching and it was absolute insanity to consider what that thing might want from her.

Whatever it wanted, it came creeping toward her, the heavy carapace forming over it scraping and crunching unevenly as it moved. It made no sense, an uneven mess of armored hell crawling her way.

"Suzy, go stand with Carter." She recognized the voice as Jonathan Crowley's, but part of his face was torn away and he was bleeding heavily, fresh crimson spreading down his left side.

He moved toward the thing, once again stepping between her and the most obvious threat.

"You're hurt."

When he turned to look at her—a sudden, violent shift of his head—he was no longer smiling. "Now!"

Crowley stepped closer toward the thing and his hands moved, fingers sliding through odd contortions as he spoke under his breath and continued to keep his mass between Suzy and the mom-strosity.

The little girl looked on, her face set in an angered expression, her body stiff and trembling.

The calcified thing barreled toward Crowley, plates of hard shell crunching and scraping and breaking away near its base as it came.

Crowley stood his ground and reached up with his hands as it hammered toward him. He braced his legs and caught the thing. By rights it should have knocked him sprawling. The mother-thing had grown a lot as it changed and likely weighed as much as a lorry, but he slammed into it and brought it to a complete halt.

From below that hard carapace several tentacles descended, wet and ending in barbed stingers. They whipped around and sought to cut into Crowley. Suzy stepped toward him seeking to help and Decamp, who had barely noticed anything while he was setting up his odd markings on the ground and preparing whatever sort of ritual he meant to perform, looked at Suzy and shook his head.

"You should stay where you are, Constable."

"He needs help."

"You'll just get in his way."

She shook her head. Crowley seemed to be standing his ground by himself, still, she didn't like the idea of leaving him so damned vulnerable. At the same time the very notion of approaching the nightmare he was struggling against was the definition of insanity.

"He's bleeding all over himself."

"He's a fast healer. And he knows what he's doing."

Crowley's hands flared with red light and he stepped back. The places where his hands had touched the hard shell of the thing were burning with light, smoking and stinking worse than burnt hair and then suddenly flaring up in an actual blaze that was nearly white.

It let out another shriek and Crowley backed up two paces as it charged for him. The shell glowed and split and emitted great boiling gouts of smoke. Even as it came closer to Crowley, Suzy could see the flames moving under that shell, burning away whatever softness might still be there.

Crowley backpedaled and Suzy followed suit.

"I need another minute, Jonathan."

"I'm doing what I can, Carter." Crowley was no longer bleeding. There were no wounds she could see on him, despite the fact that she would have sworn before the Queen herself that the man was mortally wounded.

The great, shelled thing fell forward and collapsed against the stone, parts of the shell falling inward among geysers of sparks and smoke.

"I can feel it," Decamp said. "I can feel the rift and the hidden passage."

Suzy looked toward Decamp and saw the ground in front of him shimmering, rippling, as if it were water, and in fact it appeared that the ground was melting into clear fluids of some sort.

More madness. As if to cement that fact, the little girl ran toward Crowley and let out a scream that grew deeper and louder as she moved. The sound was nearly enough to deafen and Suzy felt her bones shaking within her body.

Each transformation was different. No two ways about it. The little girl simply exploded into a crimson mess. Raw meat, shattered bone, hair and bits of clothing all wrapped around Crowley, like a wet blanket, covering him in viscera and blood.

Suzy, who considered herself a strong woman and was not wrong in her estimations, gagged as this creature attacked the man, apparently trying to force itself down his throat.

Crowley slipped backwards, his hands clutching at his face and throat, tearing at the wet mass that rippled and pumped itself against his face.

Suzy looked around. No weapons. Nothing she could do to help him. Around her the remains of what had been a mother and a father lay ruined by the man now choking on what had been a human daughter. The ground in front of Carter Decamp was different. There was a hole now, and something in that hole moved and shifted.

"No more, please. No more. I can't." She shook her head and stepped back. Her voice was broken, ruined.

Crowley fell down to his knees with an audible clacking sound.

His fingers ripped into the flesh, pulling it away from his face long enough for him to gasp in a deep breath before the viscous stuff clenched together again like a constrictor.

He was dying.

No two ways about it he'd saved her life and he was dying.

"Constable."

She looked toward Decamp and saw the blade he offered her.

"I hate to ask you, but I need a little more time or we're all dead. Take this and see if you can buy Jonathan a few moments. Be very careful, Constable. It's sharper than it looks."

He tossed the blade and she almost caught it, but the handle fell past her and bounced off the ground, making her scramble after the thing.

She picked up the slender sword. Decamp wanted her to use *this* against *that*? The blade would probably break at first stroke. Still, she had to try. Suzy advanced on the writhing, mewling, flesh-thing that enveloped Crowley.

Out of the corner of her eye Suzy caught movement. She turned as the father-thing came scrabbling toward her on its segmented, misshapen legs. The bloody ruin of its compound eye trailed red. It was almost on top of her and she struck out with the sword. To her surprise, the blade cut easily through one of the legs. Shrieking, the father-thing toppled.

Suzy spun back to Crowley. The girl-thing had enveloped him, its fluid flesh flowing over his head and shoulders. How could she attack the creature without hurting Crowley? She looked at the mass of flesh that had yet to engulf the man and spotted a round lump that seemed to be rising and falling. Was that what had become of the poor child's heart and lungs? Did she even still possess such organs?

Suzy gritted her teeth and hurried over to Crowley, almost falling as her feet slipped in blood and gore. She raised the sword and brought it down on the lump. She heard a high-pitched, hissing wail and the sheath of flesh relinquished its grip on Crowley and spun toward Suzy, expanding like the hood of a cobra.

Suzy screamed but she brandished the sword and the blade cut through the red, angry flesh, sending tatters flying.

"Jesus God," Suzy said.

"Not even close," said Crowley, slowly peeling the remaining flesh from his upper torso. "And thanks, Suzy-Q. I didn't know you had it in you."

"Don't call me that."

Crowley's grin came back, chilling and disturbing. "You can chastise me later. Mom's getting back in the game."

Suzy felt the floor shake as the carapace shrouded creature came lumbering their way. The father-thing was up again as well, lurching forward on its remaining limbs. No matter how sharp the sword was, Suzy knew it wasn't going to be enough to stop the two horrors, and Crowley could still barely stand.

"Over here you two," Decamp said. "And hurry."

Suzy put one arm around Crowley and helped him stagger toward Decamp who was standing in front of a ragged hole in the floor. Crowley said, "I'm flattered. I didn't know you cared."

"I only care about the people outside this slaughterhouse."

Suzy could hear obscene scrabbling, sloshing noises behind her and she could feel the heat coming off of the mother-thing's shell. She didn't look back. She wouldn't look back.

"Into the hole," Decamp said.

"What's down there?" said Suzy.

"I've no idea, my dear. But needs must when the devil drives."

As Suzy got closer to the hole she could smell a terrible stench rising from the opening. She said, "Oh Jesus. I don't want to go down there."

"Good thing I'm here then," said Crowley.

Then his arm was around her shoulders and he was throwing them both into the hole. Suzy felt another scream coming but then they hit a hard surface and the breath was driven from her lungs.

A moment later Decamp landed lightly beside her. He mumbled something in that weird Latin-like language he'd used before and the hole in the roof was suddenly gone. Suzy expected total darkness to envelope them, but an odd, greenish-yellow, coruscating glow came from somewhere down a long tunnel ahead of them. The walls were rounded and worn smooth by the passage of... what? She suddenly thought of the bus-size worm she had seen earlier.

"I'll take the sword back if I may," Decamp said. "You wielded it admirably."

Suzy somewhat reluctantly handed the sword over to Decamp. It had been reassuring to hold the weapon.

"Tell me something, Decamp," Suzy said. "If you can... fix this, will that family become normal again?"

Decamp shook his head. "There's nothing to be done for them, I'm afraid. And that's what the baleful influence of whatever is down here will do to everyone in West Kilbride."

Crowley said, "You know what's down here, Carter. You heard what the family from hell said. You know who is the Gate."

"I know what that can mean. We don't yet know for certain that it's true."

Suzy said, "What are you two talking about?"

"He is the Gate," Crowley said. "He knows the Gate."

"That's what those poor people were saying. What does it mean?"

"We're about to find out," said Crowley.

Suzy looked at the man. Again he was almost completely healed. What was he? Another kind of monster?

"Let's be on our way," Decamp said. "After all these centuries, it's time to finish this."

The reek that Suzy had noticed grew stronger as they moved down the tunnel. She became aware that foul, moist air was rushing up the shaft toward them. The weird, flickering light grew stronger as well.

They emerged on the edge of a great well, perhaps twenty feet in diameter. The well was full of... something. And it was moving.

Suzy staggered back, her hand going to her mouth. Her stomach clenched and she turned away and was violently ill. She didn't want to look back but she had to. Something was compelling her to do so.

The well was filled with a roiling, shifting mass of some form of matter. It wasn't flesh exactly. It looked like something caught somewhere between liquid and solid. A thick, green, viscous pool, and yet it was alive. Eyes opened and closed across its surface and tentacles formed and rose and waved before falling back into the protean mass.

"It isn't Yog-Sothoth," Decamp said. "But it is perhaps an aspect of the Old One."

A questing pseudopod came over the lip of the well and Decamp flicked the tip of the sword at it. The tentacle fell back.

"How can you be so calm?" Suzy said. "Mother of God. What is that thing?"

Decamp said, "The source of all the strife. It's trapped here, on the threshold. Halfway between our world and the outer dark. And it has been for centuries."

"*That's* what's been causing all of this?"

"Yes, it wants out and I think it's almost managed to force its way across the threshold. This is a soul well, a sort of conduit from this dimension to another."

"Who built it?" Suzy said.

"It doesn't matter," said. Crowley. "It's a way for that thing to enter this world and we have to close it."

Decamp said, "And I think I see how that can be done. Note the runes carved into the stone on the lip of the well. Those are what makes this well more than a hole in the ground."

Crowley said, "Destroy a few key runes and the door closes for good."

"Precisely."

"But once we start, that thing's going to know what we're doing and it's not going to like it."

"There is that," said Decamp.

Suzy was about to say something when she felt a sudden stabbing pain in her head. Images came rushing into her mind. Vast plains under an endless sky and huge monoliths raised to long dead stars. She stumbled and only a quick move from Decamp kept her from toppling into the well.

Decamp said, "What is it, constable?"

"I don't know. My head. I can't..."

"It's trying to get inside her like it did those people upstairs," Crowley said.

Suzy shook her head. Not that. Please God, not that. She didn't want to end up like that woman or her family.

"Whatever we're going to do we have to do it now," said Decamp.

Crowley nodded and started toward the well. "Your turn to watch my back, Carter."

Decamp followed Crowley to the well. Suzy watched them through squinted eyes. More visions were flooding her brain. She felt as if something solid was entering her head, fighting for space.

Crowley had reached the edge of the well. He knelt and put his hand on one of the stones with the strange markings. His fist began to glow and then the stone cracked.

Half a dozen tentacles came writhing up toward Crowley. Decamp struck with the sword, slashing the appendages and keeping them back. Crowley moved to another stone. A larger, thicker tentacle whipped out of the well and struck Crowley, sending him flying. It swept toward Decamp and he moved nimbly aside, severing the arm with a neat cut.

More pseudopods crawled over the lip of the well like hungry snakes. There was no way Decamp could stop them all with the sword. He reached into a pocket of his raincoat and brought out a handful of powder. He tossed it at the writhing tentacles and said a few unintelligible words. The dust burst into flames and the tentacles caught fire.

The pain in Suzy's head drove her to hands and knees. Thoughts not her own were spinning through her head. "He is the Gate," she said. "Yog Sothoth is the Gate. Yog Sothoth knows the Gate."

"Hang on Suzy-Q!" Crowley said.

A flash of anger drove the alien thoughts back. Suzy looked up and saw that Crowley was back at the edge of the well. He was working on another stone and Decamp was keeping the tentacles at bay. The second stone shattered like the first.

"One more should do it," Decamp said.

The chamber began to shake and rubble fell from the ceiling, which was lost in darkness above. A chunk of stone struck Suzy's shoulder and she was glad for the pain. It helped her fight back the thing that was still probing at her mind.

A greater mass was lifting itself from the well. A huge, sheet of the greenish matter with a hundred glaring eyes. It rolled forward like a wave, threatening to engulf the two men on the side of the soul well.

Decamp raised the sword and said something. A silver light flashed from the sword blade, cleaving into the hood of eyes. At the same moment Crowley destroyed a third stone and the gelatinous mass fell back into the well, disintegrating as it went.

"That's done it," Decamp said.

"And we need to get out of here," said Crowley.

Suzy tried to get to her feet but her legs buckled. Then Decamp and Crowley were on either side of her, supporting her, and helping her back through the tunnel. She would never clearly remember that nightmarish walk or exactly how they got back into the lower floor of Law Castle. She only knew that the pair didn't stop until they were outside of the castle and she was sitting on the grass.

It was almost morning. The castle looked as it always had. As if the events of the night had never occurred. But small fires, wailing sirens and the cries of injured people put lie to any thoughts that Suzy had somehow imagined it all.

"We're going to leave you now, Constable McNabb," Carter Decamp said. "Thank you for all of your assistance."

"What? Wait. You can't just go. Someone has to help me explain all of this. What will I tell my superiors?"

Crowley was grinning. "Tell them anything you want. Nobody will believe it anyway. And I suspect that you soon won't be able to remember most of what happened."

"What do you mean?"

"It is the nature of this sort of incursion to our world, my dear," said Decamp. "These wounds to the mind have a way of healing. People remember, but they tend to remember events more like a story."

"But it's over?" Suzy said. "Tell me it's over, Decamp."

Carter Decamp said, "Yes it's over. I think it's safe to say that Law Castle will sleep now."

REVIEWS

Title: Terror Is Our Business: Dana Roberts' Casebook of Horrors
Author: Joe Lansdale & Kasey Lansdale
Publisher: Cutting Block Books
Format: paperback / ebook
Reviewer Dave Brzeski

I've been a fan of Joe R. Lansdale's work for quite some time, so I was very happy to receive an advance review copy of this book – albeit I received it some time after the book was actually published – especially given that it features an occult detective, since I have a particular interest in that sub-genre.

It's an interesting collection with an element of work in progress, in that the format/style changes as the authors get closer to what works best. That's not to say they start out bad; it's just that certain things that seemed to work well enough at first proved to be perhaps a bit too restrictive as the series progressed.

The first four stories, written by Joe Lansdale solo, are told by Dana Roberts to the members of a club. It's not dissimilar to the way William Hope Hodgson presented his Carnacki tales, which I assume was an intentional homage of sorts. In his introduction, Joe Lansdale cites Carnacki, amongst others as an influence.

The opening tale, '*The Case of the Lighthouse Shambler*', introduces us to Dana Roberts and establishes the fact that she, unlike most occult detectives, doesn't actually believe in the supernatural – she is in fact an atheist. She takes a view that is reminiscent of that famous quote by Arthur C. Clarke, that,

"Any sufficiently advanced technology is indistinguishable from magic." That is to say that what appears supernatural is simply science we don't yet understand. That she accepts the power within occult objects and rituals is more to do with the focusing of the mind than anything magical.

We are also introduced to her assistants, Nora and Gary, not forgetting the unnamed narrator of the early tales. One does rather get the impression from this story that Dana could perhaps be a little more cautious about endangering the lives of others in her investigations.

'The Case of the Stalking Shadow', is an origin story of sorts, starting as it does with events that took place when Dana was just thirteen years old. On the one hand did like the story a lot. On the other hand there are some pretty evident problems. If, as stated in 'The Case of the Lighthouse Shambler', Dana is in her thirties in 2011 (when that story and this one were originally published), then this story has to take place in the 1990s. At one point, Dana's friend Jane describes something as "queer", as in peculiar – not a usage of the word that would have been common as recently as that. I found myself wondering if the story hadn't originally been set in an earlier era. If one ignored the fact that it's part of this series, a few small changes to references to more modern technology and fashion would easily fix it in an earlier era and I have to say it would have worked better. I was bemused to note that the story was set in Lansdale, Pennsylvania.

Thankfully, the period style is more or less gone in 'The Case of the Four Acre Haunt'. This is a haunted house story, somewhat reminiscent of Shirley Jackson's *The Haunting of Hill House* in the early stages, becoming rather more like the 1990s special effects laden film version towards the end. Unlike that dreadful film, however, the ghostly apparition doesn't show itself in lieu of actual story content. This time Dana actually goes to the extent of making sure the situation is genuinely dangerous before inviting poor Nora and Gary to join her. I'm beginning to think at this point that I could not really recommend working for Ms Roberts. This is also the case which forces Dana Roberts to accept the possibility of a soul's survival after death.

'The Case of the Angry Traveler' takes us deep into what I can only describe as Erich Von Daniken, meets Bernard Quatermass and H.P. Lovecraft in the sewers territory. I really enjoyed this one. Being given reasons to sympathise with the monster was a nice touch, even though it did actual bodily harm to Nora & Gary, not to mention the people it killed. The club based framing sequence, with the unnamed narrator was very slight this time, suggesting that Joe Lansdale was beginning to question it's worth. Indeed this is the last use of this particular trope and the narrator is never mentioned again. He's not the only character to bow out at this point.

Joe Lansdale mentions in his introduction that he tried to make the Dana Roberts tales more sober in tone than that of most of his work. This intentional reduction in humour likely played a significant part in the period feel I got reading some of the stories.

Enter Kasey Lansdale...

The story, as Kasey tells it in her introduction to the rest of the book goes like this. Michael Golden asked Joe Lansdale to contribute something to an upcoming anthology – an anthology of collaborations. Joe turned him down flat, Joe Lansdale doesn't do collaborations. Michael Golden contacted Kasey. Kasey Lansdale asked her father if he'd collaborate with her on a story. Joe said no. So Kasey sends him five pages of a story to look at and the rest is history. The fact that the rest of this book consists of collaborations between father and daughter are testament to Ms Lansdale's powers of gentle manipulation.

'*Blind Love*' doesn't feature Dana Roberts at all. It serves as an introduction to Kasey's character, Jana. The Lansdale humour is certainly back in this tale of a dating service that turns out to be even stranger than the proprietors could have imagined. It has all the hallmarks of a classic weird fiction story, but told through the filter of a young, 21st century woman.

How do I best put this?... I like bacon a lot. I also like eggs, but bacon and eggs – that's when the magic happens! In much the same way, the combination of Dana and Jana is certainly greater than the sum of its parts. The novella length, '*The Case of the Bleeding Wall*' is where this collection of enjoyable tales really starts to sing. After having survived her own encounter with the supernormal, Jana does some research online and becomes familiar with Dana Roberts and her work. She has an ex-boyfriend, now just a friend, who attends the club where Dana is a frequent guest and storyteller; she decides to go along in the hope of talking to her. It's no spoiler to reveal that they obviously do eventually connect and Jana is brought into the fold of Dana Roberts' organisation. Jana, is cast from that classic mould of sassy girl sidekick, who uses flippant humour as a shield against her being overwhelmed by the dangerous insanity she's just walked into. We've seen lots of characters like this, especially on TV shows (think Kenzie in *Lost Girl*), but Jana is much better realised. As the narrator from this point on, she provides a few laugh out loud moments of humour, which were (intentionally) lacking in the Dana Roberts solo stories. As the tale unfolds, Jana is seen to have some effect on Dana – who actually starts to show a little more emotion, and dare I say it a sense of humour of her own.

The final tale in this book, '*The Case of the Ragman's Anguish*' takes Dana and Jana into Lovecraftian territory, as they are called in to investigate a series of strange deaths in Jana's home territory which leads Dana Roberts to actually risk 'opening the way' to bring an end to the problem. Once again, the Lansdales get plenty of mileage out of the personality differences between the two protagonists. That they genuinely seem to change each other's outlook as their relationship grows is one of the main strengths.

I mentioned at the beginning of this review that the 'work in progress' element of this collection was interesting, but it can't be denied that it's possibly also a weakness. I can easily imagine some readers would have preferred the earlier tales to have been rewritten to make them fit better with the last couple. It's even possible that a few may well have preferred the style of the solo Dana Roberts stories be maintained. I certainly wouldn't go quite that far, but I was uncomfortable with the way certain elements and characters in the earlier stories were simply ditched. If, as I genuinely hope, this isn't the last we see of Dana Roberts & Jana, I would like to see Gary and Nora make a return appearance; otherwise I'm just going to worry that Dana may have got them killed in an as yet untold tale. It would also be interesting to have Jana meet the unnamed narrator of the first four stories. It seems likely that she would have, as she convinced her ex to take her along to one of the club meetings where Dana was due to tell another story.

In conclusion, this is a very enjoyable collection, well worth checking out. It's a book of two parts, the first being a more classic style occult detective, with much in common with the likes of Thomas Carnacki and Dr Silence. The second half is much more modern in style, but both are eminently readable.

Title: The Hollows: A Midnight Gunn Novel
Author: C.L. Monaghan
Publisher: Self-Published
Format: Paperback / Kindle
Reviewer: Dave Brzeski

1835: A child is born under stressful circumstances. It's a breech birth and the fate of the baby and the mother are in question as the doctor tries his best under low light conditions, caused by a total eclipse. The baby's mother lives just long enough to name him... as Halley's comet is visible in the sky, she gives him the name, Midnight.

Flash forward to 1860: Midnight Gunn is now friendly with Detective Inspector Arthur Gredge of Scotland Yard, whom he helps on some of the more puzzling cases. Midnight Gunn is not your usual sort of occult investigator. In fact he's more used to helping the police investigate non-supernatural cases with the help of his extraordinary gifts. Where many occult detective characters tend to be partnered by a Watson figure to their Sherlock Holmes, this seems more like a Batman/Commissioner Gordon relationship. A similarity shored up even more by the fact that he is now a very rich orphan and the closest thing to a father figure in his life is his faithful butler. When I mentioned this to the author, she assured me that it wasn't a knowing use of that trope as she wasn't a Batman fan. Either way, it actually made a nice change.

Where Midnight Gunn differs from the caped crusader is that he actually does have super powers of a sort. They're not very neatly laid out so the reader instantly has a handle on exactly what he can and can't do – but to some extent, Midnight is still working that out himself. He can control the shadows in mysterious ways which I will not elaborate on, for fear of being too spoilerish.

It isn't much of a spoiler, however, to reveal that the villain of the piece is Spring-Heeled Jack. That much is openly stated on the back cover blurb. Jack has appeared many times in fiction, and appears to be enjoying a revival of sorts, albeit he is as often portrayed as a hero as he is a villain.

Prior to this particular book, Monaghan had worked mainly in the paranormal romance field, so this is a bit of a departure for her – and in my opinion, a very successful one. While there's none of that soppy romance stuff here, the author does not totally abandon the emotional element – and that, if anything is one of the strengths of her writing. I challenge anyone to not fall a little in love with the waif, Polly, who Midnight Gunn adopts. I will be very disappointed if I don't get to read some stories of Polly's adventures as an adult at some point, as she's so obviously set up to become Gunn's partner, as well as his ward (Holy similarities Batman!).

Monaghan captures the feel of the period very well, albeit not without the occasional anachronistic word, or phrase. Despite a couple of small formatting glitches the book is better edited than many self-published novels I've read. Indeed, I've seen worse from the Big Five publishers. There's certainly nothing serious enough to prevent me from recommending this novel very highly indeed.

The second book in this series – *The Barghest: A Midnight Gunn Novel* is also now available.

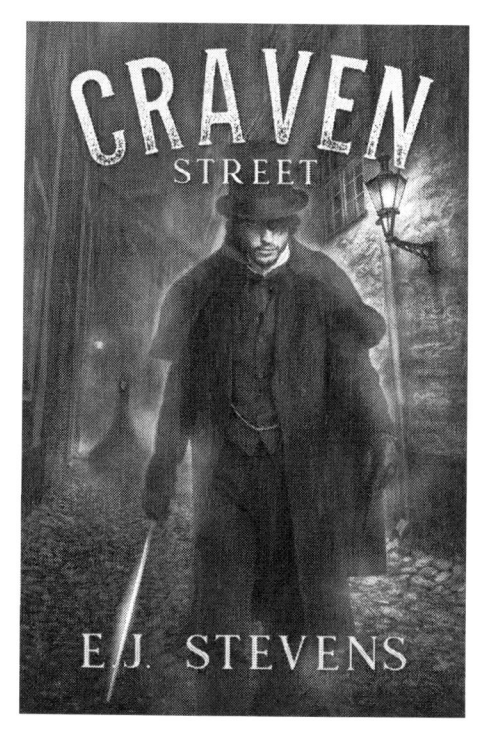

Title: Craven Street
Author: E.J. Stevens
Publisher: Sacred Oaks Press
Format: Paperback / ebook
Reviewer: Julia Morgan

Craven Street is not a stand-alone novella, but the first part of a new series of books about the adventures of The Whitechapel Paranormal Society (henceforward referred to as the WPS). As such, the story has no real resolution, just a set-up for the series of sequels. You may find, upon reading Craven Street, that you just have to buy the rest of the books. For my own part, I found it a page-turner, earnestly desiring to read what happened next.

EJ Stevens is a prolific writer of young adult and urban fantasy books, all of which are available on Amazon at a reasonable price. According to the Amazon blurb, this novella brings together characters from two of her previous series, the Whitechapel Paranormal Society series and her Ivy Granger Psychic Detective series, but it is not necessary to have read any of these in order to enjoy the novella.[1]

Set in a world where the paranormal is taken for granted, and the

---

[1] See *Occult Detective Quarterly #2* for my review of the first Ivy Granger novel, *Shadow Sight* along with the follow-up novella, *Blood and Mistletoe* – Dave Brzeski.

existence of spectres, demons and ghouls is established – though most of the human race are deliberately kept from knowing about this – it is also set in Victorian London, but, being an alternative universe version of Victorian London, there are differences. One could say there are anachronisms, but the beauty of alternative-universe fiction, is you can get away with them.

The narrative switches between Cora Drummond, the head of the WPS, and Forneus, a demon whose name is taken from the Lesser Key of Solomon. Cora is wrestling against prejudice and sabotage from male colleagues as much as she is against supernatural enemies. The WPS is a secret all female unit belonging to the Special Paranormal Research Branch of the police force. Her female colleagues are an interesting group of women, with diverse personalities and outlooks. The interactions between them are interesting, and no doubt we will have some intriguing revelations about some of them in subsequent books. I personally found the sections narrated by Forneus to be a bit irritating, as it took time away from those narrated by Cora. However, they do serve to fill us in on information that would not be available to the WPS, and gives a little insight into the workings of hell and the minds of the alternative-universe demons. It is a bit disconcerting to read that what humans see as a sub-species of demon is to Forneus 'the golden retrievers of hell', especially given the gruesome way they kill their victims.

In spite of a Lesbian romance sub-plot, the book has a straightforward style that feels like a Young Adult book, except that when the gory bits arrive, they are very gruesome indeed. The first appearance of the supernatural is very effective, being much more intense and original than the preceding led me to expect. From then on in the threats are legion.

There are a couple of flaws with the story, the early appearance of Jonathan, Cora's alluring and treacherous spirit guide was immediately of interest. But he disappears early in the book, and doesn't reappear; his function seemingly taken over by Flauros. Such was the similarity between the two that I had to track back through the book to see if Jonathan and Flauros were the same person. The WPS' male colleagues are a little overdrawn in their villainy and coarseness, which makes them not quite believable. I was greatly relieved at the introduction of a male character who was both a policeman and a decent human being. Finally, I was a little frustrated with the series introduction aspect of this novella. It left a lot of unanswered questions – the final few pages are basically an invitation to continue the series. This is obviously the intent and I must admit I am very tempted.

Title: Jonathan Dark or the Evidence of Ghosts
Author: A.K. Benedict
Publisher: Orion Books
Format: Paperback / ebook
Reviewer: Dave Brzeski

I wasn't sure about this one at first. The third person, present tense style, coupled with a shifting point of view between various characters one inevitably knows nothing about at the start did mean it took me a chapter, or two to really get into it. This is not an uncommon experience with crime novels that aren't yet part of a series, with familiar characters. There's an inevitable trade-off in such cases between drawing the reader in and giving away too much information.

Many examples of Occult Detective fiction, perhaps most of them, come from the supernatural end of the equation, and drop their investigator into a ghost/horror/urban fantasy story of some sort. What we have here is the opposite. It is first and foremost a crime novel – indeed it's marketed as such – into which the supernatural element has been added.

Where this book differs from many of this type is in the way Benedict limits the supernatural element to ghosts. Her concept of the afterlife is rather different to anything I've ever previously encountered and as such might not please those of a religious disposition. I'd really rather not go into very much detail for fear of spoilers.

As with so many mystery stories, we are introduced to the main players separately. In most crime novels these then gradually come together to form a single narrative. In this case, there are two stories going on simultaneously, albeit they do get more and more entwined as the book progresses.

The crime novel aspect, involving a complex stalker case, with an insidious secret society of corrupt officials in every walk of life takes most of the focus at first.

Marie King, the potential next victim, was born blind, but a successful operation gave her sight. She has always considered this a mistake and wears a blindfold more or less permanently. It's such a fascinating look at how such a person might cope with all of the extra information — information contradictory to expectations formed over decades of sightlessness — that I found myself wondering if Benedict had based the idea on genuine cases.

DI Jonathan Dark is a damaged detective with personal problems, and guilt over a victim he failed to save. It's a common enough trope, but Benedict tempers what could have made for an unrelentingly bleak story with skillful use of humour.

Then there's the supernatural side of things...

Frank McNally is a most unusual undertaker. Benedict is very clever in the way she shows us characters interacting, without immediately giving away the stranger aspects of what is going on. It's only as we read on that we realise that what we thought to be a pretty mundane exchange between Frank and a client is anything but.

Eventually, of course, these two separate strands of the narrative do come together, as we discover connections between the two worlds of Jonathan Dark and Frank McNally. This novel very quickly moves from being slightly confusing at the beginning to a page-turner I simply could not put down. I will be extremely disappointed if I don't eventually get to read more exploits of these characters in this very odd world.

Title: Wychwood / Wychwood: Hallowdene
Author: George Mann
Publisher: Titan Books
Format: Paperback / ebook
Reviewer: Dave Brzeski

Elspeth Reeves has just split up with her partner, lost her job and has temporarily moved back to her mother's house in the small town of Wilsby-under-Wychwood to lick her wounds. She drives straight into a murder scene.

It's not long before Elspeth — Ellie is in it up to her neck. She's a reporter, albeit a currently unemployed one and she senses a story that just might get her back into gainful employment.

George Mann is canny enough to downplay the usual press versus police tension cliché, and Ellie is soon working alongside her old childhood friend Detective Sergeant Peter Shaw, albeit they do try to keep her involvement from the attention of his superior.

One murder soon becomes two. This is no spoiler. How many book-length murder mysteries ever stop at just one these days? Where it gets interesting is that the crimes seem to be patterned after an old legend — that of the Carrion King. Mann has done such an excellent job of detailing his fictional mythology that I actually spent time Googling it after reading the book — on the off-chance that it was based on a genuine legend. That there are Carrion Kings mentioned in more than one RPG, not to mention a couple of rock albums, is pure coincidence as they are not related.

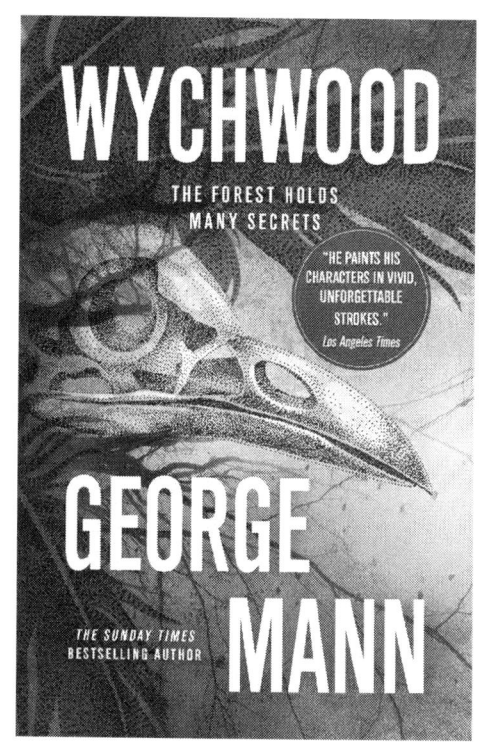

Folk horror elements are hinted at from the beginning, but Mann has been clever enough to keep the structure as strictly police procedural. This is very much more a crime novel than an occult detective novel. The supernatural element is downplayed to the extent that only Ellie, apart from the villain of the piece is seriously considering it a possibility by the end.

The book opens with the very common TV crime drama trope of a prologue, detailing the death of the first victim. Those who regale against the fact that too many crime dramas focus on women as victims, may be a little mollified to find that the victim in this case doesn't go down all that easy. It would be quite easy to use words like formulaic, or even cliché when describing parts of this book — but in the hands of a skilled writer a formula can be made to work very well. In this particular case, the writing and plotting are of a very high standard indeed.

Book two of this series, *Wychwood: Hallowdene* was already available by the time we were putting together this issue. The tagline, "The Truth Will Out", certainly gave the impression that Ellie and Peter's involvement with the abnatural was not yet over. I'd planned on reading it fairly soon, but in the end I couldn't resist dipping into it immediately.

Wychwood: Hallowdene finds Elspeth Reeves and DS Peter Shaw in a relationship, albeit a fairly casual one. Both of them need to measure their possible future together against their career ambitions.

Peter is still less ready to accept the supernatural elements of the Carrion King case than Ellie, but both have been forced to admit that there had been things that simply couldn't be explained by rational means. We know, of course, that their world view is going to be stretched even further in this book, or there'd be no purpose to it. That George Mann manages to do this and yet still keep things tidy enough that the local authorities find no reason to think anything completely beyond their experience has occurred is very impressive.

I don't really feel the need to talk too much about the actual events of this second volume in the adventures of Elspeth and Peter, except to say that I thought it was even better than the first one. I can't not mention, though, that Mann managed to make me care so much about one of the other characters in this book, that I was genuinely fearful for their future. I don't think I can recommend a book much more highly than that.

But, you ask, can Elspeth and Peter actually be considered occult detectives as such? Well, they're probably not likely to be actively seeking out the weird cases — not yet, at least, so perhaps not... but I have a feeling the abnormal may well continue to seek them out.

Describin' the Scribes

MELANIE ATHERTON ALLEN lives in Pennsylvania, in a place with just enough of a front yard to make Halloween interesting. At the time of writing, she and her boyfriend are engaged in taking down the miniature haunted house they built to amuse the neighbourhood children. Soon, she will turn her attention once more to her website, www.athertonsmagicvapour.com, and to the further adventures of Simon Wake.

ALEXIS AMES is a writer living in Colorado who first picked up a pen when she was eleven years old and hasn't put it down since. Science fiction is her preferred genre—more specifically, exploring the changing relationship between humans and technology. Her work has previously appeared in publications such as *Prismatica Magazine*, *The Corvus Review*, and *The New Accelerator*. She can be found on Twitter at @alexis_writes1, and a list of her current and upcoming stories can be found on her blog at alexisames.home.blog.

BRYCE BEATTIE loves action and adventures stories of all genres. You can learn about him at BryceABeattie.com

CLIFF BIGGERS is a comic book writer, journalist and enthusiast, as well as an author of scary fiction. He has had a wealth of experience in the comics and fandom scene since the late sixties, was a writer on comics such as *After Apocalypse* and *Earth Boys*, and has run Dr No's Comic and Games Superstore in Marietta, Georgia, USA for many years.

S.L. EDWARDS is a Texan currently living in California. He enjoys dark fiction, poetry and darker beer. With Yves Tourigny he is the co-creator of the webcomic *Borkchito: Occult Doggo Detective*. He has written a number of Joe Bartred stories, more of which will be featured in future issues of ODM, and his debut fiction collection, *Whiskey and Other Unusual Ghosts* came out from Gehenna and Hinnom Books earlier this year.

JOHN PAUL FITCH is a writer who lives in Western Australia with his wife and children. For the past decade John Paul has written fiction, comics, non-fiction, short films, and for the stage. He was shortlisted for the Australian Shadows Award for short fiction in 2013.
Find him online at https://johnpfitch.wordpress.com/2015/09/06/hello-world/ and on twitter @johnybhoy.

KELLY M. HUDSON is the author of over two dozen published short stories and two novels, all available on Amazon or at his website www.kellymhudson.com He lives in Kentucky and loves his cat and dog dearly.

IAN HUNTER was born in Edinburgh and is a children's author, short story writer, editor and poet. He is a member of the Glasgow SF Writers Circle and a Director of the Scottish Writer's Collective 'Read Raw'. He reviews for *Interzone, Shoreline of Infinity* and *Concatenation* and for the last ten years he has been poetry editor for the British Fantasy Society.

JAMES A. MOORE is the best selling and award winning author of over forty-five novels, thrillers, dark fantasy and horror alike, including the critically acclaimed *Fireworks*, The Seven Forges series, *Blood Red*, the Serenity Falls trilogy (featuring his recurring anti-hero, Jonathan Crowley) and his most recent novels, The Tides of War series (*The Last Sacrifice, Fallen Gods* and *Gates of the Dead*) Boomtown, and *Avengers: Infinity*. In addition to writing multiple short stories, he has also edited, with Christopher Golden and Tim Lebbon, the *British Invasion* anthology for Cemetery Dance Publications. With Christopher Golden and Jonathan Maberry, he is co-host of the Three Guys with Beards podcast. More information about the author can be found at his website: jamesamoorebooks.com.

CHARLES R. RUTLEDGE is the co-author of three books in the Griffin & Price supernatural suspense series, written with James A. Moore. He has written two novellas that bring Bram Stoker's *Dracula* into present day, *Dracula's Revenge* and *Dracula's Ghost*. He owns entirely too many editions of the novel Dracula, keeps actual soil from Transylvania in an envelope on his desk, and is rarely seen in daylight.

TADE THOMPSON is the author of the sci-fi novel *Rosewater* (now the first book in a trilogy), which won both the Arthur C. Clarke Award and the Nommo Award and was a finalist for the John W. Campbell Award finalist, and of The

Kitschies Golden Tentacle Award-winning novel *Making Wolf*. He also writes short stories, notably 'The Apologists' which was nominated for a British Science Fiction Association award. Born in London to Yoruba parents, he lives and works on the south coast of England where he battles an addiction to books.

I.A. WATSON stopped actively occult detecting in '09 after the Lochmerle Orphanage tragedy where the black waters rose. Once released from psychiatric care he immediately began scribbling blasphemous truths in the form of novels and short stories and has so far not been restrained again. Amongst his ramblings are a dozen or so novels and collections including *Vinnie de Soth, Jobbing Occultist* (who of course appears in this volume's tale), and more than fifty short stories, a lot of them Sherlock Holmes or occult mysteries for which people keep giving him awards – the unknowing fools!
A full list of his literary misdeeds is available at
http://www.chillwater.org.uk/writing/iawatsonhome.htm

MATTHEW WILLIS is a writer and historian with an interest in things that go bump in the night and things that go boom on the sea. Matthew's first published novel was the historical fantasy *Daedalus and the Deep*, based on a historical sea serpent sighting in the 19th century. His short stories have been published in *The New Accelerator*, *Flash Flood* and *Hell's Empire*, and he was shortlisted for the Bridport Prize in 2015. His most recent publications are two novellas of war-time Malta, *Harpoon* and *Bastion*.

Printed in Great Britain
by Amazon